SHATTERED

DICK FRANCIS

SHATTERED

G. P. PUTNAM'S SONS
NEW YORK

G. P. PUTNAM'S SONS
Publishers Since 1838
a member of
Penguin Putnam Inc.
375 Hudson Street
New York, NY 10014

Library of Congress Cataloging-in-Publication Data

Francis, Dick.
Shattered / Dick Francis.
p. cm.
ISBN 0-399-14660-1
1. Glassworkers—Fiction. 2. Glass blowing and working—Fiction.
3. Horse racing—Fiction. 4. England—Fiction. I. Title.
PR6056.R27 S55   2000   00-055937
823'.914—dc21

Printed in the United States of America

1 3 5 7 9 10 8 6 4 2

This book is printed on acid-free paper. ∞

Book design by Julie Duquet

To
Her Majesty Queen Elizabeth, The Queen Mother,
in celebration of her 100th birthday
with endless gratitude, love and every good wish, from
Dick Francis.

My thanks also
to
Stephen Zawistowski, glassblower
Stephen Spiro, professor of respiratory medicine
Tanya Williams, West Mercia Police

to
Matthew Francis, my grandson,
for the title

and to my son, Felix,
for everything

SHATTERED

FOUR OF US drove together to Cheltenham races on the day that Martin Stukely died there from a fall in a steeplechase.

It was December 31, the eve of the year 2000. A cold midwinter morning. The world approaching the threshold of the future.

Martin himself, taking his place behind the steering wheel of his BMW, set off before noon without premonition, collecting his three passengers from their Cotswold Hills bases on his way to his afternoon's work. A jockey of renown, he had confidence and a steady heart.

By the time he reached my sprawling house on the hillside above the elongated tourist-attracting village of Broadway, the air in his spacious car swirled richly full of smoke from his favorite cigar, the Montecristo No. 2, his substitute for eating. At thirty-four he was spending longer and longer in a sauna each day, but was all the same gradually losing the metabolic battle against weight.

Genes had given him a well-balanced frame in general, and an Italian mother in particular had passed on a love of cooking, and vivacity.

He quarreled incessantly with Bon-Bon, his rich, plump and talkative wife, and on the whole ignored his four small children, often frowning as he looked at them as if not sure exactly who they were. Nevertheless his skill and courage and rapport with horses took him as often as always into the winner's circle, and he drove to Cheltenham calmly discussing his mounts' chances that afternoon in two fast hurdle races and one longer 'chase. Three miles of jumping fences brought out the controlled recklessness that made him great.

He picked me up last on that fateful Friday morning, as I lived nearest to Cheltenham's racetrack.

Already on board, and by his side, sat Priam Jones, the trainer whose horses he regularly rode. Priam was expert at self-aggrandizement but not quite as good as he believed at knowing when a horse in his care had come to a performance peak. That day's steeplechaser, Tallahassee, was, according to my friend Martin on the telephone, as ready as he would ever be to carry off the day's gold trophy, but Priam Jones, smoothing his white late-middle-age thinning hair, told the horse's owner in a blasé voice that Tallahassee might still do better on softer ground.

Lounging back beside me on the rear seat, with the tip of one of Martin's cigars glowing symmetrically to ash, Tallahassee's owner, Lloyd Baxter, listened without noticeable pleasure, and I thought Priam Jones would have done better to keep his premature apologies in reserve.

It was unusual for Martin to be the one who drove Tallahassee's owner and trainer anywhere. Normally he took other jockeys, or me alone: but Priam Jones from arrogance had just wrecked his own car in a stupid rash of flat tires, thanks to his having tried to ignore head-on a newly installed deterrent no-parking set of rising teeth. It was the town's fault, he insisted. He would sue.

Priam had taken it for granted, Martin told me crossly, that he—Martin—would do the driving, and would not only take Priam himself but would also chauffeur the horse's owner, who was staying overnight with Priam for the Cheltenham meeting, having flown down from the north of England to the local Staverton airfield in a small rented air taxi.

I disliked Lloyd Baxter as thoroughly as he disliked me. Martin had warned me of the Priam tire situation ("Keep your sarcastic tongue behind your splendid teeth") and had begged me also to swamp the grumpy, dumpy millionaire owner with anesthetizing charm in advance, in case Priam Jones's fears materialized and the horse drew a blank.

I saw Martin's face grinning at me in the rearview mirror as he listened to me sympathize with the flat tires. He more than paid any debt he owed me by ferrying me about when he could, as I'd lost my driver's license for a year through scorching at ninety-five miles an hour around the Oxford bypass (fourth ticket for speeding) to take him and his broken leg to see his point-of-death old retired gardener. The gardener's heart had then thumped away insecurely for six further weeks—one of life's little ironies. My loss of license now had three months to run.

The friendship between Martin and myself, unlikely at first sight, had sprung fully grown in an instant four or more years ago, result of a smile crinkling around his eyes, echo, I gathered, of my own.

We had met in the jury room of the local crown court, chosen for jury duty to hear a fairly simple case of domestic murder. The trial lasted two and a half days. Over mineral water afterwards, I'd learned about the tyranny of weight. Though my life had nothing to do with horses, or his with the heat and chemistry of my own days, we shared, perhaps, the awareness of the physical ability that we each needed for success in our trade.

In the jury room Martin had asked with merely polite curiosity, "What do you do for a living?"

"I blow glass."

"You do *what?*"

"I make things of glass. Vases, ornaments, goblets. That sort of thing."

"Good grief."

I smiled at his astonishment. "People do, you know. People have made things of glass for thousands of years."

"Yes, but . . ." he considered, "you don't look like someone who makes ornaments. You look . . . well . . . tough."

I was four years younger than he and three inches taller, and probably equal in muscles.

"I've made horses," I said mildly. "Herds of them."

"The Crystal Stud Cup," he asked, identifying one of flat racing's more elaborate prizes. "Did you make that?"

"Not that one, no."

"Well . . . Do you have a *name?* Like, say, Baccarat?"

I smiled lopsidedly. "Not so glamorous. It's Logan, Gerard Logan."

"Logan Glass." He nodded, no longer surprised. "You have a place on the High Street in Broadway, side by side with all those antique shops. I've seen it."

I nodded. "Sales and workshop."

He hadn't seemed to take any special notice, but a week later he'd walked into my display gallery, spent an intense and silent hour there, asked if I'd personally made all the exhibits (mostly) and offered me a ride to the races. As time went by we had become comfortably accustomed to each other's traits and faults. Bon-Bon used me as a shield in battle and the children thought me a bore because I wouldn't let them near my furnace.

For half the races that day at Cheltenham things went as normal. Martin won the two-mile hurdle race by six lengths and Priam Jones complained that six lengths was too far. It would ruin the horse's position in the handicap.

Martin shrugged, gave an amused twist to his eyebrows and went into the changing room to put on Lloyd Baxter's colors of black and white chevrons, pink sleeves and cap. I watched the three men in the parade ring, owner, trainer and jockey, as they took stock of Tallahassee walking purposefully around in the hands of his groom. Tallahassee stood at odds of six to four with the bookmakers for the Coffee Forever Gold Trophy: the clear favorite.

Lloyd Baxter (ignoring his trainer's misgivings) had put his money on the horse, and so had I.

It was at the last fence of all that Tallahassee uncharacteristically tangled his feet. Easily ahead by seven lengths, he lost his concentration, hit the roots of the unyielding birch and turned a somersault over his rider, landing his whole half-ton mass upside down with the saddle tree and his withers crushing the rib cage of the man beneath.

The horse fell at the peak of his forward-to-win acceleration and crashed down at thirty or more miles an hour. Winded, he lay across the jockey for inert moments, then rocked back and forwards vigorously in his struggle to rise again to his feet.

The fall and its aftermath looked truly terrible from where I watched on the stands. The roar of welcome for a favorite racing home to a popular win was hushed to a gasp, to cries, to an endless anxious murmur. The actual winner passed the post without his due cheers, and a thousand pairs of binoculars focused on the unmoving black and white chevrons flat on the green December grass.

The racetrack doctor, though instantly attending him from his following car, couldn't prevent the fast-gathering group of paramedics and media people from realizing that Martin Stukely, though still semi-conscious, was dying before their eyes. They glimpsed the blood sliding frothily out of the jockey's mouth, choking him as the sharp ends of broken ribs tore his lungs apart. They described it, cough by groan, in their news reports.

The doctor and paramedics loaded Martin just alive into the waiting ambulance and as they set off to the hospital they worked desperately with transfusions and oxygen, but quietly, before the journey ended, the jockey lost his race.

PRIAM, NOT NORMALLY a man of emotion, wept without shame as he later collected Martin's belongings, including his car keys, from the changing room. Sniffing, blowing his nose, accompanied by Lloyd Baxter, who looked annoyed rather than grief stricken, Priam Jones offered to return me to my place of business in Broadway, though not to my home in the hills, as he intended to go in the opposite direction from there, to see Bon-Bon, to give her comfort.

I asked if he would take me on with him to see Bon-Bon. He refused. Bon-Bon wanted Priam alone, he said. She had said so, devastated, on the telephone.

Lloyd Baxter, Priam added, would now also be off-loaded at Broadway. Priam had got him the last available room in the hotel there, the Wychwood Dragon. It was all arranged.

Lloyd Baxter glowered at the world, at his trainer, at me, at fate. He should, he thought, have won the Cup. He had been robbed. Though his horse was unharmed, his feelings for his dead jockey seemed to be resentment, not regret.

As Priam, shoulders drooping, and Baxter, frowning heavily, set off ahead of us towards the car park, Martin's valet hurried after me, calling my name. I stopped, and turned towards him, and into my hands he thrust the lightweight racing saddle that, strapped firmly to Tallahassee's back, had helped to deal out damage and death.

The stirrups, with the leathers, were folded over the saddle plate, and were kept in place by the long girth wound around and around. The sight of the girth-wrapped piece of professional equipment, like my newly dead mother's Hasselblad camera, bleakly rammed into one's consciousness the gritty message that their owners would never come back. It was Martin's empty saddle that set me missing him painfully.

Eddie, the valet, was elderly, bald and, in Martin's estimation, hardworking and unable to do wrong. He turned to go back to the changing room but then stopped, fumbled in the deep front pocket of the apron of his trade and, producing a brown paper–wrapped package, called after me to wait.

"Someone gave this to Martin to give to you," he shouted, coming back and holding it out for me to take. "Martin asked me to give it back to him when he was leaving to go home, so he could pass it on to you . . . but of course . . ." He swallowed, his voice breaking. "He's gone."

I asked. "Who gave it to *him*?"

The valet didn't know. He was sure, though, that Martin himself knew, because he had been joking about its being worth a million, and Eddie was clear that the ultimate destination of the parcel had been Gerard Logan, Martin's friend.

I took the package and, thanking him, put it into my raincoat pocket, and we spent a mutual moment of sharp sadness for the gap we already felt in our lives. I supposed, as he turned to hurry back to his chores in the changing room, and I continued into the car park, that I might have gone to the races for the last time, that without Martin's input the fun might have flown.

Priam's tears welled up again at the significance of the empty saddle, and Lloyd Baxter shook his head with disapproval. Priam recovered enough, however, to start Martin's car and drive it to Broadway, where, as he'd intended, he off-loaded both me and Lloyd Baxter outside the Wychwood Dragon and himself departed in speechless gloom towards Bon-Bon and her fatherless brood.

Lloyd Baxter paid me no attention but strode without pleasure into the hotel. During the journey from the racetrack he'd complained to Priam that his overnight bag was in Priam's house. He'd gone by hired car from Staverton airfield, intending to spend the evening at Priam's now canceled New Year's Eve party, celebrating a win in the Gold Coffee Cup before flying away the following morning to his thousand-acre estate in Northumberland. Priam's assertion that, after seeing Martin's family, he would himself ferry the bag to the hotel, left Tallahassee's owner unmollified. The whole afternoon had been a disaster, he grumbled, and in his voice one could hear undertones of an intention to change to a different trainer.

My own glass business lay a few yards away from the Wychwood Dragon on the opposite side of the road. If one looked across from outside the hotel, the gallery's windows seemed to glitter with ultra-bright light, which they did from breakfast to midnight every day of the year.

I walked across the road wishing that time could be reversed to yesterday: wishing that bright-eyed Martin would march through my door suggesting improbable glass sculptures that in fact, when I made them, won both commissions and kudos. He had become fascinated by the actual composition of glass and never seemed to tire of watching whenever I mixed the basic ingredients myself, instead of always buying it the easy way—off the shelf.

The ready-made stuff, which came in two-hundred-kilo drums, looked like small opaque marbles, or large gray peas, half the size of the polished clear-glass toys. I used the simple option regularly, as it came pure and clean, and melted without flaws.

When he first watched me load the tank of the furnace with a week's supply of the round gray pebbles, he repeated aloud the listed ingredients, "Eighty percent of the mix is white silica sand from the Dead Sea. Ten percent is soda ash. Then add small specific amounts of antimony, barium, calcium and arsenic per fifty pounds of weight. If you want to color the glass blue, use ground lapis lazuli or cobalt. If you want yellow, use cadmium, which changes with heat to orange and red and I don't believe it."

"That's soda crystal glass." I nodded, smiling. "I use it all the time as it's safe in every way for eating or drinking from. Babies can lick it."

He gazed at me in surprise. "Isn't all glass safe to suck?"

"Well . . . no. You have to be exceedingly careful making things with lead. Lead crystal. Lovely stuff. But lead is mega mega poisonous. Lead silicate, that is, that's used for glass. It's a rusty red powder and in its raw state you have to keep it strictly separate from everything else and be terribly meticulous about locking it up."

"What about cut lead crystal wineglasses?" he asked. "I mean, Bon-Bon's mother gave us some."

"Don't worry," I told him with humor. "If they haven't made you ill yet, they probably won't."

"Thanks a bunch."

I went in through my heavy gallery door of beveled glass panes already feeling an emptiness where Martin had been. And it wasn't as if I had no other friends, I had a pack of beer and wine cronies for whom fizzy water and sauna sweats were on their anathema lists. Two of those, Hickory and Irish, worked for me as assistants and apprentices, though Hickory was approximately my own age and Irish a good deal older. The desire to work with glass quite often struck late in life, as with Irish, who was forty, but sometimes, as with me, the fascination arrived like talking, too early to remember.

I had an uncle, eminent in the glassblowing trade, who was also a brilliant flameworker. He could heat solid glass rods in the flame of a gas burner until among other things he could twiddle them into a semblance of lace, and make angels and crinolines and steady flat round bases for almost anything needing precision in a science laboratory.

He was amused at first that an inquisitive kid should shadow him, but was then interested, and finally took it seriously. He taught me whenever I could dodge school, and he died about the time that my inventiveness grew to match his. I was sixteen. In his will he left me plans and instructions for the building of a basic workshop, and also, much more valuably, his priceless notebooks into which he'd detailed years of unique skill. I'd built a locked safelike bookcase to keep them in, and ever since had added my own notes on method and materials needed when I designed anything special. It stood always at the far end of the workshop between the stock shelves and a bank of four tall gray lockers, where my assistants and I kept our personal stuff.

It was he, my uncle Ron, who named his enterprise Logan Glass, and he who drilled into me an embryonic business sense and an awareness that anything made by one glassblower could in general be copied by another, and that this drastically lowered the asking price. During his last few years he sought and succeeded in making pieces of uncopyable originality, working out of my sight and then challenging me to detect and repeat his methods. Whenever I couldn't, he generously showed me how; and he laughed when I grew in ability until I could beat him at his own game.

On the afternoon of Martin's death both the gallery and showroom were crowded with people looking for ways of remembering the advent of the historic millennium day. I'd designed and made a whole multitude and variety of small good-looking calendar-bearing dishes in every color combination that I knew from experience attracted the most tourist dollars, and we had sold literally hundreds of them. I'd scratched my signature on the lot. Not yet, I thought, but by the year 2020, if I could achieve it, a signed Gerard Logan calendar dish of December 31, 1999, might be worth collecting.

The long gallery displayed the larger, unusual, one-of-a-kind and more expensive pieces, each spotlit and available: the showroom was lined by many shelves holding smaller, colorful, attractive and less expensive ornaments, which could reasonably be packed into a tourist suitcase.

One side wall of the showroom rose only to waist height, so that over it one could see into the workshop beyond, where the furnace burned day and night and the little gray pebbles melted into soda crystal at a raised heat of 2400 degrees Fahrenheit.

Hickory or Irish, or their colleague Pamela Jane, took turns to work as my assistant in the workshop. One of the other two gave a running commentary of the proceedings to the customers and the third packed parcels and worked the till. Ideally the four of us took the jobs in turn, but experienced glassblowers were scarce, and my three enthusiastic assistants were still at the paperweight and penguin stage.

Christmas sales had been great but nothing like the New Year 2000. As everything sold in my place was guaranteed handmade (and mostly by me), the day I'd spent at the races had been my first respite away from the furnace for a month. I'd worked some-times into the night, and always from eight onwards in the morn-ing, with one of my three helpers assisting. The resulting exhaustion hadn't mattered. I was physically fit, and as Martin had said, who needed a sauna with 2400 degrees in one's face?

Hickory, twirling color into a glowing paperweight on the end of a slender five-foot-long steel rod called a punty iron, looked extremely relieved at my return from the races. Pamela Jane, smiling, earnest, thin and anxious, lost her place in her commentary and repeated instead, "He's here. He's here . . ." and Irish stopped packing a cobalt blue dolphin in bright white wrapping paper and sighed, "Thank God," very heavily. They relied on me too much, I thought.

I said, "Hi guys," as usual and, walking around into the workshop and stripping off jacket, tie and shirt, gave the millennium-crazy shoppers a view of a designer-label white string singlet, my working clothes. Hickory finished his paperweight, spinning the punty iron down by his feet to cool the glass, being careful not to scorch his new bright sneakers. I made, as a frivolity, a striped hollow blue-green and purple fish with fins, a geodetic type of ornament that looked impressively difficult and had defeated me altogether at fourteen. Light shone through it in rainbows.

The customers, though, wanted proof of that day's origin. Staying open much later than usual, I made endless dated bowls, plates and vases to please them, while Pamela Jane explained that they couldn't be collected until the next morning, New Year's Day, as they had to cool slowly overnight. No one seemed deterred. Irish wrote their names and told them jokes. There were hours of good nature and celebration.

Priam Jones called in fleetingly at one point. When he had been at Martin and Bon-Bon's house he'd found my raincoat lying on the back seat in the car. I was most grateful, and thanked him with New Year fervor. He nodded, even smiled. His tears had dried.

When he'd gone I went to hang up my raincoat in my locker.

Something hard banged against my knee and I remembered the package given me by Eddie, the valet. I put it on a stock shelf out of the way at the rear of the workshop and went back to satisfy the customers.

Shop-closing time was elastic but I finally locked the door behind the last customer in time for Hickory, Irish and Pamela Jane to go to parties, and for me to realize I hadn't yet opened the parcel that Priam Jones had returned in my raincoat. The parcel that had come from Martin . . . he'd sat heavily on my shoulder all evening, a laughing lost spirit, urging me on.

Full of regrets I locked the furnace against vandals and checked the heat of the annealing ovens, which were full of the newly made objects slowly cooling. The furnace, which I'd built to my uncle's design, was constructed of firebricks and fueled by propane gas under pressure from a fan. It burned day and night at never less than 1800 degrees Fahrenheit, hot enough to melt most metals, let alone burn paper. We were often asked if a memento like a wedding ring could be enclosed in a glass paperweight, but the answer was sorry, no. Liquid glass would melt gold—and human flesh—immediately. Molten glass, in fact, was pretty dangerous stuff.

I slowly tidied the workshop, counted and recounted and then enclosed the day's takings in their canvas bag ready to entrust to the night safe of the bank. Then I put on my discarded clothes and eventually took a closer look at my neglected parcel. The contents proved to be exactly what they felt like, an ordinary-looking videotape, a bit disappointing. The tape was wound fully back to the beginning, and the black casing bore no label of any sort. There was no protective sleeve. I stacked it casually beside the money, but the sight of it reminded me that my videotape player was at my home, that I'd sold my car, and that rising midnight on a thousand years' eve wasn't the best time to phone for a taxi.

Plans for my own midnight, with a neighborhood dance next door to my house, had disintegrated on Cheltenham racetrack. Maybe the Wychwood Dragon, I thought, not caring much, still had a broom cupboard to rent. I would beg a sandwich and a rug and sleep across the dark night into the new century, and early in the morning I would write an obituary for a jockey.

WHEN I WAS ready to cross to the Wychwood Dragon someone tapped heavily on the glass-paned door, and I went to open it, intending to say it was too late, the year 2000 lay fifteen minutes ahead in Broadway, even if it had been tomorrow for hours in Australia. I unlocked the door and, prompted by inexorable courtesy, faced politely an unexpected and unwanted visitor in Lloyd Baxter, telling him with a half-smothered yawn that I simply hadn't enough energy to discuss the disaster at Cheltenham or anything else to do with horses.

He advanced into the brightest area on the threshold and I saw he was carrying a bottle of Dom Pérignon and two of the Wychwood Dragon's best champagne glasses. The heavily disapproving expression, despite these pipes of peace, was still in place.

"Mr. Logan," he said formally, "I know no one at all in this place except yourself, and don't say this isn't a time for rejoicing, as I agree with you in many ways . . . not only because Martin Stukely is dead but because the next century is likely to be even more bloody than the last and I see no reason to celebrate just a change of date, particularly as there's no doubt the date is incorrect to begin with." He took a breath. "I therefore decided to spend the evening in my room . . ." He stopped abruptly, and I would have finished the tale for him, but instead I merely jerked my head for him to come right in, and closed the heavy door behind him.

"I'll drink to Martin," I said.

He looked relieved at my acquiescence, even though he thought little of me and was old enough to be my father. Loneliness, though, still propelling him, he set the glasses on the table beside the till, ceremoniously popped the expensive cork and unleashed the bubbles.

"Drink to whatever you like," he said in depression. "I suppose it was a bad idea, coming here."

"No," I said.

"I could hear the music, you see . . ."

Music in the distance had forced him out of his lonely room. Music powerfully attracted the gregarious human race. No one welcomed two thousand years in silence.

I looked at my watch. Only nine minutes to ring-the-bells time.

Regardless of cynical withdrawals from organized enjoyments, regardless even of thrusts of raw unprocessed grief, I found there was inescapable excitement after all in the sense of a new chance offered, a fresh beginning possible. One could forgive one's own faults.

New numbers themselves vibrated with promise.

Five minutes to ring-the-bells . . . and fireworks. I drank Lloyd Baxter's champagne and still didn't like him.

Tallahassee's owner had changed, thanks to his transferred bag, into formal clothes, complete with black tie. His almost Edwardian type of grooming seemed to intensify rather than lighten his thunderous personality.

Even though I'd been introduced to him at least two years earlier, and had drunk his fizz on happier occasions, I'd never before bothered to read his face feature by feature. Rectifying that, I remembered that he'd earlier had thick strong dark hair, but as his age had advanced from fifty there were gray streaks that to my eyes had multiplied quite fast. His facial bone structure was thick and almost Cro-Magnon, with a powerful-looking brow and a similar no-nonsense jaw.

Perhaps in the past he had been lean-and-hungry, but as the twentieth century rolled away he had thickened around the neck and stomach and taken on the authoritative weight of chairmen. If he looked more like an industrialist than a landowner, it was because he'd sold his majority share in a shipping line to buy his racehorses and his acres.

He disapproved, he'd told me severely, of young men like myself who could take days off work whenever they cared to. I knew he considered me a hanger-on who sponged on Martin, regardless of Martin's insisting it was more likely to be the other way around. It seemed that when Lloyd Baxter formed a set of opinions he was slow to rearrange them.

Distantly, out in the cold night, bells in England pealed the passing of the all-important moment, celebrating the artificial date change and affirming that humankind could impose its own mathematics on the unresponsive planet. Lloyd Baxter raised his glass to drink to some private goal, and I, following his gesture, hoped merely that I would see January 2001 in safety. I added in fact, with banal courtesy, that I would drink to his health outside, if he'd forgive me my absence.

"Of course," he said, his voice in a mumble.

Pulling open the gallery door, I walked out into the street still holding my golden drink, and found that dozens of people had felt impelled in the same way. A host, myself included, had been moved by an almost supernatural instinct to breathe free new air under the stars.

The man who sold antique books in the shop next to my gallery shook my hand vigorously, and with uncomplicated goodwill wished me a happy new year. I smiled and thanked him. Smiling was easy. The village, a fairly friendly place at any time, greeted the new year and the neighbors with uncomplicated affection. Feuds could wait.

Up the hill a large group of people had linked arms and were swaying across the road singing "Auld Lang Syne" with half the words missing, and a few cars crept along slowly, headlights full on, horns blaring, with enthusiastic youths yelling from open windows. Up and down High Street local sophistication found its own level, but everywhere with a benign slant of mind.

Perhaps because of that, it was longer than I'd intended before I reluctantly decided I should return to my shop, my ready-for-the-bank takings and my unwelcome visitor, whose temper wouldn't have been improved by my absence.

Declining with regret a tot of single malt from the bookseller, I ambled along to Logan Glass feeling the first twitch of resignation for the lack of Martin. He had known always that his job might kill him, but he hadn't expected it. Falls were inevitable but they would happen "some other time." Injuries had been counted a nuisance that interfered with winning. He would "hang up his boots," he'd told me lightheartedly, the minute he was afraid to put them on.

It was the *thought* of fear that bothered him, he'd once said.

I pushed open the heavy door preparing my apologies and found that an entirely different sort of action was essential.

Lloyd Baxter lay facedown, unmoving and unconscious, on my showroom floor.

Dumping my empty glass rapidly on the table that held the till I knelt anxiously beside him and felt for a pulse in his neck. Even though his lips were bluish he hadn't somehow the look of someone dead, and there was to my great relief a slow perceptible *thud-thud* under my fingers. A stroke, perhaps? A heart attack? I knew very little medicine.

What an appallingly awkward night, I thought, sitting back on my heels, for anyone to need to call out the medics. I stood up and took a few paces to the table which held the till and all the business machines, including the telephone. I dialed the come-at-once number without much expectation, but even on such a New Year's Eve, it seemed, the emergency services would respond, and it wasn't until I'd put down the receiver on their promise of an instant stretcher that I noticed the absence beside the till of the ready-for-the-bank canvas bag. It had gone. I searched for it everywhere, but in my heart I knew where I'd left it.

I swore. I'd worked hard for every cent. I'd sweated. My arms still ached. I was depressed at that point as well as furious. I began to wonder if Lloyd Baxter had done his best, if he'd been knocked out trying to defend my property against a thief.

The black unidentified videotape had gone as well. The wave of outrage common to anyone robbed of even minor objects shook me into a deeper anger. The tape's loss was a severe aggravation, even if not on the same level as the money.

I telephoned the police without exciting them in the least. They were psyched up for bombs, not paltry theft. They said they would send a detective constable in the morning.

Lloyd Baxter stirred, moaned and lay still again. I knelt beside him, removed his tie, unfastened his belt and in general rolled him slightly onto his side so that he wasn't in danger of choking. There were flecks of blood, though, around his mouth.

The chill of the deep night seeped into my own body, let alone Baxter's. The flames of the furnace roared captive behind the trapdoor that rose and fell to make the heat available, and finally, uncomfortably cold, I went and stood on the treadle that raised the trap, and let the heat flood into the workshop to reach the showroom beyond.

Normally, even in icy winter, the furnace in constant use gave warmth enough, supplemented by an electric convection heater in the gallery, but by the time help arrived for Baxter I had wrapped him in my jacket and everything else handy, and he was still growing cold to the touch.

The ultra-efficient men who arrived in the prompt ambulance took over expertly, examining their patient, searching and emptying his pockets, making a preliminary diagnosis and wrapping him in a red warming blanket ready for transport. Baxter partially awoke during this process but couldn't swim altogether to the surface of consciousness. His gaze flickered woozily once across my face before his eyes closed again into a heavier sleep.

The paramedics did some paperwork and had me provide them with Baxter's name, address and as much as I knew (practically nothing) of his medical history. One of them was writing a list of all the things they had taken from Lloyd, starting with a Piaget gold watch and ending with the contents of a pocket of his pants—a handkerchief, a bottle of pills and a businesslike hotel room key in the shape of a ball-and-chain deterrent to forgetfulness.

I didn't even have to suggest that I should return the key myself to the hotel; the paramedics suggested it themselves. I rattled it into my own pants without delay, thinking vaguely of packing Lloyd Baxter's things into his much-traveled suitcase and more positively of sleeping in his bed, since the paramedics were adamant that he would have to stay in the hospital all night.

"What's wrong with him?" I asked. "Has he had a heart attack? Or a stroke? Has he been . . . well, attacked and knocked out?"

I told them about the money and the tape.

They shook their heads. The most senior of them discounted my guesses. He said that to his experienced eyes Lloyd Baxter wasn't having a nonfatal heart attack (he would be awake, if so) nor a stroke, nor were there any lumpy bruises on his head. In his opinion, he announced authoritatively, Lloyd Baxter had had an epileptic fit.

"A *fit?*" I asked blankly. "He's seemed perfectly well all day."

The medics nodded knowledgeably. One of them picked up the pill bottle whose contents were listed as phenytoin and said he was certain that this was the preventative for epilepsy.

"Epilepsy"—the chief medic nodded—"and who'll bet that he was overdue with a dose? We have all the other symptoms here. Alcohol." He gestured to the depleted bottle of Dom. "Late night without sleep. Stress . . . isn't he the one whose jockey was done for at the races today? Then there's the slow pulse and bluish lips, the blood flecks from where he's bitten his tongue . . . and did you notice that his pants are wet? They urinate, you know."

CHAPTER 2

THE RESIDENT DRAGON of the Wychwood Dragon
Hotel being its fierce lady manager, I could ooze in and out of
the halls unseen (as it were), owing both to the collection of
small colored glass animals marching around her dressing table,
and to her occasional invitations to bed. The glass animals weren't
so much trophies as apologies, however, as she was fortunately resigned to accepting that a thirty years' difference in age was a fair
enough reason for me to say no. Her habit of calling me "lover"
in public was embarrassment enough, though, and I knew that
most of Broadway believed she ate me with eggs for breakfast.

Anyway, no one questioned my takeover of Lloyd Baxter's
room. In the morning I packed his belongings and, explaining all

to the Dragon, arranged for the hotel to send them to the hospital. Then I walked down and across to the workshop, where Martin, though vivid in my mind, refused to fly as a statement in glass. Inspiration operated at its own good speed, and many a time I'd found that trying to force it didn't work.

The furnace roared in its firebox. I sat beside the stainless-steel table (called a marver) on which I should have been rolling eternity into basic balls of liquid glass, and thought only of Martin alive in the body, Martin laughing and winning races, and Martin's lost message on videotape. Where was that tape, what did it contain and who thought it worth stealing?

These profitless thoughts were interrupted by the doorbell ringing early at nine o'clock, when we'd said we'd open at ten.

On the doorstep stood no recognizable customer but a young woman in a vast sloppy sweater hanging around her knees, topped by a baseball cap over a shock of brassily dyed streaky hair. We stared at each other with interest, her brown eyes alive and curious, her jaw rhythmic with chewing gum.

I said politely, "Good morning."

"Yeah. Yeah." She laughed. "Happy New Century and all that rubbish. Are you Gerard Logan?"

Her accent was Estuary, Essex or Thames: take your pick.

"Logan." I nodded. "And you?"

"Detective Constable Dodd."

I blinked. "Plainclothes?"

"You may laugh," she said, chewing away. "You reported a theft at twelve thirty-two this A.M. Can I come in?"

"Be my guest."

She stepped into the gallery spotlights and glowed.

From habit I dramatized her in glass in my mind, an abstract essence as a conduit of feeling and light, exactly the instinctive process I'd tried in vain to summon up for Martin.

Oblivious, Detective Constable Dodd produced a down-to-earth warrant card identifying her in uniform and adding a first name, Catherine. I handed the warrant card back and answered her questions, but the police opinion was already firm. Too bad I'd left a bagful of money lying around, she said. What did I expect? And videotapes came by the dozen. No one would think twice about snapping one up.

"What was on it?" she asked, pencil poised over a notepad.

"I've no idea." I explained how it had come to me originally in a brown-paper parcel.

"Pornography. Bound to be." Her pronouncement was brisk, world-weary and convinced. "Unidentified." She shrugged. "Would you know it from any other tape if you saw it again?"

"It hadn't any labels."

I dug the wrapping out of the rubbish bin and gave her the wrinkled and torn paper. "This came to me by hand," I said. "There's no postmark."

She took the paper dubiously, enclosed it in a further bag, got me to sign across the fold and tucked it away somewhere under the extra-loose sweater.

My answers to her questions about the stolen money caused her eyebrows to rise over the amount, but she obviously thought

I'd never again see the canvas bag or the mini-bonanza inside. I still had checks and credit card slips, of course, but most of my tourist customers paid in cash.

I told her then about Lloyd Baxter and his epileptic fit. "Maybe he saw the thief," I said.

She frowned. "Maybe he *was* the thief. Could he have faked the fit?"

"The paramedics didn't seem to think so."

She sighed. "How long were you out in the street?"

"Bells. 'Auld Lang Syne,' fireworks, happy new thousand years . . ."

"Getting on for half an hour?" She consulted her notebook. "You phoned the ambulance service at twelve twenty-seven."

She wandered through the showroom looking at the small colorful vases, the clowns, sailing boats, fishes and horses. She picked up a haloed angel and disapproved of the price sticker under the feet. Her swath of hair fell forward, framing her intent face, and I again clearly saw the bright analytical intelligence inside the sloppy hippie-type disguise. She was through and through a police officer, not primarily a come-hither female.

Replacing the angel with decision on the shelf, she folded her notebook, stored it out of sight and with body language announced that the investigation, despite its lack of results, was over. It was the go-to-work version of Constable Dodd that prepared to step into the street.

"Why?" I asked.

"Why what?" She concentrated on her change of character.

"Why the too-big sweater and the baseball cap?"

She flashed me an aware, amused glance and turned back to the world outside. "You happened to have been robbed on my allotted beat. My assignment in Broadway is to spot the gang stealing cars on bank holidays in this area. Thanks for your time."

She grinned with cheerfulness and shuffled off down the hill, pausing to talk to a homeless-looking layabout sitting in a shop doorway, huddling against the chill of morning.

A pity the hippie and the hobo hadn't been car-thief spotting at midnight, I thought vaguely, and telephoned to the hospital to inquire about Baxter.

Awake and grumbling, I gathered. I left a message of goodwill.

Bon-Bon next.

She wailed miserably into my ear. "But darling Gerard, *of course* I didn't tell Priam not to bring you with him. How could you believe it? You are the *first* person Martin would want to come here. Please, please come as soon as you can, the children are crying and everything's dreadful." She drew a shaky breath, the tears distorting her voice. "We were going to a midnight party . . . and the baby-sitter came and said she wanted her full money anyway, even if Martin was dead, can you believe it? And Priam talked about the inconvenience of finding another jockey halfway through the season. He's an old fool and he kept patting me . . ."

"He was seriously upset," I assured her. "A matter of tears."

"Priam?"

I frowned at the memory, but the tears had looked real.

"How long did he stay with you?" I asked.

"Stay? He didn't stay long. Ten to fifteen minutes, maybe. My mother descended on us while he was here, and you've met her, you know what she's like. Priam was mostly in Martin's den, I think. He kept saying he had to be back for evening stables, he couldn't sit still." Bon-Bon's despair overflowed. "Can't you *come*? Please, please come. I can't deal with my mother by myself."

"As soon as I've done one job, and found some transport. Say . . . about noon."

"Oh yes, I forgot your bloody car. Where are you? Did you get home?"

"I'm in my workshop."

"I'll come and fetch you . . ."

"No. First, fill your mama with gin and let the children loose on her, then shut yourself in Martin's den and watch the tapes of him winning three Grand Nationals but don't drive anywhere while you're so upset. I'll find transport, but at the worst we could persuade your remarkable parent to lend me Worthington and the Rolls."

Bon-Bon's mother's versatile chauffeur raised his eyebrows to heaven frequently at Marigold's odd requirements, but had been known to drive a roofless Land Rover at breakneck speed at night across stubble fields, headlights blazing in the dark, while his employer stood balancing behind him with a double-barreled shotgun loosing off at mesmerized rabbits over his head. Martin said he'd been afraid to watch, but Worthington and Marigold had achieved a bag of forty and freed her land of a voracious pest.

Worthington, bald and fifty, was more an adventure than a last resort.

ON NEW YEAR'S Day 2000 in England the world in general came to a stop. Saturday's running of one of the best steeple-chasing afternoon programs of the whole midwinter season was stuck in a silly halt because the people who worked the betting machines wanted to stay at home. There was no racing—and no football—to entertain the nonworkers on or off the television.

Logan Glass astounded the other residents of Broadway by opening its doors to the day-before's customers, who arrived to collect their overnight-cooled souvenirs. To my own astonishment two of my assistants turned up, even though bleary-eyed, saying they couldn't leave me to pack the whole delivery job alone; so it was with speed and good humor that my new century began. I looked back later at the peace of that brief morning with a feeling of unreality that life could ever have been so safe and simple.

PAMELA JANE, TWITTERY, anxious, stick-thin and wanly pretty, insisted on driving me to Bon-Bon's place herself, leaving me in the driveway there and departing with a wave, hurrying back to the shop, as she'd left Irish alone there.

Martin and Bon-Bon had agreed at least on their house, an eighteenth-century gem that Marigold had helped them buy. I admired it every time I went there.

A small van stood on the gravel, dark blue with a commercial name painted on it in yellow: THOMPSON ELECTRONICS. I supposed it was because I'd been working myself that I didn't immediately remember that that day was a national holiday; definitely a moratorium for television repair vans.

Chaos was too weak a word to describe what I found inside Martin's house. For a start, the front door was visibly ajar and, when I touched it, it swung wide, although it was only the kitchen door the family left hospitably unlocked, both for friends and for visiting tradesmen.

Beginning to feel a slight unease, I stepped through the heavily carved front doorway and shouted, but without response, and a pace or two later I learned why I had misgivings.

Bon-Bon's mother, Marigold, frothy gray hair and floaty purple dress in disarray as usual, lay unconscious on the stairs. Worthington, her eccentric chauffeur, sprawled like a drugged medieval guard dog at her feet.

The four children, out of sight, were uncannily quiet, and the door to Martin's room, his den, was closed on silence.

I opened this door immediately and found Bon-Bon there, lying full-length on the wood block floor. Again, as with Lloyd Baxter, I knelt to feel for a pulse in the neck, but this time with sharp anxiety; and I felt the living *ga-bump ga-bump* with a deeper relief. Concentrating on Bon-Bon, I saw too late in peripheral sight a movement behind my right shoulder . . . a dark figure speeding from where he'd been hiding behind the door.

I jerked halfway to standing but wasn't quick enough on my feet. There was a short second in which I glimpsed a small metal gas cylinder—more or less like a quarter-sized fire extinguisher. But this cylinder wasn't red. It was orange. It hit my head. Martin's den turned gray, dark gray, and black. A deep well of nothing.

I RETURNED SLOWLY TO a gallery of watchers. To a row of eyes dizzily in front of my own. I couldn't think where I was or what was happening. It had to be bad, though, because the children's eyes looked huge with fright.

I was lying on my back. Into the blank spaces of memory slowly crept the picture of an orange gas cylinder in the hands of a figure in a black head mask with holes cut out for eyes.

As a return to awareness grew clearer I focused on Bon-Bon's face and tried to stand up. Bon-Bon, seeing this minor revival, said with great relief, "Thank God you're all right. We've all been gassed and we've all been sick since we woke up. Totter to the loo next door, there's a chum. Don't throw up in here."

I had a headache, not nausea. My head had collided with the outside of a metal gas cylinder, not with the contents. I felt too lethargic to explain the difference.

Worthington, notwithstanding the muscular physique he painstakingly developed by regular visits to a punch-bag gym, looked pale and shaky and far from well. He held each of the two youngest children by the hand, though, giving them what comfort and confidence he could. In their eyes he could do everything, and they were nearly right.

Bon-Bon had once mentioned that Worthington's top value

to her mother was his understanding of bookmakers' methods, because, as Marigold herself disliked walking along between the rows of men shouting the odds, Worthington got her the best prices. A versatile and compulsive good guy, Worthington, though he didn't always look it.

Only Marigold herself was now missing from the sick parade. I asked about her, and the eldest of the children, a boy called Daniel, said she was drunk. She was snoring on the stairs, the elder girl said. So pragmatic, 2000-year children.

While I peeled myself slowly off the wood blocks Bon-Bon, with annoyance, remarked that her doctor had announced he no longer made house calls, even for those recovering from bereavement. He said all would be well with rest and fluid. "Water," he'd said.

"Gin," corrected one of the children dryly.

I thought it scandalous that Bon-Bon's doctor should have refused to tend her and had a go at him myself. Capitulating with apologetic grace, he promised he would "look in," New Year's Day holiday notwithstanding. He hadn't understood Mrs. Stukely, he excused himself. He didn't realize she'd been *attacked*. She'd been partly incoherent. Had we informed the police?

It did seem obvious that robbery had been the purpose of the mass anesthesia. Three television sets with integral tape players were missing. Bon-Bon had been angry enough to count things.

Also gone was a separate video player on which she'd been watching Martin, together with dozens of tapes. Two laptop computers, with printers and racks of filing disks, were missing too, but Worthington prophesied that the police would offer little hope of recovering these things, as Martin had apparently not recorded any identifying numbers anywhere.

Bon-Bon began crying quietly from the strain of it all and it was Worthington, recovering and worth his weight in video-tapes, who talked to the overburdened local police station. My constable, Catherine Dodd, he found, was attached to a different branch. Detectives, however, would arrive on the Stukely doorstep soon.

Not surprisingly, the THOMPSON ELECTRONICS van had gone.

Marigold went on snoring on the stairs.

Worthington made calming sandwiches of banana and honey for the children.

Feeling queasy, I sat in Martin's black leather chair in his den, while Bon-Bon, on an opposite sofa, dried her complicated grief on tissues and finally gave no complete answer to my repeated question, which was, "What was on the tape that Martin meant to give me after the races, and where did it come from? That's to say, who gave it to Martin himself at Cheltenham?"

Bon-Bon studied me with wet eyes and blew her nose. She said, "I know Martin wanted to tell you something yesterday, but he had those other men in the car, and I know he wanted to talk to you without Priam listening, so he planned to take you home last, after the others, even though you live nearest to the racetrack . . ." Even in distress she looked porcelain pretty, the plumpness an asset in a curvy black wool suit cut to please a living husband rather than a mourning neighborhood.

"He trusted you," she said finally.

"*Mm.*" I'd have been surprised if he hadn't.

"No, you don't understand." Bon-Bon hesitated and went on slowly. "He knew a secret. He wouldn't tell me what it was. He said I would fret. But he wanted to tell *someone.* We did discuss *that,* and I agreed it should be you. *You* should be his backup. Just in case. Oh dear . . . He had what he wanted you to know put onto a plain old-fashioned recording tape, not onto a CD or a computer disk, and he did that, I think, because whoever was giving him information preferred it that way. I'm not sure. And also it was easier to play, he said. Better on video than computer because, darling Gerard, you know I never get things right when it comes to computers. The children laugh at me. I can play a videotape easily. Martin wanted me to be able to do that if he died, but of course . . . of *course* . . . he didn't think he'd die, not really."

I asked, "Could you yourself make a home movie on a video-tape?"

She nodded. "Martin gave me a video camera for Christmas. It makes your own home films but I've hardly had time to learn how to use it."

"And he didn't say *anything* about what was on that tape he meant for me?"

"He was awfully careful not to."

I shook my head in frustration. The tape stolen from the glass showroom was surely the one with the secret on it. The one passed to Martin, then to Eddie the valet, and then to me. Yet if the Broadway thieves, or thief, had viewed it—and they'd had all night to do so—why were they needing to rob Martin's house ten hours later?

Did the tape taken from the showroom actually contain Martin's secret?

Perhaps not.

Was the second robbery carried out by a *different* thief, who didn't know about the first one?

I had no answers, only guesses.

Marigold at that point tottered into the den as if coming to pieces in all directions. I had been used to Marigold for the four years since Martin had straightfacedly presented me to his buxom mother-in-law, a magnified version of his pretty wife. Marigold could be endlessly witty or tiresomely belligerent according to the gin level, but this time the effect of gas on alcohol seemed to have resulted in pity-me pathos, a state that aroused genuine sympathy, not serve-you-right.

In Bon-Bon's house it was the police that turned up first, and Bon-Bon's children who described down to the laces on his shoes the clothes worn by their attacker. He had stared with wide eyes through his black head mask while he'd pointed the orange cylinder at them and squirted a nearly invisible but fierce mist, sweeping from face to face and knocking them out before they'd realized what was happening. Asked about it, Daniel, the eldest child, described the black-masked man having something white tied over his face underneath. An elementary gas mask, I surmised. Something to prevent the robber from inhaling his own gas.

Worthington had been attacked most strongly and had fallen unconscious first, and Bon-Bon—in the den—last. The gas had perhaps been exhausted by the time I arrived; a direct bang on the head had sufficed.

Worthington had been right in guessing the police would offer no hope of Bon-Bon ever again seeing the missing goods. She felt less pain than I would have expected over the loss of tapes showing Martin winning the Grand National because, as she explained, she could get duplicates.

Scarcely had the police notebooks been folded away than Bon-Bon's doctor hurried in without apology, giving the impression he was making an exception, out of the goodness of his heart.

It was the color orange that slowed him into frowns and more thorough care. He and the police all listened to Daniel, brought out paper, and took notes. The doctor told the departing detectives to look for villains with access to the anesthetic gas cyclopropane, which came in orange cylinders, and wasn't much used because of being highly flammable and explosive.

Slowly, after decently thorough peerings into eyes and throats and careful stethoscope chest checks, each of the family was judged fit to go on living. Sweet Bon-Bon, when her house was finally free of official attention, sat sprawling on the office sofa telling me she was utterly exhausted and needed help. Specifically she needed *my* help and Martin would have asked for it.

So I stayed and looked after things, and because of that I saved myself at least another sore head, as thieves broke into my house on the hill that night and stole everything that could remotely be called a videotape.

On Monday, after an early-morning session in the workshop making new little items for stock, I went to Cheltenham races again (by taxi) to talk to Martin's valet, Eddie Payne.

Ed or Eddie (he answered to both) was ready to help, he said, but he couldn't. He'd spent all weekend thinking it over and he said, his gaze darting over my shoulder and back again to my face, he couldn't—however hard he tried—remember any more than he'd told me on Friday. I thought back to the moment of empathy between us, when we had each realized what we'd lost. That moment of genuine emptiness had gone.

The difference between Friday and Monday was a fierce-eyed woman approaching forty, now standing a pace or two behind me, a woman Ed referred to as his daughter. He slid a second glance at her expressionlessly and like a ventriloquist not moving his lips, said to me almost too quietly for me to hear, "*She* knows the man who gave Martin the tape."

The woman said sharply, "What did you say, Dad? Do speak up."

"I said we'd miss Martin badly," Eddie said, "and I'm due back in the changing room. Tell Gerard—Mr. Logan—what he wants to know, why don't you?"

He walked away with a worried shuffle, apologetically saying to me as he went, "Her name's Rose; she's a good girl really."

Rose, the good girl, gave me such a bitter flash of hate that I wondered what I'd ever done to annoy her, as I hadn't known of her existence until moments earlier. She was angularly bony and had mid-brown hair with frizzy sticking-out curls. Her skin was dry and freckled, and although her clothes looked too big for the thin body inside, there was about her an extraordinary air of magnetism.

"Er . . . Rose . . . ," I started.

"Mrs. Robins," she interrupted abruptly.

I cleared my throat and tried again.

"Mrs. Robins, then, could I buy you some coffee, or a drink in the bar?"

She said, "No, you could *not*." She bit the words off with emphasis. She said, "You'd do better to mind your own business."

"Mrs. Robins, did you see who gave a brown paper–wrapped parcel to Martin Stukely at Cheltenham races last Friday?"

Such a simple question. She primped her lips together tightly, swiveled on her heel, and walked away with an air of not intending to come back.

After a short pause, I followed her. Looking down from time to time at my racecard as any prospective punter would, I trickled along in her wake as she made for the ranks of bookmakers' pitches in front of the open-to-the-public Tattersalls stands. She stopped at a board announcing ARTHUR ROBINS, PRESTWICK, ESTABLISHED 1894, and talked to an Elvis Presley lookalike with heavy black side whiskers, who was standing on a box, leaning down to take money from the public and dictating his transactions to a clerk, who was punching the bets into a computer.

Rose Robins, established long after 1894, had a fair amount to say. The Elvis lookalike frowned, listening, and I retreated: I might have strength and reasonable agility but Rose's contact made my muscle power look the stuff of kindergartens. Whichever Robins filled the shoes of Arthur nowadays, if he were the Elvis lookalike, he weighed in with grandfather-gorilla shoulders.

Patiently I climbed the stands and waited while the Arthur Robins, Est. 1894, bookmakers—three of them—took bets on the final two races of the afternoon, and then I watched their chief, the Elvis lookalike, pack up the board and take charge of the money bag and walk towards the exit with Rose and his two helpers beside him. I watched them go out of sight. As far as I could tell, they all left the racetrack. As a group, they equaled an armored tank.

From experience with Martin, I knew that jockeys' valets finished their work after most of the crowds had gone home. A valet was the man who helped the jockeys change rapidly between races. He also looked after and cleaned their gear, saddles, britches, boots and so on, so it was all ready for the next time they raced. Martin had told me that a single valet would look after a whole bunch of jockeys and the valets would work as a team to cover all the race meetings. While Eddie packed up his hamper of saddles, kit and clothes for laundering, I waited with hope for him to reappear out of the changing room at the end of his day.

When he came out and saw me, he was at first alarmed, and then resigned.

"I suppose," he said, "Rose wouldn't tell you."

"No," I agreed. "So would you ask her something, for Martin's sake?"

"Well . . ." He hesitated. "It depends."

I said, "Ask her if the tape Martin gave you was the one he thought it was."

He took a few seconds to work it out.

"Do you mean," he asked doubtfully, "that my Rose thinks Martin had the wrong tape?"

"I think," I confessed, "that if Martin's tape ever surfaces after all the muddle and thieving, it'll be a matter of luck."

He protested self-righteously that he'd given me Martin's tape in good faith. I insisted that I believed him. No more was said about Rose.

Eddie knew, as did the whole racing world after that day's newspapers, that Martin's funeral was planned for Thursday, provided no jinx upset Wednesday's inquest. Eddie, eyes down, mumbled a few words about seeing me there, he supposed, and in discomfort hurried away to the inner realms of the changing rooms, from where the public with awkward questions were banned.

Rose Robins and her enmity added complexity to an already tangled situation.

I caught a bus from the racetrack which wound its way from village to village and, in the end, to Broadway. In spite of my having spent all the time tossing around in my mind the unexpected involvement of Eddie's scratchy daughter I came to no more satisfactory or original conclusion than that someone had given some tape or other to Martin, who had given it to Eddie, who had given it to me, who had carelessly lost it to a thief.

Still drifting in outer space was whatever confidential data Martin had meant to entrust to me. In some respects that didn't matter, and never would, just as long as the hidden nugget of information didn't heat up or collide with an inconvenient truth. Additionally, as I had no road map to the ingredients of the nugget, I had no way of either foreseeing or preventing trouble.

Unrealistically, I simply hoped that Martin's secret would remain forever hidden in uncharted orbit, and all of us could return to normal.

It was after five-thirty by the time I reached the doors of Logan Glass, and again my assistants were there, two of them making paperweights with enthusiasm and the third keeping shop. Bon-Bon had telephoned, they told me, saying she was begging me to go on organizing her household in return for transport; at least until after the funeral, and, much to the amusement of my assistants, the transport she sent that afternoon wasn't her own runabout, but was Marigold's Rolls.

Whenever we were alone together, I sat beside Worthington as he drove. He had offered me the comfort and prestige of the rear seat usually taken by his employer, but I felt wrong there. Moreover, on the showing of the last few days, if I sat in the back he tended both to call me "sir" and to favor respectful silence instead of pithy and irreverent observation. When I sat in the front, Marigold was "Marigold"; when in the back, "Mrs. Knight." When I sat beside her chauffeur, he showed his inner self.

In addition to being bald, fifty and kind to children, Worthington disliked the police force as a matter of principle, referred to marriage as bondage and believed in the usefulness of being able to outkick any other muscle man in sight. It wasn't so much as a chauffeur that I now valued Worthington at my elbow, but as a prospective bodyguard. The Elvis lookalike had radiated latent menace at an intensity that I hadn't met before and didn't like; and for a detonator there was fierce, thorny Rose, and it was with her in mind that I casually asked Worthington if he'd ever placed a bet at the races with Arthur Robins, Est. 1894.

"For a start," he said with sarcasm, fastening his seat belt as if keeping to the law were routine, "the Robins family don't exist. That bunch of swindlers known as Arthur Robins are mostly Veritys and Webbers, with a couple of Browns thrown in. There hasn't been a bona-fide Arthur Robins *ever*. It's just a pretty name."

Eyebrows raised in surprise, I asked, "How do you know all that?"

"My old man ran a book," he said. "Fasten your seat belt, Gerard, the cops in this town would put eagles out of business. Like I said, my old man was a bookmaker, he taught me the trade. You've got to be real sharp at figures, though, to make a profit, and I never got quick enough. But Arthur Robins, that's the front name for some whizzers of speed merchants. Don't bet with them, that's my advice."

I said, "Do you know that Eddie Payne, Martin's valet, has a daughter called Rose who says her last name is Robins and who's on cuddling terms with an Elvis Presley lookalike taking bets for Arthur Robins?"

Worthington, who had been about to start the car outside Logan Glass to drive us to Bon-Bon, sat back in his seat, letting his hands fall laxly on his thighs.

"No," he said thoughtfully, "I didn't know that." He thought for a while, his forehead troubled. "That Elvis fellow," he said finally, "that's Norman Osprey. You don't want to mix with *him*."

"And Rose?"

Worthington shook his head. "I don't know her. I'll ask around." He roused himself and started the car.

B Y T H U R S D A Y , T H E day of Martin's funeral, the police as predicted hadn't found one identifiable videotape in a country awash with them.

On the day before the funeral a young woman on a motor-bike—huge helmet, black leather jacket, matching pants, heavy boots—steered into one of the five parking spaces at the front of Logan Glass. Outside in the January chill she pulled off the helmet and shook free a cap of fair fine hair before walking without swag-ger into the gallery and showroom as if she knew the way well.

I was putting the pre-annealing final touches to a vase, with Pamela Jane telling a group of American tourists how it was done, but there was something attention-claiming about the motorcyclist, and as soon as I thought of her in terms of glass, I knew her infallibly.

"Catherine Dodd," I said.

"Most people don't recognize me." She was amused, not piqued.

With interest I watched the tourists pack somewhat closer to-gether as if to elbow out the stranger in threatening clothes.

Pamela Jane finished her spiel and one of the American men said the vases were too expensive, even if they were handmade and handsome. He collected nods and all-around agreement, and there was relief in the speed with which the tourists settled instead on simple dolphins and little dishes. While Hickory wrapped the parcels and wrote out bills, I asked the motorcyclist if there were any news of my lost tape.

She watched me handle the vase in heatproof fiber and put it to cool in the annealing oven.

"I'm afraid," said Detective Constable Dodd in plain—well, plainer—clothes, "your tape is gone for good."

I told her it held a secret.

"What secret?"

"That's the point, I don't know. Martin Stukely told his wife he was giving me a secret on tape for safekeeping—that's a bit of a laugh—in case he was killed in a car crash, or something like that."

"Like a steeplechase?"

"He didn't expect it."

Catherine Dodd's detective mind trod the two paths I'd reluc-tantly followed myself since Norman Osprey and his Elvis side-burns had appeared on my horizon. First, *someone* knew Martin's secret, and second, *someone,* and maybe not the same someone, could infer that, one way or another, that secret was known to me. Someone might suppose I'd watched that tape during the evening of Martin's death, and for safety had wiped it off.

I hadn't had a tape player on the Logan Glass premises, but the Dragon over the road made one available generously to the paying guests, and she distributed brochures by the hundred advertising this.

"If I'd had a tape player handy," I said, "I probably *would* have run that tape through early in the evening, and if I thought it awful I *might* have wiped it off."

"That's not what your friend Martin wanted."

After a brief silence I said, "If he'd been sure of what he wanted he wouldn't have fiddled about with tapes, he would just have *told* me this precious secret." I stopped abruptly. "There are too many *ifs*. How about you coming out for a drink?"

"Can't. Sorry. I'm on duty." She gave me a brilliant smile. "I'll call in another day. And oh! There's just one loose end." She produced the ever essential notebook from inside her jacket. "What are your assistants' names?"

"Pamela Jane Evans and John Irish and John Hickory. We leave off John for the men and use their last names, as it's easier."

"Which is the elder?"

"Irish. He's about ten years older than both Hickory and Pamela Jane."

"And how long have they all worked for you?"

"Pamela Jane about a year, Irish and Hickory two to three months longer. They're all good guys, believe me."

"I do believe you. This is just for the records. This is actually . . . er . . . what I dropped in for."

I looked at her straightly. She all but blushed.

"I'd better go now," she said.

With regret I walked with her as far as the door, where she paused to say good-bye as she didn't want to be seen with me too familiarly out in the street. She left, in fact, in the bunch of winter tourists, all of them overshadowed by the loud voice of a big man who judged the whole afternoon a waste of time and complained about it all the way back to the group's warm tour bus. His broad back obscured my view of the departure of Detective Constable Dodd, and I surprised myself by minding about that quite a lot.

On Bon-Bon's telephone, the night before Martin's funeral, I learned from the Dragon herself that Lloyd Baxter had deemed it correct to fly down for "his jockey's last ride" (as he put it) but hadn't wanted to stay with Priam Jones, whom he was on the point of ditching as his trainer. The Dragon chuckled and went on mischievously, "You didn't have to go all that way to stay with Bon-Bon Stukely, if you didn't fancy sleeping in your burgled house, lover boy. You could have stayed here with me."

"News gets around," I said dryly.

"You're always news in this town, lover, didn't you know?"

In truth I did know it, but I didn't feel it.

On the evening before Martin's funeral Priam Jones telephoned, meaning to talk to Bon-Bon, but reaching me instead. I had been fielding commiserations for her whenever I was around. Marigold, Worthington and even the children had grown expert at thanks and tact. I thought how Martin would have grinned at the all-around grade-A improvement in his family's social skills.

Priam blustered on a bit, but was, I gathered, offering himself as an usher in the matter of seating. Remembering his spontaneous tears I put him on the list and asked him if, before he'd picked me up from my home on Friday morning, Martin had by any chance mentioned that he was expecting delivery of a tape at the races.

"You asked me that the day after he died," Priam said impatiently. "The answer is still yes, he said we wouldn't leave the racetrack until he'd collected some package or other to give to you. And I did give it to you, don't you remember? I brought it back to Broadway after you'd left it in your raincoat in the car . . . Well, I'll see you tomorrow, Gerard. Give my regards to Bon-Bon."

Also on the evening before Martin's funeral, Eddie Payne went to his local Catholic church and in the confessional recited his past and present sins, asking for pardon and absolution. He told me this with self-righteousness when I intercepted his condolences to Bon-Bon. He'd tried and tried to get someone else to do his racetrack work, he said, but such was life, he hadn't succeeded, and he'd have to miss the funeral, and it grieved him sorely as he'd been Martin's racetrack valet for six or seven years. Eddie, to my disparaging ear, had plucked up half a bottle of dutch courage before stretching out his hand to the phone, and wouldn't remain long in a state of grace owing to his distance from the fact that he could have more easily got stand-ins to free him to go to that particular funeral than if it had been for his own grandmother.

On the same evening, before Martin's funeral (though I didn't learn of it until later), Ed Payne's daughter, Rose, described to a small group of fascinated and ruthless knaves how to force Gerard Logan to tell them the secret he'd been given at Cheltenham races.

CHAPTER 3

ON THE FIRST Thursday of January, the sixth day of the next thousand years, I, with Priam Jones and four senior jump jockeys, carried Martin into church in his coffin and later delivered him to his grave.

The sun shone on frosty trees. Bon-Bon looked ethereal, Marigold stayed fairly sober, Worthington took off his chauffeur's cap, baring his bald pate in respect, the four children knocked with their knuckles on the coffin as if they could wake their father inside, Lloyd Baxter read a short but decent eulogy and all the racing world, from the Stewards of the Jockey Club to the men who replaced the divots, everyone crowded into the pews in church and packed the wintry churchyard grass outside, standing on the moss-grown ancient slabs of stone. Martin had been respected, and respects were paid.

The new burial ground lay on a hillside a mile away by hearse and heavy limousines. Among banks of flowers there Bon-Bon cried as the man who'd quarreled with her daily sank into the quiet embracing earth, and I, who'd stage-managed the second farewell party in a month (my mother the other), prosaically checked that the caterers had brought enough hot toddy and that the choristers were paid, along with other mundane greasings of the expensive wheels of death.

After the hundreds who had turned up for Martin had drunk and eaten and had kissed Bon-Bon and left, I sought her out to say my own good-bye. She was standing with Lloyd Baxter, asking about his health. "*Do* take the pills," she was saying, and he with embarrassment promised he would. He nodded to me coldly as if he had never brought Dom Pérignon to me for company.

I congratulated Baxter on his eulogy. He received the praise as his due, and stiffly invited me to dine with him in the Wychwood Dragon.

"Don't go," Bon-Bon exclaimed to me, alarmed. "Stay here one more night. You and Worthington have tamed the children. Let's have this one more night of peace."

Thinking of Martin, I excused myself to Baxter and stayed to help Bon-Bon, and after midnight, when only I was awake, I sat in Martin's squashy chair in his den and thought intently of him. Thought of his life and of what he'd achieved, and thought eventually about that last day at Cheltenham, and about the videotape and whatever he'd had recorded on it.

I had no minutest idea what he could have known that needed such complex safekeeping. I did see that, much as I thought Bon-Bon a darling and as sweet as her name, she wasn't the most reticent person on earth. To Bon-Bon a secret would be safe until her next nice chat with her best friend. Many of hers and Martin's shouting matches had been the result of Bon-Bon repeating publicly what she'd been privately told or overheard about some horse or other's prospects.

I slouched in Martin's chair, deep in regret. One had so few close friends in life. None to spare. His personality filled the room to the extent that it seemed that if I turned I would see him standing by his bookcase, looking up some race's result in the form book. The feeling of his presence was so intense that I actually swiveled his chair around to see, but of course there were only books, row on row, and no Martin.

It was time, I supposed, to make sure the outside doors were locked and to sleep away the last hours in Martin's house. I'd lent him a couple of books a few weeks earlier on ancient glass-making techniques, and as they were lying on the long table by the sofa, it seemed a good time to pick them up to take home without bothering Bon-Bon too much. One of the things I would most miss was, I thought nostalgically, Martin's constant interest in historic difficult-to-make goblets and bowls.

In the morning, saying good-bye, I mentioned I was taking the books. "Fine, fine," Bon-Bon said vaguely. "I wish you weren't going."

She was lending me Worthington to drive me in her white runabout to Broadway. "If you weren't getting your butt out of that house pronto," Worthington said bluntly as we drove away, "Bon-Bon would catch you like a Venus flytrap."

"She's unhappy," I protested.

"Sticky, attractive, and once caught, you can't escape." Worthington grinned. "Don't say I haven't warned you."

"And Marigold?" I teased him. "How's the Marigold flytrap?"

"I can leave her any day I want," he protested, and drove for miles smiling, as if he believed it.

Stopping to unload me at my gallery door in Broadway, he said more seriously, "I got a low-life investigator to ask about that woman, Rose." He paused. "He didn't get much further than you did. Eddie Payne thinks she saw who gave that damned tape to Martin, but I wouldn't rely on it. Eddie's afraid of his own daughter, if you ask me."

I agreed with him on that, and we left it there. My three assistants welcomed me back to a regular workday, and I taught Hickory—as I'd taught Pamela Jane before Christmas—how to collect a third gather of glass, so hot that it was red and semi-liquid, and fell in a heavy teardrop shape that drooped towards the floor (and one's feet) if one didn't marver it fast enough on the steel table. He knew how to press its lengthened tip into long heaps of dustlike colors before returning the revolving head into the heat of the furnace to keep the now-heavy chunk of glass at working temperature. I showed him how to gather glass neatly on the end of a blowing iron, before lifting it into the air ready to blow, and how to keep the resulting slightly ballooned shape constant while he continued to develop his ideas towards a final goal.

Hickory watched the continuous process with anxious eyes and said that, like Pamela Jane when she'd tried it, he couldn't go the whole way.

"Of course not. Practice handling three gathers. You can do two now easily."

A gather was the amount of molten glass that could be brought out of the tank at one time on the tip of the steel punty rod. A gather could be of any size, according to the skill and strength of the glassblower. Glass in bulk, very heavy, demanded muscle.

Owing to the space limitation of tourist suitcases, few pieces of "Logan Glass" sold in the shop were of more than three gathers. Pamela Jane, to her sorrow, had never quite mastered the swing-upwards-and-blow technique. Irish, in spite of enthusiasm, would never be a top-rated glassblower. Of Hickory, though, I had hopes. He had ease of movement and, most important, a lack of fear.

Glassblowers were commonly arrogant people, chiefly because the skill was so difficult to learn. Hickory already showed signs of arrogance but if he became a notable expert he would have to be forgiven. As for myself, my uncle (as arrogant as they came) had insisted that I learn humility first, second and third, and had refused to let me near his furnace until I'd shed every sign of what he called "cockiness."

"Cockiness" had broken out regularly after his death, humbling me when I recognized it. It had taken perhaps ten years before I had it licked, but vigilance would be necessary for life.

Irish had grown accustomed to brewing the large jugs of hot

tea to replace the sweat lost to the furnace. I sat on a box and drank thirstily and all day watched my apprentice improve considerably, even though, with exhausted rests, there was generally a lot of swearing and a whole heap of shattered glass.

There were, of course, few customers to interrupt the lesson and by five o'clock on this bleakly cold January afternoon I sent my three helpers home and with gloom did some long-overdue paperwork. The cash stolen on New Year's Eve left a depressing hole in what was otherwise a cheerful season. It wasn't difficult after a while to lay aside the minus figures and pick up the books I'd lent to Martin.

My favorite of all historic goblets was a glowing red cup, six and a half inches high (16.5 centimeters), constructed around the year three hundred and something A.D. (a fair time ago, when one looked back from two thousand). It was made of lumps of glass, held fast in an intricate gold cage (a technique from before blowing was invented), and would appear green in different lights. Flicking through the early pages in one of the books, I came across the goblet's picture with my usual pleasure and a few pages later smiled over the brilliant gold and blue glass Cretan sunrise necklace that I'd once spent days copying. Sleepily, I by accident let the book begin to slide off my knees towards the smooth brick floor and, by luck, caught it without damage to its glossy construction.

Relieved at the catch, and berating myself for such clumsiness in not holding on more tightly to a valued treasure, I didn't notice at first a thin buff envelope that lay at my feet. With a reaction accelerating from puzzlement to active curiosity I laid the old book down carefully and picked up the new-looking envelope, which I supposed had been held within the leaves and had fallen out when I made my grab.

The envelope from inside my book was addressed by computer printer not to me but to Martin Stukely, Esq., Jockey.

I had no qualms at all in taking out the single-page letter inside, and reading it.

Dear Martin,
You are right, it is the best way. I will take the tape, as you want,
to Cheltenham races on New Year's Eve.
This knowledge is dynamite.
Take care of it.
Victor Waltman Verity.

The letter too was written on a computer, though the name given as signature had been printed in a different font. There was no address or telephone number on the letter itself, but faintly across the stamp on the envelope there was a round postmark. After long concentration with a magnifying glass, the point of origin seemed to me only "xet" around the top and "evo" around the bottom. The date alone was easily readable, though looking anemic as to ink.

The letter had been sent on 17. xii.99.

December 17. Less than a month ago.

xet

evo

There weren't after all many places in Great Britain with an *x* in their name, and I could think of nowhere else that fitted the available letters other than Exeter, Devon.

When I reached Directory Inquiries, I learned that there was indeed a Victor Verity in Exeter. A disembodied voice said, "The number you require is . . ." I wrote it down, but when I called Victor Verity I spoke not to him, but to his widow. Her dear Victor had passed away during the previous summer. Wrong Verity.

I tried Inquiries again.

"Very sorry," said a prim voice, not sounding it, "there is no other Victor or V. Verity in the Exeter telephone area which covers most of Devon."

"How about an ex-directory number?"

"Sorry, I can't give you that information."

Victor Waltman Verity was either ex-directory or had mailed his letter far from home.

Cursing him lightly I glanced with reluctance at the money job half done on my computer . . . and there, of course, lay the answer. Computers. Internet.

The Internet among other miracles might put an address to a name anywhere, that's to say it would if I could remember the open sesame code. I entered my Internet-access number and typed in my password, and sat hopefully, flicking mentally through possibilities as the machine burped and whined until a connection was made.

After a while a website address drifted into my mind, but it was without certainty that I tried it: www.192.com.

192.com was right.

I started a search for Verity in Devon, and as if eager to be of service, the Internet, having surveyed every fact obtainable in the public domain (such as the electoral registers), came up with a total of twenty-two Devon-based Veritys, but none of them any longer was Victor.

Dead end.

I tried Verity in Cornwall: sixteen but still no Victor.

Try Somerset, I thought. Not a Victor Verity in sight.

Before reaching to switch off, I skimmed down the list and at the end of it noticed that at No. 19 Lorna Terrace, Taunton, Somerset, there lived a Mr. *Waltman* Verity. Good enough to try, I thought.

Armed with the address I tried Directory Inquiries again, but ran up against the same polite barrier of virtual nonexistence. Ex-directory. Sorry. Too bad.

Although Saturday was a busier day in the showroom, my thoughts returned continuously to Taunton and Victor Waltman Verity.

Taunton . . . Having nothing much else urgently filling my Sunday, I caught a westbound train the next morning, and asked directions to Lorna Terrace.

Whatever I expected Victor Waltman Verity to look like, it was nothing near the living thing. Victor Waltman Verity must have been all of fifteen.

The door of No. 19 was opened by a thin woman dressed in pants, sweater and bedroom slippers, with a cigarette in one hand and big pink curlers in her hair. Thirty something, perhaps forty, I thought. Easygoing, with a resigned attitude to strangers on her doorstep.

"Er . . . Mrs. Verity?" I asked.

"Yeah. What is it?" She sucked smoke, unconcerned.

"Mrs. Victor Waltman Verity?"

She laughed. "I'm Mrs. Waltman Verity, Victor's my son." She shouted over her shoulder towards the inner depths of the narrow terraced house. "Vic, someone to see you," and while we waited for Victor Waltman Verity to answer the call, Mrs. Verity looked me over thoroughly from hair to sneakers and went on enjoying a private giggle.

Victor Waltman Verity appeared quietly from along the narrow hallway and regarded me with curiosity mixed, I thought, with the possibility of alarm. He himself was as tall as his mother, as tall as Martin. He had dark hair, pale gray eyes and an air of knowing himself to be as intelligent as any adult. His voice, when he spoke, was at the cracked stage between boy and man, and his face had begun to grow from the soft lines of childhood into adult planes.

"What've you been up to, young Vic?" his mother asked, and to me she said, "It's bloody cold out here. Want to come in?"

"Er," I said. I was suffering more from the unexpected than the cold, but she waited for no answer and walked back past the boy until she was out of sight. I pulled the envelope sent to Martin out of a pocket and immediately set the alarm racing above the curiosity in young Victor.

"You weren't supposed to find me," he exclaimed, "and in any case, you're dead."

"I'm not Martin Stukely," I said.

"Oh." His face went blank. "No, of course, you aren't." Puzzlement set in. "I mean, what do you want?"

"First of all," I said plainly, "I'd like to accept your mother's invitation."

"Huh?"

"To be warm."

"Oh! I get you. The kitchen is warmest."

"Lead on, then."

He shrugged and stretched to close the door behind me, and then led the way down beside the staircase to the heart of all such terrace houses, the space where life was lived. There was a central table covered with a patterned plastic cloth, four attendant unmatched upright chairs and a sideboard deep in clutter. A television set stood aslant on a draining board otherwise stacked with unwashed dishes, and checked vinyl tiles covered the floor.

In spite of the disorganization there was bright new paint and nothing disturbingly sordid. I had an overall impression of yellow.

Mrs. Verity sat in one of the chairs, rocking on its back legs and gulping smoke as if she lived on it.

She said pleasantly enough, "We get all sorts of people here, what with Vic and his wretched Internet. We'll get a full-sized genie one of these days, I shouldn't wonder." She gestured vaguely to one of the chairs, and I sat on it.

"I was a friend of Martin Stukely," I explained, and I asked Vic what was on the videotape that he had sent or given to Martin at Cheltenham.

"Yes, well, there wasn't a tape," he said briefly. "I didn't go to Cheltenham."

I pulled his letter to Martin out of the envelope and gave it to him to read.

He shrugged again and handed it back when he'd reached the end.

"It was just a game. I made up the tape." He was nervous, all the same.

"What knowledge was it that was dynamite?"

"Look, none." He grew impatient. "I told you. I made it up."

"Why did you send it to Martin Stukely?"

I was careful not to let the questions sound too aggressive, but in some way that I didn't understand, they raised all his defenses and colored his cheeks red.

His mother said to me, "What's all this about a tape? Do you mean a *video*tape? Vic hasn't got any videotapes. We're going to get a new video machine any day now, then it will be different."

I explained apologetically. "Someone did give Martin a videotape at Cheltenham races. Martin gave it to Ed Payne, his valet, to keep safe, and Ed gave it to me, but it was stolen before I could see what was on it. Then all the videotapes in Martin Stukely's house and all the videotapes in my own house were stolen too."

"I hope you're not suggesting that *Vic* stole anything, because I can promise you he wouldn't." Mrs Verity had grasped one suggestion wrongly and hadn't listened clearly to the rest, so she too advanced to the edge of anger, and I did my best to retreat and placate, but her natural good humor had been dented, and her welcome had evaporated. She stubbed out a cigarette instead of lighting another from it, and stood up as a decisive signal that it was time I left.

I said amiably to young Victor, "Call me," and although he shook his head I wrote my mobile number on the margin of a Sunday newspaper.

Then I stepped out of No. 19 Lorna Terrace and walked unhurriedly along the street pondering two odd unanswered questions.

First, how did Victor happen to come to Martin's attention?

Second, why had neither mother nor son asked my name?

LORNA TERRACE CURVED sharply to the left, taking No. 19 out of sight behind me.

I paused there, wondering whether or not to go back. I was conscious of not having done very well. I'd set off expecting to unearth the mysteries of the videotape, if not with ease, then actually without extreme trouble. Instead I seemed to have screwed up even what I'd thought I understood.

Irresolutely I wasted time and missed the train I'd thought of catching. I might be OK at glass, but not excellent at Sherlock Holmes. Dim Doctor Watson, that was me. It grew dark and it took me a long time to reach Broadway. Luckily, I found a willing neighbor on the train to give me a lift from the station.

Without Martin, I reflected with depression, I was either going to spend a fortune on cabs or thumb a thousand lifts. There were still eighty-one days before I could apply to get my license-to-speed out of the freezer.

I thanked my generous companion with a wave as he drove away, and fishing out a small bunch of keys, I plodded towards the gallery door. Sunday evening. No one about. Brilliant lights shining from Logan Glass.

I hadn't learned yet to beware of shadows. Figures in black materialized from the deep entrance to the antique bookshop next door and from the dark line of the trash bins put out ready for collection on Monday morning.

I suppose there were four of them leaping about in the dark; an impression, not an accurate count. Four was profligate, anyway. Three, two, maybe only one could have done the job. I guessed they'd been waiting there for a long time and it hadn't improved their temper.

I hadn't expected another physical attack. The memory of the orange cylinder of cyclopropane had faded. The cylinder, I soon found, had delivered a less painful message than the one on my doorstep. This one consisted of multiple bashes and bangs and of being slammed two or three times against the lumpy bit of Cotswold stone wall that joined the bookshop to my own place.

Disorientated by the attack itself, I heard demands as if from a distance that I should disclose information that I knew I didn't have. I tried to tell them. They didn't listen.

All that was annoying enough, but it was their additional aim that lit my own inner protection furnace and put power into half-forgotten techniques of kickboxing left over from my teens.

It seemed that a straightforward pulping was only half their purpose, as a sharp excited voice specifically instructed over and over again, "Break his wrists. Go on. *Break his wrists. . . .*" And later, out of the dark, the same voice exulting, "That got him."

No, it bloody didn't. Pain screeched up my arm. My thoughts were blasphemy. Strong, whole and flexible wrists were as essential to a glassblower as to a gymnast on the Olympic high rings.

Two of the black-clad agile figures waved baseball bats. One with heavily developed shoulders was recognizably Norman Osprey. Looking back later from a huddled sort of collapse on the sidewalk, I saw that only one of those two had the bright idea of holding my fingers tightly together in a bunch against the wall before getting his colleague to aim just below them with the bat.

I had too much to lose and I hadn't been aware of how desperately one could fight when it was the real thing. My wrists didn't get broken but my watch stopped in pieces from a direct hit. There were lumps and bruised areas all over everywhere. A few cuts. Torn skin. Enough. But my fingers worked, and that was all that mattered.

Maybe the fracas would have ended with me taking a fresh hole in the ground beside Martin, but Broadway wasn't a ghost town in a western desert; it was somewhere that people walked their dogs on a Sunday evening, and it was a dog-walker who yelled at my attackers, and with three toothy Dobermans barking and pulling at their leashes, got the shadowy figures to change their minds smartly and vanish as fast as they'd come.

"Gerard *Logan!*" The tall dog-walker, astounded, bending to look at me, knew me by sight, as I did him. "Are you all right?"

No, I wasn't. I said, "Yes," as one does.

He stretched down to help me to my feet, when all I really wanted to do was lie on a soft mattress.

"Shall I call the police?" he asked, though he wasn't a police lover; far from it.

"Tom . . . Thanks. But no police."

"What was it all about?" He sounded relieved. "Are you in trouble? That looked to me like payback business."

"Muggers."

Tom Pigeon, who knew a thing or two about the rocky sides of life, gave me a half-smile, half-disillusioned look, and shortened the leashes of his hungry life preservers. More bark than bite, he'd assured me once. I wasn't certain I believed it.

He himself looked as if he had no need to bark. Although not heavily built and without a wrestler's neck, he had unmistakable physical power, and, at about my own age, a close–cut dark pointed beard that added years of menace.

Tom Pigeon told me there was blood in my hair and said if I would give him my keys he would open the door for me.

"I dropped them," I said and leaned gingerly against the lumpy bit of wall. The dizzy world revolved. I couldn't remember ever before feeling so pulverized or so sick, not even when I'd fallen to the bottom of the scrum in a viciously unfriendly school rugby match and had my shoulder blade broken.

Tom Pigeon persevered until he kicked against my keys and found them by their clinking. He unlocked and opened the gallery door and with his arm around my waist got me as far as the threshold. His dogs stayed watchfully by his legs.

"I better not bring the canines in among your glass, had I?" he said. "You'll be all right now, OK?"

I nodded. He more or less propped me against the door frame and made sure I could stand up before he let go.

Tom Pigeon was known locally as "The Backlash," chiefly on account of being as quick with his wits as his fists. He'd survived unharmed eighteen months inside for aggravated breaking and entering and had emerged as a toughened hotshot, to be spoken of in awe. Whatever his dusty reputation, he had definitely rescued me, and I felt in an extraordinary way honored by the extent of his aid.

He waited until I could visibly control things and stared shrewdly into my eyes. It wasn't exactly friendship that I saw in his, but it was . . . in a way . . . recognition.

"Get a pit bull," he said.

I STEPPED INTO MY bright lights and locked the door against the violence outside. Pity I couldn't as easily blot out the woes of battery. Pity I felt so stupid. So furious. So wobbly, so dangerously mystified.

In the back reaches of the workshop there was running water for rinsing one's face, and a relaxing chair for recovery of all kinds of balance. I sat and ached a lot, and then phoned the taxi firm, who apologized that this Saturday and Sunday had already overstretched their fleet, but they would put me on their priority list from now on . . . yeah . . . yeah . . . never mind . . . I could have done with a double cyclopropane, shaken, with ice. I thought of Worthington, tried for him on the phone, got Bon-Bon instead.

"Gerard darling. I'm so *lonely*." She sounded indeed in sorrowing mode, as her elder son would have put it. "Can't you come over to cheer me up? Worthington will come to fetch you, and I'll drive you home myself. I promise."

I said with regret that I didn't want to give her "flu" (which I hadn't got) and simply went on doing very little through a highly unsatisfactory evening. Worthington's flytrap vision itched. I loved Bon-Bon as a friend, but not as a wife.

At about ten-thirty I fell asleep in the soft chair and half an hour later was awakened again by the doorbell.

Disorientated as I woke, I felt stiff, miserable and totally unwilling to move.

The doorbell rang insistently. I went on feeling shivery and unwilling, but in the end I wavered upright and creaked out of the workshop to see who wanted what at such an hour. Even then, after the dire lessons I'd been given, I hadn't enough sense to carry with me a weapon of defense.

As it happened, my late-evening visitor looked pretty harmless. In addition, she was welcome. More than that, I thought that with a kiss or two and a hug she might prove therapeutic.

Detective Constable Catherine Dodd took her finger off the doorbell when she saw me, and smiled with relief when I let her in.

"We had reports from two separate Broadway residents," she said first. "They apparently saw you being attacked outside here.

But we had no complaint from yourself, even though you were hardly walking, it seemed . . . so anyway, I said I would check on you on my way home."

She again wore motorcycle leathers, and had parked her bike at the curb. With deft speed, as before, she lifted off her helmet and shook her head to loosen her fair hair.

"One of the reports," she added, "said that your attacker had been Tom Pigeon, with his dogs. That man's a damned pest."

"No, no. It was he who got rid of the pests. Really depressing pests."

"Could you identify them?"

I made a noncommittal gesture and meandered vaguely through the showroom to the workshop, pointing to the chair for her to sit down.

She looked at the chair and at the sweat I could feel on my forehead, and sat on the bench normally the domain of Irish, Hickory and Pamela Jane. Gratefully I sank into the soft armchair and half answered her who? and why? queries, not knowing whether they had a police basis or were ordinary curiosity.

She said, "Gerard, I've seen other people in your state."

"Poor them."

"Don't laugh, it's hardly funny."

"Not tragic, either."

"Why haven't you asked my colleagues for more help?"

Well, I thought, why not?

"Because," I said lightly, "I don't know who or why, and every time I think I've learned something, I find I haven't. Your colleagues don't like uncertainty."

She thought that over with more weight than it deserved.

"Tell *me,* then," she said.

"Someone wants something I haven't got. I don't know what it is. I don't know who wants it. How am I doing?"

"That makes nonsense."

I winced and turned it into a smile. "It makes nonsense, quite right." And in addition, I thought to myself with acid humor, I have the Dragon and Bon-Bon on my watch-it list, and policewoman Dodd on my wanted-but-can-I-catch-her list, and Tom Pigeon and Worthington on my save-my-skin list, Rose Payne/Robins on my black-mask-possible list and young Victor Waltman on my can't-or-won't-tell list.

As for Lloyd Baxter and his epilepsy, Eddie Payne keeping and delivering videotapes, Norman Osprey running a book with the massive shoulders of 1894, and dear scatty Marigold, often afloat before breakfast and regularly before lunch, all of them could have tapes on their mind and know every twist in the ball of string.

Constable Dodd frowned, faint lines crossing her smooth clear skin, and as it seemed to be question time I said abruptly, "Are you married?"

After a few seconds, looking down at her ringless hands, she replied, "Why do you ask?"

"You have the air of it."

"He's dead."

She sat for a while without moving, and then asked, "And you?" in calm return.

"Not yet," I said.

Silence could sometimes shout. She listened to what I would probably ask quite soon, and seemed relaxed and content.

The workshop was warmed as always by the furnace, even though the roaring fire was held in control for nights and Sundays by a large screen of heat-resistant material.

Looking at Catherine Dodd's face above the dark close-fitting leather I most clearly now saw her in terms of glass: saw her in fact so vividly that the urge and desire to work at once couldn't be stifled. I stood and unclipped the fireproof screen and put it to one side, and fixed instead the smaller flap, which opened to allow access to the tankful of molten glass.

I pressed extra time into the light switch, overriding the midnight cutoff, and with boringly painful movements took off my jacket and shirt, leaving only normal working gear of bare arms and singlet.

"What are you doing?" She sounded alarmed but had no need to be.

"A portrait," I said. "Sit still." I turned up the heat in the furnace and sorted out the punty blowing irons I would need, and fetched a workable amount of glass manganese powder which would give me black in color eventually.

"But your bruises . . . ," she protested. "Those marks. They're terrible."

"I can't feel them."

I felt nothing indeed except the rare sort of excitement that came with revelation. I'd burned myself often enough on liquid glass and not felt it. That Sunday night the concept of one detective darkly achieving insight into the sins of others, and then the possibility that good could rise above sin and fly, these drifting thoughts set up in me in effect a mental anesthesia, so that I could bleed and suffer on one level and feel it only later after the flame of imagination had done its stuff. Sometimes in the disengagement from this sort of thing, the vision had shrunk to disappointment and ash, and when that happened I would leave the no-good piece on the marver table and not handle it carefully into an annealing oven. After a while, its unresolved internal strains would cause it to self-destruct, to come to pieces dramatically with a cracking noise; to splinter, to fragment . . . to shatter.

It could be for onlookers an unnerving experience, to see an apparently solid object disintegrate for no visible reason. For me the splitting apart symbolized merely the fading and insufficiency of the original thought. On that particular Sunday I had no doubts or hesitation, and I gathered glass in muscle-straining amounts that even on ordinary days would have taxed my ability.

That night I made Catherine Dodd in three pieces that later I would join together. I made not a literal lifelike sculpture of her head, but an abstract of her daily occupation. I made it basically as a soaring upward spread of wings, black and shining at the base, rising through a black, white and clear center to a high rising pinion with streaks of gold shining to the top.

The gold fascinated my subject.

"Is it *real* gold?"

"Iron pyrites. But real gold would melt the same way . . . only I used all I had a week ago."

I gently held the fragile top wing in layers of heatproof fiber and laid it carefully in one of the six annealing ovens, and only then, with all three sections safely cooling, could I hardly bear the strains in my own limbs and felt too like cracking apart myself.

Catherine stood up and took a while to speak. Eventually she cleared her throat and asked what I would do with the finished flight of wings and I, coming down to earth from invention, tried prosaically (as on other such occasions) just to say that I would probably make a pedestal for it in the gallery and light it with a spotlight or two to emphasize its shape.

We both stood looking at each other as if not knowing what else to say. I leaned forward and kissed her cheek, which with mutual small movements became mouth to mouth, with passion in there somewhere, acknowledged but not yet overflowing.

Arms around motorcycle leathers had practical drawbacks. My own physical aches put winces where they weren't wanted, and with rueful humor she disengaged herself and said, "Maybe another time."

"Delete the maybe," I said.

CHAPTER 4

ALL THREE OF my assistants could let themselves in through the gallery with a personal key, and it was Pamela Jane alone whom I saw first with a slit of eyesight when I returned unwillingly to consciousness at about eight o'clock on Monday morning. I'd spent the first hour after Catherine had gone considering the comfort of a Wychwood Dragon bed (without the Dragon herself) but in the end from lack of energy had simply flopped back into the big chair in the workshop and closed my eyes on a shuddering and protesting nervous system.

Catherine herself, real and abstract, had kept me warm and mobile through the darkest hours of night, but she'd left long before dawn, and afterwards sleep, which practically never knitted up any raveled sleave of care, had made things slightly worse.

Pamela Jane said, horrified, "Honestly, you look as if you'd been hit by a steamroller. Have you been here all night?"

The answer must have been obvious. I was unshaven, for a start, and any movement set up quite awful and stiffened reactions. One could almost hear the joints creak. Never again, I promised myself.

I hadn't considered how I was going to explain things to my little team. When I spoke to Pamela Jane, even my voice felt rough.

"Can you . . ." I paused, cleared my throat and tried again. "Pam . . . jug of tea?"

She put her coat in her locker and scurried helpfully around, making the tea and unbolting the side door, which we were obliged to use as a fire escape if necessary. By the advent of Irish I was ignoring the worst, and Hickory, arriving last, found me lifting the three wing sections of the night's work out of the ovens and carefully fitting them together before fusing them into place. All three of my helpers wished they'd seen the separate pieces made. One day, I agreed with them, I would make duplicates to show them.

They couldn't help but notice that I found too much movement a bad idea, but I could have done without Hickory's cheerful assumption it was the aftermath of booze.

The first customer came. Life more or less returned to normal. Irish began building a plinth in the gallery to hold the wings. If

I concentrated on blowing glass, I could forget four black jersey-wool masks with eyeholes.

Later in the morning Marigold's Rolls drew up outside and occupied two of the parking spaces, with Worthington at the wheel looking formal in his badge-of-office cap.

Marigold herself, he reported through his wound-down window, had gone shopping with Bon-Bon in Bon-Bon's car. Both ladies had given him the day off and the use of the Rolls, and he appreciated their generosity, he said solemnly, as he was going to take me to the races.

I looked back at him in indecision.

"I'm not going," I said. "And where am I not going?"

"Leicester. Jump racing. Eddie Payne will be there. Rose will be there. Norman Osprey will be there with his book. I thought you wanted to find out who gave the videotape to Martin. Do you want to know what was on it, or who stole it, and do you want to know who gassed me with the kids and the ladies, or do you want to stay here quietly and make nice little pink vases to sell to the tourists?"

I didn't answer at once and he said judiciously, making allowances, "Mind you, I don't suppose you want another beating like you got last night, so stay here if you like and I'll mooch around by myself."

"Who told you about last night?"

He took off his cap and wiped his bald crown with a white handkerchief.

"A little bird told me. A not so little bird."

"Not . . . a pigeon?"

"Quick, aren't you." He grinned. "Yeah, a Pigeon. It seems he thinks quite a bit of you. He phoned me specially at Bon-Bon's. He says to put it around that in future any hands laid on you are laid on him."

I felt both grateful and surprised. I asked, "How well do you know him?"

He answered obliquely. "You know that gardener of Martin's that was dying? That you lost your license for, speeding to get him there in time?"

"Well, yes, I remember."

"That gardener was Tom Pigeon's dad."

"He didn't die, though. Not then, anyway."

"It didn't matter. Are you coming to Leicester?"

"I guess so."

I went back into the workshop, put on my outdoor clothes and told Irish, Hickory and Pamela Jane to keep on making paperweights while I went to the sports. They had all known Martin alive, as my friend, and all of them in brief snatches, and in turn, had been to his sending off. They wished me luck with many winners at the races.

I sat beside Worthington for the journey. We stopped to buy me a cheap watch, and to pick up a daily racing newspaper for the runners and riders. In a section titled "News Today" on the front page I read, among a dozen little snippets, that the Leicester Stewards would be hosts that day to Lloyd Baxter (owner of star jumper Tallahassee) to honor the memory of jockey Martin Stukely.

Well, well.

After a while I told Worthington in detail about my visit to Lorna Terrace, Taunton. He frowned over the more obvious inconsistencies put forward by mother and son, but seemed struck to consternation when I said, "Didn't you tell me that the bookmaking firm of Arthur Robins, established 1894, was now owned and run by people named Webber, Brown . . . and Verity?"

The consternation lasted ten seconds. "And the mother and son in Taunton were Verity!" A pause. "It must be a coincidence," he said.

"I don't believe in coincidences like that."

Worthington slid a silent glance my way as he navigated a roundabout, and after a while said, "Gerard . . . if you have any clear idea of what's going on . . . what is it? For instance, who were those attackers in black masks last night, and what did they want?"

I said, "I'd think it was one of them who squirted you with cyclopropane and laid me out with the empty cylinder . . . and I don't know who that was. I'm sure, though, that one of the black masks was the fragrant Rose."

"I'm not saying she wasn't, but why?"

"Who else in the world would scream at Norman Osprey— or anyone else, but I'm pretty sure it was him—to break my wrists? Rose's voice is unmistakable. And there is the way she moves . . . and as for purpose . . . partly to put me out of business, wouldn't you say? And partly to make me give her what I haven't got. And also to stop me from doing what we're aiming to do today."

Worthington said impulsively, "Let's go home, then."

"You just stay beside me, and we'll be fine."

Worthington took me seriously and bodyguarded like a professional. We confirmed one of the black-mask merchants for certain simply from his stunned reaction to my being there and on my feet when anyone with any sense would have been knocking back aspirins on a sofa with an ice pack. Martin himself had shown me how jump jockeys walked around sometimes with broken ribs and arms and other injuries. Only broken legs, he'd said, postponed actual riding for a couple of months. Bruises, to him, were everyday normal, and he dealt with pain by putting it out of his mind and thinking about something else. "Ignore it," he'd said. I copied him at Leicester as best I could.

When he saw me, Norman Osprey had stopped dead in the middle of setting up his stand, his heavy shoulders bunching; and Rose herself made the mistake of striding up to him in a carefree bounce at that moment, only to follow his disbelieving gaze and lose a good deal of her self-satisfaction. What she said explosively was "bloody hell."

If one imagined Norman Osprey's shoulders in black jersey, he was recognizably the figure who'd smashed my watch with his baseball bat, while aiming at my wrist. I'd jerked at the vital moment and I'd kicked his shin very hard indeed. The sharp voice urging him to try again, had, without doubt, been Rose's.

I said to them jointly, "Tom Pigeon sends his regards."

Neither of them looked overjoyed. Worthington murmured something to me urgently about it not being advisable to poke a wasps' nest with a stick. He also put distance between himself and Arthur Robins, Est. 1894, and, with unobvious speed, I followed.

"They don't know exactly what they're looking for," I pointed out, slowing down. "If they knew, they would have asked for it by name last night."

"They might have done that anyway, if Tom Pigeon hadn't been walking his dogs." Worthington steered us still farther away from Norman Osprey, looking back all the same to make certain we weren't being followed.

My impression of the events of barely fifteen hours earlier was that damage, as well as information, had been the purpose. But if Tom Pigeon hadn't arrived, and if it had been to save the multiple wrist bones that Martin had said never properly mended, and if I *could* have answered their questions, then would I . . . ?

Sore as I already felt all over, I couldn't imagine any piece of knowledge that Martin might have had that he thought was worth my virtual destruction . . . and I didn't like the probability that they—the black masks—wrongly believed that I did know what they wanted, and that I was being merely stubborn in not telling them.

Mordantly I admitted to myself that if I'd known for certain what they wanted and if Tom Pigeon hadn't arrived with his dogs, I wouldn't at that moment be strolling around any racetrack, but would quite likely have told them *anything* to stop them, and have been considering suicide from shame. And I was *not* going to confess that to anyone at all.

Only to Martin's hovering presence could I even admit it. Bugger you, pal, I thought. What the sod have you let me in for?

L LOYD BAXTER LUNCHED at Leicester with the Stewards. His self-regarding nature found this admirable invitation to be merely his due. He told me so, condescendingly, when our paths crossed between parade ring and stands.

To Lloyd Baxter the meeting was unexpected, but I'd spotted him early and waited through the Stewards' roast beef, cheese and coffee, talking to Worthington outside, and stiffening uncomfortably in the cold wind.

Cold weather emphasized the Paleolithic-like weight of Baxter's facial structure and upper body, and even after only one week (though a stressful one) his hair seemed definitely to have grayed a further notch.

He wasn't pleased to see me. I was sure he regretted the whole Broadway evening, but he concentrated hard on being civil, and it was churlish of me, I dare say, to suspect that it was because I knew of his epilepsy. Nowhere in print or chat had his condition been disclosed, but if he were afraid I would not only broadcast but snigger, he had made a judgment of my own character which hardly flattered.

Worthington melted temporarily from my side and I walked with Lloyd Baxter while he oozed compliments about the Stewards' lunch and discussed the worth of many trainers, excluding poor old Priam Jones.

I said mildly, "It wasn't his fault that Tallahassee fell at Cheltenham."

I got an acid reply. "It was Martin's fault. He unbalanced him going into the fence. He was too confident."

Martin had told me that *it*—whatever *it* might be—was, with a disgruntled owner, normally the jockey's fault. "Pilot error." He'd shrugged philosophically. "And then you get the other sort of owner, the cream to ride for, the ones who understand that horses aren't infallible, who say, 'That's racing,' when something shattering happens, and who comfort the jockey who's just lost them the win of a lifetime. . . . And believe me," Martin had said, "Lloyd Baxter isn't one of those. If I lose for him, it is, in his opinion, my fault."

"But," I said without heat to Lloyd Baxter during his trainer-spotting at Leicester, "if a horse falls, it surely isn't the trainer's fault? It wasn't Priam Jones's fault that Tallahassee fell and lost the Coffee Cup."

"He should have schooled him better."

"Well," I reasoned, "that horse had proved he could jump. He'd already won several races."

"I want a different trainer." Lloyd Baxter spoke with obstinacy: a matter of instinct, I saw.

Along with lunch the Stewards had given Tallahassee's owner an entry ticket to their guests' vantage viewing box. Lloyd Baxter was already apologizing for shedding me at the entrance when one of the Stewards, following us, changed our course.

"Aren't you the glass man?" he boomed genially. "My wife's

your greatest fan. We have lumps of your stuff all over our house. That splendid horse you did for her . . . you came to rig its spotlights, didn't you?"

I remembered the horse and the house with enough detail to be invited into the Stewards' guests' viewing balcony, not entirely to Lloyd Baxter's delight.

"This young man's a genius, according to my wife," the Steward said to Baxter, ushering us in. The genius merely wished he felt less weak.

Lloyd Baxter's poor opinion of the Steward's wife's judgment was written plain on his heavy features, but perhaps it did eventually influence him, because, after the cheering for the next winner had faded, he surprised me very much by resting his hand lightly on my arm to indicate that I should stay and hear what he felt like telling me. He hesitated still, though, so I gave him every chance.

"I've often wondered," I said mildly, "if you saw who came into my showroom on New Year's Eve. I mean, I know you were ill . . . but before that . . . when I'd gone out into the street, did anyone come?"

After a long pause, he faintly nodded. "Someone came into that long gallery you have there. I remember he asked for you and I said you were out in the street . . . but I couldn't see him properly as my eyes . . . my sight develops zigzags sometimes . . ." He stopped, but I continued for him.

"You surely have pills."

"Of course I do!" He was irritated. "But I'd forgotten to take them because of the terrible day it had been, and I hate those very small air taxis to begin with, and I do want a different trainer." His voice died away, but his troubles had been laid out clearly enough for a chimpanzee to understand.

I asked if, in spite of the zigzag aura, he could describe my unknown visitor.

"No," he said. "I told him you were in the street and the next time I was properly awake I was in hospital." He paused while I regretted the cut-short sequence, and then with diffidence he said slowly, "I am aware that I should thank you for your reticence. You could still cause me much embarrassment."

"There's no point in it," I said.

He spent a while studying my face as in the past I'd learned his. The result surprised me. "Are you ill?" he said.

"No. Tired. Didn't sleep well."

"The man who came," he said abruptly, making no other comment, "was thin and had a white beard and was over fifty."

The description sounded highly improbable as a thief, and he must have seen my doubt because he added to convince me, "When I saw him, I immediately thought of Priam Jones, who's been saying for years he's going to grow a beard. I tell him he'd look weedy."

I nearly laughed: the picture was true.

Baxter said the white-bearded man reminded him chiefly of a university professor. A lecturer.

I asked, "Did he speak? Was he a normal customer? Did he mention glass?"

Lloyd Baxter couldn't remember. "If he spoke at all, I heard him only as a jumble. Quite often things seem wrong to me.

They're a sort of warning. Often I can control them a little, or at least prepare . . . but on that evening it was happening too fast."

He was being extraordinarily frank, I thought. I wouldn't have expected so much trust.

"That man with the whisker job," I said. "He must have seen the beginning at least of your . . . er . . . seizure. So why didn't he help you? Do you think he simply didn't know what to do, so ran away from trouble, as people tend to, or was it he who made off with the loot . . . er . . . that money, in the canvas bag?"

"And the videotape," Baxter said.

There was an abrupt breath-drawing silence. Then I asked, "What videotape?"

Lloyd Baxter frowned. "He asked for it."

"So you gave it to him?"

"No. Yes. No. I don't know."

It became clear that in fact Lloyd Baxter's memory of that evening in Broadway was a scrambled egg of order into chaos. It wasn't certain that any university lecturer in any white beard existed outside fiction.

While we occupied for another ten uninterrupted minutes the most private place on a racetrack—the Stewards' friends' viewing balcony in between races—I managed to persuade Lloyd Baxter to sit quietly and exchange detailed memories of the first few minutes of 2000, but try as he might, he still clung to the image of the scrawny man in the white beard who probably— or maybe it was some other man at some other time—asked for a videotape . . . perhaps.

He was trying his best. His manner to me had taken a ninety-degree angle of change, so that he'd become more an ally than a crosspatch.

One of the things he would never have said in the past was his reassessment of my and Martin's friendship. "I see I was wrong about you," he admitted, heavily frowning. "Martin relied on you for strength, and I took it for granted that it was the other way round."

"We learned from each other."

After a pause he said, "That fellow in the white beard, he was real, you know. He did want a videotape. If I knew more than that, I would tell you."

I finally believed him. It was just unlucky that Baxter's fit had struck at the wrong random moment; unlucky from white-beard's point of view that Baxter had been there at all; but it did now seem certain that during the time I was out in the street seeing the year 2000 arrive safely, a white-bearded, thin middle-aged professor-type individual had come into my showroom and had said something about a videotape, and had left before I returned, taking the tape, and incidentally the money, with him.

I hadn't seen any white-bearded figure out in the street. It had been a week too late for the Ho-ho-ho joker from the North Pole. Lloyd Baxter said he couldn't tell whether or not the beard was real or left over from Santa Claus.

When we parted we shook hands for the first time ever. I left him with the Stewards and fell into step with Worthington, who was shivering outside and announcing he was hungry. Accordingly we smelled out some food, which he galloped through with endless appetite.

"Why don't you eat?" he demanded, chomping.

"Habit," I said. A habit caught from a scales-conscious jockey. Martin seemed to have influenced my life more than I'd realized.

I told Worthington while he saw off two full plates of steak-and-kidney pie (his and mine) that we were now looking for a thin man, late middle-age, white beard, who looked like a college lecturer.

Worthington gazed at me earnestly while loading his fork with pastry. "That," he pointed out, "doesn't sound at all like someone who would steal a bagful of money."

"I'm surprised at you, Worthington," I teased him. "You of all people I thought would know that beards aren't automatic badges of honesty! So how does this sit with you? Suppose Mr. White-Beard gives a tape to Martin, which Martin gives to Eddie Payne, who handed it on to me. Then when Martin died, Mr. White-Beard decided to take his videotape back again, so he found out where the tape would be . . . that's to say he turned up in Broadway. He found the tape and took it back, and on impulse he also whisked up the bag of money that I'd stupidly left lying around, and in consequence he cannot tell anyone that he has his tape back."

"Because he would be confessing he'd stolen the cash?"

"Dead right."

My bodyguard sighed and scraped his plate clean. "So what next?" he said. "What happened next?"

"I can only guess."

"Go on, then. Guess. Because it wasn't some old guy that gassed us with that cyclopropane. Young Daniel described the sneakers that the gas man wore, and nobody but a teenager, I don't think, would be seen dead in them."

I found I disagreed. Eccentric white-beards might wear anything. They might also make erotic tapes. They might also tell someone the tape was worth a fortune, and that it was in Gerard Logan's hands. A few little lies. Diversionary tactics. Beat up Logan, make him ready to cough up the tape, or, failing that, whatever information had been on it.

What had Martin been going to give me for safekeeping?

Did I any longer really want to know?

If I didn't know, I couldn't tell. But if they believed I knew and wouldn't tell . . . dammit, I thought, we've almost been through that already, and I couldn't expect Tom Pigeon and Dobermans to rescue me every time.

Not knowing the secret on the tape was perhaps worse than knowing it. So somehow or other, I decided, it wasn't enough to discover who took it, it was essential after all to find out what they expected as well as what they'd actually got.

Once Worthington's hunger had retreated temporarily and we had lost our money on a horse Martin should have ridden, we walked back to where the serried ranks of bookmakers were shouting their offers for the getting-out stakes, the last race.

With Worthington's well-known muscle as guarantee of immunity from onslaught, we arrived in the living-and-breathing space of the 1894 Arthur Robins operation 2000. Norman Osprey's raucous voice soared unself-consciously above his neighbors' until he realized we were listening, at which point a sudden silence gave everyone else a chance.

Close enough to see the scissor marks on the Elvis sideburns, I said, "Tell Rose . . ."

"Tell her yourself," he interrupted forcefully. "She's just behind you."

I turned without haste, leaving Worthington at my back. Rose glared, rigid with a hatred I didn't at that point understand. As before, the dryness of her skin echoed the lack of generosity in her nature, but earlier, at our first and last racetrack encounter, neither of us held the subsequent memory of fists, stone walls, baseball bats, a smashed watch and a whole bunch more of assaults-to-the-person, all orchestrated and encouraged as Sunday evening entertainment for the troops.

Being as close to her as a couple of yards gave my outraged skin goose bumps, but she seemed to think a black mask and leotard had made her invisible.

I asked again the question she had already refused to answer.

"Who gave a videotape to Martin Stukely at Cheltenham races?"

She answered this time that she didn't know.

I said, "Do you mean you didn't see anyone give Martin a parcel, or that you saw the transfer but didn't know the person's name?"

"Dead clever, aren't you," Rose said sarcastically. "Take your pick."

Rose, I thought, wasn't going to be trapped by words. At a guess she had both seen the transfer and knew the transferrer, but even Torquemada would have had trouble with her, and I hadn't any thumbscrews handy in Logan Glass.

I said without much hope of being believed, "I don't know where to look for the tape you want. I don't know who took it and I don't know why. I haven't got it."

Rose curled her lip.

As we walked away Worthington sighed deeply with frustration.

"You'd think Norman Osprey would be the 'heavy' in that outfit. He has the voice and the build for it. Everyone thinks of him as the power behind Arthur Robins 1894. But did you see him looking at Rose? She can make any blunder she likes, but I'm told she's still the brains. She's the boss. She calls the tune. My low-life investigator gave me a bell. He finds her very impressive, I'm afraid to say."

I nodded.

Worthington, a practiced world traveler, said, "She hates you. Have you noticed?"

I told him I had indeed noticed. "But I don't know why."

"You'd want a psychiatrist to explain it properly, but I'll tell you for zilch what I've learned. You're a man, you're strong, you look OK, you're successful at your job and you're not afraid of her; and I could go on, but that's for starters. Then she has you roughed up, doesn't she, and here you are looking as good as new, even if you aren't feeling it, and sticking the finger up in her face, more or less, and believe me, I'd've chucked a rival down the stairs for less, if they as much as yawned in my presence."

I listened to Worthington's wisdom, but I said, "I haven't done her any harm."

"You threaten her. You're too much for her. You'll win the tennis match. So maybe she'll have you killed first. She won't kill you herself. And don't ignore what I'm telling you. There are people who really have killed for hate. People who've wanted to win."

Not to mention murders because of racism or religious prejudice, I thought, but it was still hard to imagine it applying to oneself—until one had felt the watch smash, of course.

I expected that Rose would have told Eddie Payne, her father, that I was at the races, but she hadn't. Worthington and I lay in wait for him after the last race and easily ambushed him in a pincer movement when he came out of the changing rooms on his way to his car.

He wasn't happy. He looked from one to the other of us like a cornered horse, and it was as if to a fractious animal that I soothingly said, "Hi, Ed. How's things?"

"I don't know anything I haven't told you," he protested.

I thought if I cast him a few artificial flies, I might startle and hook an unexpected fish; a trout, so to speak, sheltering in the reeds.

So I said, "Is Rose married to Norman Osprey?"

His face lightened to nearly a laugh. "Rose is still Rose Payne but she calls herself Robins and sometimes *Mrs.* Robins when it suits her, but she doesn't like men, my Rose. Pity, really, but there it is."

"But she likes to rule them?"

"She's always made boys do what she wants."

"Were you with her yesterday evening?" I asked him the question casually, but he knew instantly what I meant.

"I didn't lay a finger on you," he said quickly. "It wasn't me." He looked from me to Worthington and back again, this time with puzzlement. "Look," he said wheedlingly, as if begging for forgiveness, "they didn't give you a chance. I told Rose it wasn't fair . . ." He wavered to a stop.

With interest I asked, "Do you mean that you yourself wore a black mask in Broadway yesterday evening?" and almost with incredulity saw in his face an expression of shame that he had.

"Rose said we would just frighten you." He stared at me with unhappy eyes. "I tried to stop her, honest. I never thought you'd be here today. So it can't have been as bad as it looked . . . but I know it was *awful*. I went to confession first to ask forgiveness . . ."

"So there was you and Rose." I said it matter-of-factly, though stunned beneath. "And Norman Osprey, and who else? One of Norman Osprey's bookmaking clerks, was it?"

"No. Not them."

Horror suddenly closed his mouth. He had already admitted far too much from his daughter's point of view, and if the other so far unidentified black-mask shape were one of the other two clerks working with Norman Osprey at Arthur Robins, Est. 1894, Eddie was no longer going to admit it easily.

I tried another fly.

"Do you know anyone who could lay their hands on anesthetics?"

A blank.

Try again.

"Or anyone with a white beard, known to Martin?"

He hesitated over that, but in the end shook his head.

I said, "Do you yourself know anyone with a white beard who looks like a university lecturer?"

"No." His reply was positive, his manner shifty.

"Was the brown-paper parcel you gave me at Cheltenham the selfsame one that Martin gave you earlier in the day?"

"Yes." He nodded this time with no need for thought. "It was the same one. Rose was furious. She said I should have stuck onto it when Martin died, and I shouldn't have mentioned it; we should have kept it ourselves and then there wouldn't have been all this fuss."

"Did Rose know what was in it?"

"Only Martin knew for sure. I did more or less ask him what was in it but he just laughed and said the future of the world, but it was a joke, of course."

Martin's joke sounded to me too real to be funny.

Ed hadn't finished. "A couple of weeks before Christmas," he said, still amused, "Martin said that what he was giving Bon-Bon—a few of the jockeys were talking about presents for their wives and girlfriends while they were changing to go home—it wasn't a big deal—what he was giving Bon-Bon was a gold-and-glass antique necklace, but he was laughing and he said he would have to get you to make him a much cheaper and modern copy. He said you had a videotape to tell you how. But next minute he changed his mind because Bon-Bon wanted new fur-lined boots, and anyway he was mostly talking about the King George VI

Chase at Kempton on December 26 and how much weight he'd have to take off by not eating turkey . . . I mean, he was always worried about his weight, like most of them are."

"He talked to you a lot," I commented. "More than most."

Ed didn't think so. He liked to chat with the boys, he said. He could tell us a thing or two about them. He winked on it, as if all jockeys were real sexual rogues, and with this confidence his manner more or less returned to the calm and efficient valet I'd met through Martin.

Worthington, driving us home, summed up the day's haul of information. "I'd say Martin and the white-bearded guy were serious with this tape."

"Yes," I agreed.

"And somehow or other, through her father, Rose may have imagined that that tape showed how to make an antique necklace."

I said doubtfully, "It must be more than that."

"Well . . . perhaps it actually says where the necklace can be found."

"A treasure hunt?" I shook my head. "There's only one valuable antique gold-and-glass necklace that I know of, and I do know a fair amount about antique glass, and it's in a museum. It's priceless. It was probably designed in Crete, or anyway somewhere round the Aegean Sea sometime about three thousand five hundred years ago. It's called the Cretan Sunrise. I did make a copy of it, though, and I once lent it to Martin. I also made a videotape to explain the methods I used. I lent that to Martin too and he still has it—or rather, heaven knows where it is now."

"What if there's another one?" Worthington asked.

"Are you talking about *two tapes* now? Or two necklaces?"

"Why not two tapes?" Worthington reasoned, as if it had suddenly become likely. "Rose could have muddled them up."

I thought it just as likely that it was Worthington and I who'd muddled everything up, but we arrived safely at Bon-Bon's house richer with at least two solid new facts: first, that Rose, Norman Osprey and Eddie Payne had spent their Sunday evening in Broadway; and second, that an elderly, thin, white-bearded, university-lecture-type man had walked into my shop as the new century came in with bells, and had not stayed to help Lloyd Baxter with his epileptic fit.

As we scrunched to a halt on Bon-Bon's gravel, Marigold came with wide-stretched arms out of the front door to greet us.

"Bon-Bon doesn't need me anymore," she announced dramatically. "Get out the maps, Worthington. We're going skiing."

"Er . . . when?" her chauffeur asked, unsurprised.

"Tomorrow morning of course. Fill up the gas tanks. We'll call at Paris on the way. I need new clothes."

Worthington looked more resigned than I felt. He murmured to me that Marigold bought new clothes most days of the week and prophesied that the skiing trip would last less than ten days overall. She would tire of it quickly, and come home.

Bon-Bon was taking the news of her mother's departure with well-hidden relief, and asked me with hope whether "the upsetting videotape business" was now concluded. She wanted calm in her life, but I had no idea if she would get it. I didn't tell her of Rose's existence or the distinct lack of calm she represented.

I asked Bon-Bon about White-Beard. She said she'd never seen or heard of him. When I explained who he was, she telephoned to Priam Jones, who though with his self-esteem badly hurt by Lloyd Baxter's ditching of him, regretted he couldn't help.

Bon-Bon tried several more trainers, but thin, elderly, white-bearded owners of racehorses seemed not to exist. After she'd tired of it she persuaded her mother to let Worthington continue our journey, to take me where I wanted. I kissed her gratefully and chose to go straight home to my hillside house and flop.

Worthington liked skiing, he said as we drove away. He liked Paris. He liked Marigold. He regularly admired her more bizarre clothes. Sorry, he said, about leaving me with the lioness, Rose. Good luck, he said cheerfully.

"I could throttle you," I said.

While Worthington happily chuckled at the wheel, I switched on my mobile phone again to call Irish at his home to find out how the day had finally gone in the shop, but before I could dial the number the message service called, and the disembodied voice of young Victor W. V. said briefly in my ear, "Send your e-mail address to me at vicv@freenet.com."

Holy hell, I thought, Victor had things to say. Flopping could wait. The only computer I owned that handled e-mail was in Broadway. Worthington with resignation changed direction, at length stopping by my main glass door and insisting he come in with me, to check the place for black masks and other pests.

The place was empty. No Rose in wait. Worthington returned with me to the Rolls, shook my hand, told me to look after myself and left lightheartedly, again prophesying his swift return well within two weeks.

Almost at once I missed the muscle man, missed him as a safety umbrella and as a source of a realistic view of life. Paris and skiing attracted powerfully. I sighed over my inescapable bruises, roused my sleeping computer into action, connected it to the Internet, and sent an e-mail message to Victor, with my address.

I'd expected to have to wait a good long time to hear from Victor, but almost immediately, which meant he had been sitting at his computer, waiting, the screen of my laptop demanded, "Who are you?"

I typed and sent, "Martin Stukely's friend."

He asked, "Name," and I told him, "Gerard Logan."

His reply was "What do you want?"

"How did you know Martin Stukely?"

"I've known him for years, saw him often at the races with my granddad."

I wrote, "Why did you send that letter to him? How had you heard of any tape? Please tell me the truth."

"I heard my aunt telling my mother."

"How did your aunt know?"

"My aunt knows everything."

I began to lose faith in his common sense, and I remembered him saying he was playing a game.

"What is your aunt's name?" I expected nothing much: certainly not the breath-taker that came back.

"My aunt's name is Rose. She keeps changing her last name.

She's my mother's sister." There was barely an interval before his next remark. "I'd better log off now. She's just come!"

"Wait." Stunned by that revelation I rapidly typed, "Do you know of a thin old man with a white beard?"

A long time after I'd settled for no answer, three words appeared.

"Doctor Force. Good-bye."

CHAPTER 5

To MY CONSIDERABLE delight Catherine Dodd again stood her motorbike by my curb and pulled off her helmet before walking across the sidewalk to the door I held open for her. It seemed natural to us both to kiss hello, and for her to stand in front of the soaring flight of wings that I had barely finished lighting.

"It's tremendous." She meant it. "It's too good for Broadway."

"Flattery will get you an awfully long way," I assured her, and took her into the workshop, where it was warmest.

The sheet printed of my e-mail conversation with Victor lay folded on the marver table and I passed it to her to read. "What do you think?" I asked.

"I think you need better painkillers."

"No . . . Think about Victor."

She sat this time in the armchair on my promise that on the next day I would walk down the hill looking in secondhand and antique furniture shops to buy another one.

"If," I amended to the promise, "if you will come and sit in it."

She nodded as if it were an "of course" decision and read Victor's e-mail. When she'd finished she laid the sheet on her black leather–clad knees and asked her own questions.

"OK," she said. "First of all, remind me, who is Victor?"

"The fifteen-year-old grandson of Ed Payne, Martin Stukely's racetrack valet. Ed gave me the videotape that was stolen from here, which you came to see about. Victor sent this letter to Martin." I gave her the letter to read, which raised her eyebrows in doubt.

"Victor said he was playing games," I acknowledged.

"You can't believe a word he says!" Catherine agreed.

"Well, yes you can, actually. He's made a game of actual bits of fact. Or anyway, he's done what everyone does at some point— he's heard one thing and thought it meant another."

"The wrong end of the stick?" Catherine suggested. "How about the right end?"

"Well . . . the stick as I see it, then." I stopped for a minute or two to make coffee, which in spite of her being off duty she said she preferred to wine. No milk, no sugar, cool rather than hot.

"Have to begin with a 'suppose,' " I said.

"Suppose away."

"Start with a white-bearded man who looks like a university

lecturer and who might be called Doctor Force. Suppose that this Doctor Force has somehow got to know Martin. Doctor Force has some information he wants to put into safekeeping so he takes it to Cheltenham races and gives it to Martin."

"Crazy." Catherine sighed. "Why didn't he put it in a bank?"

"We'll have to ask him."

"And you are crazy too. How do we find him?"

"It's you," I pointed out, smiling, "that is the police officer."

"Well, I'll try." She smiled back. "And what then?"

"Then Doctor Force went to the races as planned. He gave his tape to Martin. After Martin crashed, our Doctor Force must have gone through a lot of doubt and worry, and I'd guess he stood around near the changing rooms wondering what to do. Then he saw Ed Payne give the tape in its brown-paper parcel to me, and he knew it was the right tape as he'd packed it himself."

"You should join the police," Catherine teased. "So OK, Doctor Force finds out who you are and takes himself here to Broadway, and when you leave your door unlocked for a spell in the new-age air, he nips in and takes back his own tape."

"Right."

"And steals your cash on impulse."

"Right. But up to that point he hasn't realized that there is someone else in the depths of the shop; and that's Lloyd Baxter, who proceeds to have an epileptic fit."

"Upsetting for Doctor White-Beard Force." She spoke dryly. I nodded. "He did a bunk."

Catherine said thoughtfully, "One of our detective constables interviewed Lloyd Baxter in hospital. Mr. Baxter said he didn't see anyone at all come into the showroom."

"Lloyd Baxter didn't care about getting the tape back, nor the money either. He did care very much about keeping his illness as private as possible."

Catherine showed irritation. "However can we solve cases if people don't give us the facts?"

"You must be used to it."

She said that being used to something wrong didn't make it right. The starchy disapproval common to her profession had surfaced briefly. Never forget, I told myself, that the inner crime fighter is always there, always on duty, and always part of her. She shook herself free of the moment and made a visible gear change back to a lighter approach.

"OK." She nodded. "So Doctor Force has his tape back. Fine. So who squirted anesthetic at the Stukelys and took their TVs, and who ransacked your own house, and beat you up last night? And I don't really understand how this boy Victor got involved."

"I can't answer everything, but think Rose."

"Pink?"

"Rose. She is Ed Payne's daughter, and Victor's aunt. She's sharp-featured, sharp-tongued, and I think is on the edge of criminal. She jumps a bit to conclusions, and she's all the more dangerous for that."

"For instance?"

"For instance . . . I'd guess it was she who stole all the video-tapes in Bon-Bon's house and mine because they could possibly have been mixed up with the one I brought from the racetrack."

"But heavens!" Catherine exclaimed. "Tapes do so easily get mixed up."

"Rose probably thought so too. I would think it likely that Rose chatters to her sister (Victor's mother) quite a lot and I think it's fairly certain that Victor did overhear her when she said she knew of a tape worth a fortune."

If only Martin had explained what he was doing! There was too much guesswork, and definitely too much Rose.

Sighing, Catherine gave me back Victor's printout and stood up, saying with apparent reluctance, "I have to go. I was so glad to find you here, but I've promised to be with my parents tonight. I was wondering, though, if you by any chance want to go to your house now, then—um—you don't need a license to ride pillion."

She necessarily shed the police half of herself. I got on the bike and clasped her close around her waist, having more or less strapped on her spare helmet, which was too small and into wobble. We set off insecurely, but the bike had guts enough to take us both up the hills without stuttering, and she was laughing when she stopped by the weedy entrance to my drive.

I thanked her for the ride. She roared off still laughing. I was conscious of wishing that Worthington, or failing him, Tom Pigeon and his Dobermans, were by my side, but there were no thorny briar Roses lying in wait this time. When I unlocked a side door and let myself in, it seemed that the house gave back in peace the years the Logan family had prospered there, father, mother and two sons, each in a different way. I was the only one left, and with its ten rooms still filled with sharp memories, I'd made no move to find a smaller or more suitable lair. One day, perhaps. Meanwhile the house felt like home in all senses: home to me, the home of all who'd lived there.

I walked deliberately through all the rooms thinking of Catherine, wondering both if she would like the place, and whether the house would accept her in return. Once in the past the house had delivered a definite thumbs-down, and once I'd been given an ultimatum to smother the pale plain walls with brightly patterned paper as a condition of marriage, but to the horror of her family I'd backed out of the whole deal, and as a result, I now used the house as arbiter and had disentangled myself from a later young woman who'd begun to refer to her and me as "an item" and to reply to questions as "we." *We* think.

No, we don't think.

I knew that several people considered me heartless. Also promiscuous, also fickle. Catherine would be advised not to get herself involved with that fellow whose reputation was as brittle as his glass. I knew quite well what the gossips said, but it wasn't going to be to please any gossip that the house and I one day would settle on a mate for life.

The burglars who'd taken all my videotapes hadn't made a lot of mess. There had been television sets with video recorders in three rooms: in the kitchen, and in each of the sitting rooms in which for nearly ten years my mother and I had lived our semi-separate lives.

As I hadn't yet done anything about the rooms since her death, it seemed as if she would soon come out of her bedroom, chiding me for having left my dirty clothes on the floor.

There wasn't a single tape left anywhere that I could find. My parent had had a radically different taste from me in films and recorded TV programs, but it no longer mattered. Out of my own room I'd lost a rather precious bunch of glassblowing instruction tapes that I might be able to replace if I could find copies. I'd been commissioned to make some of them myself for university courses. Those courses were basic and mostly dealt with how to make scientific equipment for laboratories. I couldn't imagine those teaching tapes being the special target of any thief.

In the kitchen there had been game shows, tennis, American football and cooking. All gone. The police had suggested I list them all. What a hope!

There wasn't much left to tidy, except for patches of dust and a couple of dead spiders here and there, where once the TVs had stood.

With the Rose-induced bruises growing gradually less sore, I slept safely behind bolted doors, and in the morning walked (as usual while sans car) downhill to Logan Glass, getting there before Irish, Hickory and Pamela Jane. Relief was the emotion I chiefly felt about the soaring wings; relief that somehow someone hadn't managed to smash them overnight.

Irish's pedestal and my lighting system had combined to make accidental breakage very difficult, but one couldn't easily guard against hurricane or ax.

I made a fleet of little ornamental sailing ships all morning and bought a comfortable armchair at lunchtime which minimized every remaining wince. Followed by a brown-overalled chair pusher (with chair), I returned to Logan Glass and rearranged the furniture. My assistants grinned knowingly.

I straightened out the worst of Hickory's growing hubris by giving him a sailing boat as an exercise, which resulted in a heap of sad lumps of stunted mast and a mainsail that no breeze would ever fill.

Hickory's good looks and general air of virility would always secure him jobs he couldn't do. In less than the first week of his attractive company I'd learned more of his limitations than his skills, but every customer liked him and he was a great salesman.

"It's all right for *you*," he now complained, looking from the little boat I'd made in demonstration to the heap of colored rubble he'd painstakingly achieved, "you know what a sailing boat *looks* like. When I make them they come out flat."

Half the battle in all I did, as I tried to explain to him without any "cockiness" creeping in, was the draftsman's inner eye that saw an object in three-dimensional terms. I could draw and paint all right, but it was the three-dimensional imagination that I'd been blessed with from birth that made little sailboats a doddle.

As Hickory's third try bit the dust amid commiserating murmurs from the rest of us, the telephone interrupted the would-be star glassblower's explanation of how drops of water had unfairly fallen on his work at the crucial moment and splintered it, which was definitely not his fault. . . .

I didn't listen. The voice on the line was Catherine's.

"I've been a police officer all morning," she said. "Did you really get another chair?"

"It's here waiting for you."

"Great. And I've collected some news for you. I'll be along when I go off duty, at six o'clock."

To fill in time I e-mailed Victor, expecting to have to wait for a reply, as he should have been at school, but as before, he was ready.

He typed, "Things have changed."

"Tell me."

There was a long gap of several minutes.

"Are you still there?" he asked.

"Yes."

"My dad's in jail."

E-mail messages crossed the ether without inflection. Victor's typed words gave no clues to his feelings.

I sent back, "Where? What for? How long? I'm very sorry."

Victor's reply had nothing to do with the questions.

"I hate her."

I asked flatly, "Who?"

A pause, then, "Auntie Rose, of course."

I itched for faster answers but got only a feeling that if I pressed too hard I would lose him altogether.

Without the tearing emotion I could imagine him trying to deal with, he wrote, "He's been there ten weeks. They sent me to stay with my uncle Mac in Scotland when the trial was on, so I wouldn't know. They told me my dad had gone on an Antarctic expedition as a chef. He is a chef, you see. He got sent down for a year, but he'll be out before that. Will you go on talking to me?"

"Yes," I sent back. "Of course."

A long pause again, then "Rose sneaked on Dad." I waited, and more came. "He hit Mom. He broke her nose and some ribs." After an even longer pause, he sent, "E-mail me tomorrow," and I replied fast, while he might still be on-line, "Tell me about Doctor Force."

Either he'd disconnected his phone line or didn't want to reply, because Doctor Force was a nonstarter. Victor's silence lasted all day.

I went back to the teaching session. Hickory finally fashioned a boat that might have floated had it been full-size and made of fiberglass with a canvas sail. He allowed himself a smirk of satisfaction, which none of us begrudged him. Glassblowing was a difficult discipline even for those like Hickory, who apparently had everything on their side—youth, agility, imagination. Hickory put the little boat carefully in the annealing oven, knowing I would give him the finished ornament to keep, in the morning.

By six I'd managed to send them all home, and by six plus twenty-three Detective Constable Dodd was approving the new armchair and reading Victor Waltman Verity's troubles.

"Poor boy," she said.

I said ruefully, "As he hates his aunt Rose for grassing on his pa, he might not tell me anything else himself. Sneaking appears to be a mortal sin, in his book."

"Mm." She read the printed pages again, then cheerfully said, "Well, whether or not you have Victor's help, your Doctor Force is definitely on the map." It pleased her to have found him. "I chased him through a few academic *Who's Who*s with no results. He's not a university lecturer, or not primarily, anyway. He is, believe it or not, a medical doctor. Licensed, and all that." She handed me an envelope with a grin. "One of my colleagues spends his time chasing struck-off practitioners. He looked for him, and in the end he did find him."

"Is he struck off?" It would make sense, I thought, but Catherine shook her head.

"No, not only is he not struck off, he was working in some research lab or other until recently. He took a lot of finding, because of that. It's all in this envelope."

"And is he fiftyish with a white beard?"

She laughed. "His date of birth will be in the envelope. A white beard's expecting too much."

Both of us at that point found that there were more absorbing facets to life than chasing obscure medics.

I suggested food from the takeout; she offered another pillion ride up the hill: we saw to both. I'd left central heating on for comfort, and Catherine wandered all over the house, smiling.

"I've been warned that you'll dump me," she said casually.

"Not in a hurry."

I still held the envelope of Doctor Force details, and I opened it then with hope, but it told me very few useful facts. His name was Adam Force, age fifty-six, and his qualifications came by the dozen.

I said blankly, "Is that all?"

She nodded. "That's all, folks, when it comes to facts. As to hearsay—well—according to a bunch of rumors he's a brilliant researcher who has published star-spangled work since his teens. No one could tell my colleague about a white beard. He didn't speak to anyone who'd actually met the subject."

I asked, "Does Doctor Force have an address?"

"Not in these notes," she answered. "In the *Who's Who* we used, it gives only the information provided by the people themselves. Those reference books leave people out if they don't want to be in."

"Utterly civilized."

"No, very annoying."

She didn't sound very annoyed, however, as she knew all about the Internet. The next morning, she decided, we could catch him on the Web.

We ate the takeout food, or a little of it, owing to a change of appetite, and I switched up the heating a little in my bedroom without any need for explanation.

She'd shed somewhere in her life whatever she had ever suffered in the way of overpowering shyness. The Catherine who came into my bed came with confidence along with modesty, an intoxicating combination as far as I was concerned. We both knew enough, anyway, to give to each other as much pleasure as we received, or at least enough to feel slumberous and fulfilled in consequence.

The speed of development of strong feelings for one another didn't seem to me to be shocking but natural, and if I thought about the future it unequivocally included Catherine Dodd. "If you wanted to cover the pale plain walls with brightly patterned paper, go ahead," I said.

She laughed. "I like the peace of pale walls. Why should I want to change them?"

I said merely, "I'm glad you don't," and offered her thirst quenchers. Like Martin, it seemed she preferred fizzy water to alcohol, though in her case the cause wasn't weight but the combination of a police badge and a motorbike. She went soberly home before dawn, steady on two wheels. I watched her red rear light fade into what was left of the night and quite fiercely wanted her to stay with me instead.

I walked restlessly downhill through the slow January dawn, reaching the workshop well before the others. The Internet, though, when I'd accessed it, proved less obliging about Adam Force than the address of Waltman Verity in Taunton. There had been a whole clutch of Veritys. Adam Force wasn't anywhere in sight.

Hickory arrived at that point, early and eager to take his precious sailboat out of the Lehr annealing oven. He unbolted the oven door and lifted out his still-warm treasure. Although he would get the transparent colors clearer with practice, it wasn't a bad effort, and I told him so. He wasn't pleased, however. He wanted unqualified praise. I caught on his face a fleeting expression of contempt for my lack of proper appreciation of his ability. There would be trouble ahead if he tackled really difficult stuff, I thought; but as I'd done once in the past with someone of equal talent, I would give him good references when he looked for a different teacher, as, quite soon now, he would.

I would miss him most in the selling department for results and in the humor department for good company.

Irish, more humble about his skills, and Pamela Jane, twittery and positively self-deprecating, came sweeping in together in the cold morning and gave the sailboat the extravagant admiration Hickory thought it deserved. Harmony united the three of them as usual, but I hadn't much faith in its lasting much longer.

Watched and helped by all three of them I spent the day replacing the minaret-shaped scent bottles we'd sold at Christmas, working fast at eight pieces an hour, using blue, turquoise, pink, green, white and purple in turn and packing the finished articles in rows in the ovens to cool. Speed was a commercial asset as essential as a three-dimensional eye, and winter in the Cotswold Hills was the time to stock up for the summer tourists. I consequently worked flat out from morning to six in the evening, progressing from sailboats via scent bottles to fishes, horses, bowls and vases.

At six in the evening when my semi-exhausted crew announced all six ovens to be packed, I sent them off home, tidied the workshop and put everything ready for the morrow. In the evening Catherine Dodd, straight off duty, rode her bike to Broadway, collected a pillion passenger and took him to his home. Every night possible that week Detective Constable Dodd slept in my arms in my bed but left before the general world awoke, and, during that time, no one managed to stick an address on Adam Force.

Glassblowing aside, by Friday afternoon, three days after Worthington and Marigold had joyfully left for Paris, the weekend held no enticements, as Catherine had departed on Friday morning as promised to a school-friends' reunion.

On the same Friday, aching, I dare say, from the absence of their daily quarrel, Bon-Bon filled her need of Martin by driving his BMW, bursting at the seams with noisy children, to pick me up at close of day in Broadway.

"Actually," Bon-Bon confessed as we detoured to my hill house for mundane clean shirts and socks, "Worthington didn't like you being out here alone."

"Worthington didn't?"

"No . . . He phoned from somewhere south of Paris and specially told me a whole gang of people jumped on you in Broadway last Sunday evening when there were dog-walkers about, and this place of yours out here is asking for trouble, he said. He also said Martin would have taken you home."

"Worthington exaggerated," I protested, but after we'd all unloaded at Bon-Bon's house, I used the evening there to invent a game for the children to compete in, a game called "Hunt the orange cylinder and the shoelaces."

Bon-Bon protested. "But they told everything they know to the police! They won't find anything useful."

"And after that game," I said, gently ignoring her, "we'll play 'Hunt the letters sent to Daddy by somebody called Force' and there are prizes for every treasure found, of course."

They played until bedtime with enthusiasm on account of the regular handouts of gold coin treasure (money), and when they'd noisily departed upstairs I laid out their final offerings all over Martin's desk in the den.

I had watched the children search uninhibitedly in places I might have left untouched so that their haul was in some ways spectacular. Perhaps most perplexing was the original of the letter Victor had sent a copy of to Martin.

Dear Martin, it said, and continued word for word as far as the signature, which didn't say Victor Waltman Verity in computer-print, but was scrawled in real live handwriting, Adam Force.

"The kids found that letter in a secret drawer in Martin's desk," Bon-Bon said. "I didn't even know there was a secret drawer, but the children did."

"Um," I pondered. "Did any of these other things come out of the drawer?"

She said she would go and ask, and presently returned with Daniel, her eleven-year-old eldest, who opened a semi-hidden drawer in the desk for us with an easy twiddle, and asked if it were worth another handout. He hadn't emptied the drawer, he explained, as he'd found the letter straightaway, the letter that was the point of the whole game, the letter sent to Daddy by someone called Force.

Of course, no one had found any trace of an orange cylinder or of recognizable laces for sneakers.

I gladly handed over another installment of treasure, as the hidden drawer proved to stretch across the whole width of the desk under the top surface, and to be about four inches deep. Daniel patiently showed me how it opened and closed. Observant and quick-witted, he offered other discoveries with glee, especially when I gave him a coin for every good hiding place with nothing in it. He found four. He jingled the coins.

Bon-Bon, searching the desk drawer, found with blushing astonishment a small bunch of love letters from her that Martin
had saved. She took them over to the black leather sofa and wept
big slow tears, while I told her that her son knew the so-called
secret drawer wasn't a secret at all but was a built-in feature of the
modern desk.

"It's designed to hold a laptop computer," I told Bon-Bon.
"Martin just didn't keep a laptop in it, as he used that table-
top one over there, the one with the full keyboard and the
screen."

"How do you know?"

"Daniel says so."

Bon-Bon said through her tears, "How disappointing it all is,"
and picked up a tissue for mopping.

I, however, found the laptop drawer seething with interest, if
not with secrets, as apart from Adam Force's letter to Martin,
there was a photocopy of Martin's letter to Force, an affair not
much longer than the brief reply.

It ran:

Dear Adam Force,
I have now had time to consider the matter of your formulae and
methods. Please will you go ahead and record these onto the video-
tape as you suggested and take it to Cheltenham races on New
Year's Eve. Give it to me there, whenever you see me, except,
obviously, not when I'm on my way out to race.
Yours ever,
Martin Stukely.

I stared not just at the letter, but at its implications.

Daniel looked over my shoulder, and asked what formulae were. "Are they secrets?" he said.

"Sometimes."

When Bon-Bon had read the last loving letter and had dried her tears, I asked her how well Martin had known Doctor Adam Force.

With eyes darkened from crying, she said she didn't know. She regretted desperately all the hours the two of them had spent in pointless arguing. "We never discussed anything without quarreling. You know what we were like. But I *loved* him . . . and he loved *me,* I know he did."

They had quarreled and loved, both intensely, throughout the four years I'd known them. It was too late to wish that Martin had confided more in her, even in spite of her chattering tongue, but together for once they had decided that it should be I and not Bon-Bon who held Martin's secret for safekeeping.

What secret? *What secret?* dear God.

Alone in the den since Bon-Bon and Daniel had gone upstairs to the other children, I sorted through everything in the drawer, putting many loose letters in heaps according to subject. There were several used old checkbooks with sums written on the stubs but quite often not dates or payees. Martin must have driven his accountant crazy. He seemed simply to have thrust tax papers, receipts, payments and earnings haphazardly into his out-of-sight drawer.

Semi-miracles occasionally happen, though, and on one stub, dated November 1999 (no actual day), I came across the plain name Force (no Doctor, no Adam). On the line below there was the single word BELLOWS, and in the box for the amount of money being transferred out of the account there were three zeros, 000, with no whole numbers and no decimal points.

Searches through three other sets of stubs brought to light a lot of similar unfinished records: Martin deserved secrets, curse him, when he wrote so many himself.

The name Force appeared again on a memo pad, when a Martin handwriting scrawl said, "Force, Bristol, Wednesday if P. doesn't declare Legup at Newton Abbot."

Legup at Newton Abbot . . . Say Legup was a horse and Newton Abbot the racetrack where he was entered . . . I stood up from Martin's desk and started on the form books in his bookcase, but although Legup had run in about eight races in the fall and spring over four or five years, and seldom, as it happened, on Wednesdays, there wasn't any mention of days he'd been entered but stayed at home.

I went back to the drawer.

A loose-leaf notebook, the most methodically kept of all his untidy paperwork, appeared as a gold mine of order compared with all the rest. It listed, with dates, amounts given by Martin to Eddie Payne, his racetrack valet, since the previous June 1. It included even the day he died, when he'd left a record of his intentions.

As there was, to my understanding, a pretty rigid scale of pay from jockeys to valets, the notebook at first sight looked less important than half the neglected rest, but on the first page Martin had doodled the names of Ed Payne, Rose Payne, Gina Verity and Victor. In a box in a corner, behind straight heavy bars, he'd written Waltman. There were small sketches of Ed in his apron, Gina in her curlers, Victor with his computer and Rose . . . Rose had a halo of spikes.

Martin had known this family, I reflected, for almost as long as Ed had been his valet. When Martin had received the letter from Victor Waltman Verity, he would have known it was a fifteen-year-old's game. Looking back, I could see I hadn't asked the right questions, because I'd been starting from the wrong assumptions.

With a sigh I put down the notebook and read through the letters, most of which were from the owners of horses that Martin's skill had urged first past the post. All the letters spoke of the esteem given to an honest jockey and none of them had the slightest relevance to secrets on videotapes.

A 1999 diary came next, though I found it not in the drawer but on top of the desk, put there by one of the children. It was a detailed jockey's diary, with all race meetings listed. Martin had circled everywhere he'd ridden, with the names of his mounts. He had filled in Tallahassee on the last day of the century, the last day of his life.

I lolled in Martin's chair, both mourning him and wishing like hell that he could come back alive just for five minutes.

My mobile phone, lying on the desk, gave out its brisk summons and, hoping it was Catherine, I pushed "send."

It wasn't Catherine.

Victor's cracked voice spoke hurriedly.

"Can you come to Taunton on Sunday? Please say you will

catch the same train as before. I'm running out of money for this phone. Please say yes."

I listened to the urgency, to the virtual panic.

I said, "Yes, OK," and the line went dead.

I would have gone blithely unwarned to Taunton on that Sunday if it hadn't been for Worthington shouting in alarm over crackling lines from a mountaintop.

"Haven't you learned the first thing about not walking into an ambush?"

"Not Victor," I protested. "He wouldn't lure me into a trap."

"Oh yeah? And does the sacrificial lamb understand he's for the chop?"

Lamb chop or not, I caught the train.

CHAPTER 6

Tom Pigeon, who lived within walking distance with his three energetic Dobermans, strolled to the gallery door of Logan Glass late on Saturday morning and invited me out for a beer in a local pub. Any bar, but not the Dragon's across the road, he said.

With the dogs quietly tied to a bench outside, Tom Pigeon drank deep on a pint in a crowded dark inn and told me that Worthington thought that I had more nerve than sense when it came to the Verity-Paynes.

"*Mm*. Something about a wasps' nest," I agreed. "When, exactly, did he talk to you?"

Tom Pigeon looked at me over the rim of his glass as he

swallowed the dregs. "He said you were no slouch in the brain box. He told me this morning." He smiled. "He phoned from Gstaad. Only the best for his lady employer, of course."

He ordered a second pint while I still dawdled about on my first. His slightly piratical dark little pointed beard and his obvious physical strength turned heads our way. I might be of his age and height, but no one sidled away at my approach, or found me an instinctive threat.

"It was only a week ago tomorrow," he said, "that they hammered you until you could hardly stand."

I thanked him for my deliverance.

He said, "Worthington wants you to stay away from any more trouble of that sort. Especially, he said, while he's in Switzerland."

I listened, though, to the Tom Pigeon view of that course of inaction. He sounded as bored with the safe road to old age as Worthington himself had been the day he had goaded me to go to Leicester races.

"Worthington's coming across like a father," Tom said.

"A bodyguard," I commented wryly, "and I miss him."

Tom Pigeon said casually but with unmistakable sincerity, "Take me on board instead."

I reflected briefly that Tom's offer wasn't what Worthington had intended to spark off, and wondered what my dear constable Dodd would think of my allying myself to an ex–jail occupant with a nickname like Backlash. I said regardless, "Yes, if you'll do what I ask . . ."

"Maybe."

I laughed and suggested how he might spend his Sunday. His eyes widened and came to vivid approving life. "Just as long as it's legal," he bargained. "I'm not going back in the slammer."

"It's legal," I assured him; and when I caught the train the following morning I had a new rear defender in the guards' van, accompanied by three of the most dangerous-looking black dogs that ever licked one's fingers.

There was only one possible train combination to travel on that would achieve the same time of arrival at Lorna Terrace as I'd managed the previous Sunday. It would be the time that Victor meant. Tom had wanted to rethink the plan and go by car. He would drive, he said. I shook my head and changed his mind.

Suppose, I'd suggested, this is not the ambush that Worthington feared, but just the frantic need of a worried boy. Give him a chance, I'd said.

We would compromise, though, about the awkward return journey. We would rent a car with driver to follow us from Taunton station, to shadow us faithfully, to pick us up when we wanted and finally drive us to Broadway and home.

"Expensive," Tom Pigeon complained.

"I'm paying," I said.

Victor himself was waiting on the Taunton platform when the train wheels ran smoothly into the station. I'd traveled near the front of the train so as to be able to spot and to pass any little unwelcoming committee where I had plenty of space to assess them, but the boy seemed to be alone. Also, I thought, anxious. Also cold in the January wind. Beyond that, an enigma.

Tom's dogs, traveling at the rear of the train, slithered down onto the platform and caused a sharp local division between dog lovers and those with antifang reservations.

I reckoned, or anyway hoped, that Victor himself wouldn't know Tom or his dogs by sight, even though Rose and the rest of her family probably would, after the rout of the black masks in Broadway.

I needed no black mask to meet Victor, but learning from the plainclothes police, I wore a baseball cap at the currently with-it angle above a navy-blue tracksuit topped with a paler blue sleeveless padded jacket. Normal enough for many, but different from my usual gray pants and white shirt.

Bon-Bon's children having sniggered behind their hands, and Tom having swept his gaze over me blankly as if I had been a stranger, I walked confidently and silently in my sneakers to Victor's back and said quietly in his ear, "Hello."

He whirled around and took in my changed appearance with surprise, but chief of his emotions seemed to be straightforward relief that I was there at all.

"I was afraid you wouldn't come," he said. "Not when I heard them saying how they'd smashed you up proper. I don't know what to do. I want you to tell me what to do. They tell me lies." He was shaking slightly, more with nervousness, I guessed, than with cold.

"First of all, we get off this windy platform," I said. "Then you tell me where your mother thinks you are."

Down in front of the station the driver I'd engaged was polishing a dark blue estate car large enough for the occasion. Tom Pigeon came out of the station with his dogs, made contact with the driver and loaded the Dobermans into the big rear space designed for them.

Victor, not yet realizing that the car and dogs had anything to do with him, answered my question and a dozen others. "Mom thinks I'm at home. She's gone to see my dad in jail. It's visiting day. I listened to her and my auntie Rose planning what they would say to me, and they made up some story about Mom going to see a woman with a disgusting illness that I wouldn't like. Every time she goes to see Dad they make up another reason why I stay at home. Then, when I listened some more, I heard them say they're going to try again, after Mom sees Dad, to make you tell them where the tape is you had from Granddad Payne. They say it's worth millions. My auntie Rose says its all nonsense for you to say you don't know. Please, please tell her where it is, or what's on it, because I can't bear her *making* people tell her things. I've heard them twice up in our attic screaming and groaning and she just laughs and says they have toothache."

I turned away from Victor so that he shouldn't see the absolute horror that flooded my mind and assuredly appeared on my face. Just the idea of Rose using teeth for torture melted at once any theoretical resistance I might have thought to be within my own capacity.

Teeth.

Teeth and wrists and hell knew what else . . .

The need intensified to a critical level to find out what secrets I was supposed to know, and then to decide what to do with the knowledge. Victor, I thought, might be able to dig from the semi-conscious depths of his memory the scraps I still needed if I were to glue together a credible whole. I had pieces. Not enough.

I asked with an inward shudder, "Where is your auntie Rose today? Did she too visit your dad?"

He shook his head. "I don't know where she is. She didn't go to the jail because Dad's not talking to her since she shopped him." He paused, and then said passionately, "I wish I belonged to an ordinary family. I wrote to Martin once and asked if I could stay with him for a while but he said they didn't have room. I begged him. . . ." His voice cracked. "What can I do?"

It seemed clear that Victor's need for someone to advise him stretched very far back. It wasn't odd that he was now close to breakdown.

"Come for a ride?" I suggested with friendliness, and held open for him the door behind the estate car driver. "I'll get you back home before you're missed, and before that we can talk about what you need."

He hesitated only briefly. He had, after all, brought me there to help him, and it appeared he was reaching out to someone he trusted even though his family considered that person to be an enemy. Victor couldn't invent or act at this level of desperation.

If this were an ambush, then Victor was the lamb who didn't know it.

I asked him if he knew where I could find Adam Force. The question caused a much longer hesitation and a shake of the head. He knew, I thought, but perhaps telling me came under the category of squealing.

Tom Pigeon sat beside the driver, making him nervous simply by being himself. Victor and I sat in the rear passenger seats with the dogs behind us, separated from us by a netting divider. The driver, taciturn from first to last, set off as soon as we were all aboard and headed at first through winding Somerset country roads and then out to the wide expanses of Exmoor. Even in the summer, I imagined, it would be a bare and daunting place, grim with sunny dreams unfulfilled and long skylines blurring into drizzly mist. On that Sunday in January the cloudless air was bright, cold and crisp and on the move. The driver pulled off the road onto an area consolidated for tourist parking, and with a few spare words pointed to a just perceptible path ahead, telling me it led onto trackless moorland if I went far enough.

He would wait for us, he said, and we could take our time. He had brought a packed picnic lunch for all of us, as I had arranged.

Tom Pigeon's dogs disembarked and bounded free ecstatically, sniffing with unimaginable joy around heather roots in rich dark red earth. Tom himself stepped out of the car and stretched his arms and chest wide, filling his lungs with deep breaths of clean air.

Victor's face, transformed by the exchange of terrace-house-Taunton for wide-open sky, looked almost carefree, almost happy.

Tom and his black familiars set off fast along the track and were soon swallowed into the rolling scenery. Victor and I followed him but eventually more slowly, with Victor pouring out his devastating home life and difficulties, as I guessed he'd never done before.

"Mom's all right," he said. "So's Dad really, except when he comes home from the pub. Then if Mom or I get too near him he belts us one." He swallowed. "No, I didn't mean to say that. But last time he broke her ribs and her nose and her face was black all down one side; and when Auntie Rose saw it she went to the cops, and it was funny, really, because other times I'd seen *her* hit my dad. She's got fists like a boxer when she gets going. She can deal it out until the poor buggers beg her to stop, and that's when she laughs at them, and often when she's clouted them once or twice more, she'll step back a bit and smile . . . And then sometimes she'll *kiss* them." He glanced at me anxiously, sideways, to see what I made of his aunt Rose's behavior.

I thought that possibly I'd got off fairly lightly at the hands of the black masks, thanks to Rose having met her equal in ferocity, my friend with his dogs ahead now on the moor.

I asked Victor, "Has Rose ever attacked you, personally?"

He was astonished. "No, of course not. She's my aunt."

I'd give him perhaps another two years, I thought, before his aunt looked on him as a grown man, not a child.

We walked another length of track while I thought how little I understood of the psychology of women like Rose. Men who enjoyed being beaten by women weren't the sort that attracted Rose. For her to be fulfilled they had to hate it.

The track had narrowed until I was walking in front of Victor, which made talking difficult, but then suddenly the ground widened into a broader flat area from which one could see distant views in most directions. Tom Pigeon stood out below us, his Dobermans zigzagging around him with unfettered joy.

After watching them for several moments I gave life to an

ear-splitting whistle, a skill taught me by my father and brother, who had both been able to accomplish the near-impossible of summoning taxis in London in the rain.

Tom stopped fast, turned towards me from lower down the rolling hills, waved acknowledgment, and began to return to where I stood. His dogs aimed towards me without a single degree of deviation.

"Wow," Victor said, impressed. "How do you do that?"

"Curl your tongue." I showed him how, and I asked him again to tell me more about Doctor Force. I needed to talk to him, I said.

"Who?"

"You know damn well who. Doctor Adam Force. The man who wrote the letter you copied and sent to Martin."

Victor, silenced, took a while to get going again.

In the end he said, "Martin knew it was a game."

"Yes, I'm sure he did," I agreed. "He knew you well, he knew Adam Force, and Adam Force knows you." I watched Tom Pigeon trudge towards us up the hill. "You may know their secret, that one that was on the tape everyone's talking about."

"No," Victor said, "I don't."

"Don't lie," I told him. "You don't like liars."

He said indignantly, "I'm not lying. Martin knew what was on the tape, and so did Doctor Force, of course. When I sent that letter to Martin I was just pretending to be Doctor Force. I often pretend to be other people, or sometimes animals. It's only a game. Sometimes I talk to people who don't really exist."

Harvey the rabbit, I thought, and I'd been engine drivers and jockeys in my time. Victor would grow out of it soon, but not soon enough for now in January 2000.

I asked him how he had obtained a copy of Doctor Force's letter, which he had sent to Martin with his own name attached instead of Force's.

He didn't reply but just shrugged his shoulders.

I asked him yet again if he knew where I could find his Doctor Force, but he said dubiously that Martin had for sure written it down somewhere.

Probably he had. Victor knew where, but he still wasn't telling that either. There had to be some way of persuading him. Some way of bringing him to the point of wanting to tell.

Tom Pigeon and his three bouncing companions reached us at the flattened viewing area, all clearly enjoying the day.

"That's some whistle," Tom commented admiringly, so I did it again at maximum loudness, which stunned the dogs into pointing their muzzles in my direction, their noses twitching, their eyes alert, Tom patting them, with their stumpy tails wagging excessively.

Walking back towards the car Victor did his breathy best at a whistle that would equally affect the dogs, but they remained unimpressed. Water in dishes and handfuls of dog biscuits, brought from home by their owner, suited them better as a prelude to lying down for a doze.

Tom himself, the driver, Victor and I ate sandwiches inside the car, out of the wind, and afterwards sleep came easily to the other three. I left the car and walked back slowly along the track sorting out and simplifying Victor's muddling game of pretense and reducing the Verity-Payne videotape roundabout to probabilities. Still, the absolutely first thing to do next, I concluded, was to find Adam Force, and the path to him still lay with Victor.

What I needed was to get Victor to trust me so instinctively that his most deeply secret thoughts would pop out of him without caution. Also I needed to get him to that state fast, and I didn't know if that sort of total brainwash were possible, let alone ethical.

When there was movement around the car I returned to tell the yawning passengers that according to my new cheap watch it was time to leave if we were to get back to Lorna Terrace in advance of the time that Victor was expecting his mom.

Tom walked off to find comfort behind bushes, and jerked his head for me to go with him.

Contingency planning was in his mind. The day had gone too smoothly. Had I considered a few "What ifs"?

We considered them together and returned to the car, where the taciturn driver had taken a liking to Victor and was deep in esoteric chat about computers.

The contentment of the day high on the moor slowly sank and evaporated as the estate car inevitably drew nearer to Lorna Terrace. Victor's nervous tremor reasserted itself and he watched me anxiously for signs of thrusting him back into his unsatisfactory life. He knew pretty well that at fifteen he would be at the mercy of the courts, and that the courts' mercy would undoubtedly be to consign him to the care of his mother. Gina, his mother, even a Gina chain-smoking in large pink curlers, would quite likely be

seen as the badly-done-by parent of a thankless child. Gina Verity, unlike her sister Rose, who couldn't help radiating a faint air
of menace, would be seen by any court in the way that I had seen
her at first, as a relaxed, tolerant and fond mother doing her best
in difficult circumstances.

The driver stopped the car where Tom Pigeon asked him,
which was around the bend that kept him out of sight of No. 19.
Victor and I disembarked at that point, and I sympathized very
much with the misery and hopelessness reappearing in the droop
of his shoulders. I went with him to the front door of No. 19,
which as in many terraced houses opened from a concrete path
across a small square front garden of dusty grass. Victor produced
a key from a pocket and let us in, leading me as before down the
passage to the bright little kitchen where life was lived, and
where I had promised to stay as company until his mother came
back, even though she might not like it.

The door from the kitchen brought Victor to a standstill of
puzzlement and unease.

He said, "I'm sure I bolted the door before I went out." He
shrugged. "Anyway, I know I bolted that gate from the backyard
into the lane. Mom gets furious if I forget it."

He opened the unbolted kitchen door and stepped out into a
small high-walled square of backyard. Across the weeds and dead-
looking grass a tall brown-painted door was set into the high
brick wall, and it was this door that freshly upset Victor by again
not having its bolts, top and bottom, firmly slid into place.

"Bolt them now," I said urgently about the door from the
lane, but Victor stood still in front of me in puzzlement and

dismay, and although understanding flashed like lightning through my mind, I couldn't get around Victor fast enough. The door from the lane opened the moment I stepped towards it across the grass from the kitchen.

Rose had come into the backyard from the lane. Gina and the quasi gorilla Norman Osprey marched out triumphantly from the house. Both Rose and Osprey were armed with a cut-off section of garden hose. Rose's piece had a tap on it.

Victor at my side stood like a rock, not wanting to believe what he was seeing. When he spoke, the words addressed to his mother were a scramble of "You've come back early."

Rose prowled like a hunting lioness between me and the door to the lane, swinging the heavy brass tap on the supple green hose, and almost licking her lips.

Gina, for once without curlers and pretty as a result, tried to justify the prospect ahead by whining to Victor that his caged father had told her to eff off, he wasn't in the mood for her silly chatter. In her anger she told Victor for the first time that his father was "inside," and deserved it.

"He can be a mean brute, your dad," Gina said. "And when we'd gone all that way! So Rose drove me home again, and that bitch next door told me you'd sneaked off craftily to the station, because she followed, as she was going that way anyhow, and you met that fellow, that one over there, that Rose says is stealing a million from us. How *can* you, young Vic? So Rose says this time she'll make him tell us what we want to know, but it's no thanks to you, Rose says."

I heard only some of it. I watched Victor's face, and saw with relief his strong alienation from Gina's smug voice. The more she said, the more he didn't like it. Teenage rebellion visibly grew.

The present and future scene here hadn't been exactly one of the "what ifs" that Tom and I had imagined in the bushes, but now what if . . . if I could think it out fast enough . . . if I could use Victor's horrified reaction to his mother's outpouring . . . if I could put up with a bit of Rose's persuasion . . . then perhaps—on top of the carefree day on the moor—perhaps Victor would indeed feel like telling me what I was sure he knew. Perhaps the sight of his aunt Rose's cruelty in action would impel him to offer a gift in atonement . . . to offer me the one thing he knew I wanted. Maybe the prize was worth a bit of discomfort. So get on with it, I told myself. If you're going to do it, do it fast.

Last Sunday, I thought, the black masks had jumped me unawares. It was different this Sunday. I could invite the assault head-on, and I did, at a run towards the door to the lane, straight towards Rose and her swinging tap.

She was fast and ruthless and managed to connect twice before I caught her right arm and bent it up behind her, her face close to mine, her dry skin and freckles in sharp focus, hate and sudden pain drawing her lips back from her teeth. Gina, yelling blasphemy, tore at my ear to free her sister.

I caught a glimpse of Victor's horror an instant before Norman Osprey lashed out at me from behind with his own length of hose. Rose wrenched herself out of my grip, pushed Gina out of her way and had another swing at me with her tap. I managed a circular kickbox which temporarily put the gorilla Norman facedown on the grass, and in return got another fearful clout from Rose along the jaw, which ripped the skin open.

Enough, I thought. Far and away too much. Blood dripped everywhere. I used my only real weapon, the piercing whistle for help, which Tom and I in the bushes had agreed meant "come at once."

What if I whistle and he doesn't come . . . ?

I whistled again, louder, longer, calling not for a taxi in the rain in London, but quite likely for life without deformity and certainly for self-respect. I couldn't have told Rose from direct knowledge where to find that videotape, but if I'd needed to badly enough I would have invented something. Whether or not she would have believed me was another matter and one I hoped not to find out.

I fortunately also didn't find out what conclusion Rose intended for her Sunday afternoon sports. There was a vast crashing and tinkling noise and Tom's voice roaring at his dogs, and then three snarling Doberman pinschers poured like a torrent out of the house's wide-open kitchen door into the confined space of the backyard.

Tom carried an iron bar he'd borrowed from local town railings. Norman Osprey backed away from him, his hose soft and useless in opposition, his Sunday pleasure no longer one long laugh.

Rose, the quarry of the dogs, turned tail and ignominiously left the scene through the gate into the lane, sliding through a small opening and pulling it shut behind her.

Trusting that the dogs knew me well enough to keep their fangs to themselves, I walked among them and slid the bolts across on the wall-to-lane door, blocking Rose's immediate way back.

Gina screeched at Tom only once and without much conviction, Tom's fierce physical closeness reducing her protests to nil. She was silent even when she discovered Tom's mode of entry had been to smash open her front door. She didn't try to stop her son when he ran past her along the passage from backyard to front, and called to me in the few steps before I reached the road.

Tom and the Dobermans were already out on the sidewalk on their way back to the car.

I stopped at once when Victor called me, and waited until he came up. Either he would tell me or he wouldn't. Either the hose and tap had been worth it, or they hadn't. Payoff time.

"Gerard . . ." He was out of breath, not from running but from what he'd seen in the yard. "I can't bear all this. If you want to know . . . Doctor Force lives in Lynton," he said. "Valley of Rocks Road."

"Thanks," I said.

Victor unhappily watched me use tissues scrounged from his mother's kitchen to blot the oozing blood on my face. I said, "There's always e-mail, don't forget."

"How can you even speak to me?"

I grinned at him. "I still have all my teeth."

"Look out for Rose," he warned me anxiously. "She never gives up."

"Try to arrange to live with your grandfather," I suggested. "It would be safer than here."

Some of his misery abated. I touched his shoulder in parting and walked along Lorna Terrace to where Tom Pigeon waited.

Tom looked at my battered face and commentated, "You were a hell of a long time whistling."

"Mm." I smiled. "Silly of me."

"You delayed it on purpose!" he exclaimed in revelation. "You let that harpy hit you."

"You get what you pay for, on the whole," I said.

Most bruises faded within a week, Martin had said, and also this time on the Monday I got a doctor to stick together the worst of the cuts with small adhesive strips.

"I suppose you walked into another black-masked door," guessed Constable Dodd, horrified. "Rose may not frighten you but, from what I've heard, she'd terrify me."

"Rose didn't bother about a mask," I said, putting together a spicy rice supper on Monday evening in the kitchen of my house on the hill. "Do you like garlic?"

"Not much. What are you planning to do about Rose Payne? You should go to the Taunton police and make a complaint against her for assault. That wound might even constitute GBH."

Grievous Bodily Harm, I thought. Not half as grievous as she had intended.

"What would I tell them—a thin woman beat me up so a

friend of mine with a criminal record smashed down her front door and set his dogs on her?"

She was not amused but simply repeated, "So what are you going to do about her?"

I didn't answer directly. I said instead, "Tomorrow I'm going to Lynton in Devon and I'd rather she didn't know." I frowned over a green pepper. "It's a wise man as knows his enemies," I asserted, "and I do know our Rose."

"In the biblical sense?"

"God forbid!"

"But Rose Payne is only one person," Catherine said, drinking fizzy water routinely. "There were four black masks, you said."

I nodded. "Norman Osprey, bookmaker, he was Number Two, and Ed Payne, who was Martin Stukely's racetrack valet and is Rose's father, he was Number Three and he's sorry for it, and all those three know I recognized them. One other seemed familiar to me at the time but I can't have been right. He was a clutcher setting me up for the others and I think of him as Number Four. He was behind me most of the time."

Catherine listened in silence and seemed to be waiting.

Skidding now and then across a half-formed recollection went the so-far unidentified figure that I called simply Blackmask Four, and I remembered him most for the inhumanity he took to his task. It had been Norman Osprey who'd smashed my watch, but it had been Blackmask Four who'd bunched my fingers for him. For all Norman Osprey's awesome strength, in retrospect it was Blackmask Four who'd scared me most, and who now, eight days later, intruded fearsomely into my dreams, nightmares in which Blackmask Four intended to throw me into the 1800 degrees Fahrenheit of the liquid glass in the tank in the furnace.

That night, while Constable Dodd slept peacefully in my arms, it was she whom Blackmask Four threw to a burning death.

I awoke sweating and cursing Rose Payne with words I'd rarely used before, and I felt more reluctant than ever to leave Catherine to the risks of her plainclothes operation.

"Come back safe yourself this time," she said worriedly, zooming off in the dawn, and I, with every intention of carrying out her instructions, walked down to my blameless furnace and did the day's work before my three helpers arrived.

The day before they had joked about my recurring Monday bruises, which Irish had sworn were the result of pub brawls. I hadn't disillusioned them, and on the Tuesday cheerfully left them practicing dishes for the day while I walked out of the village for a mile to catch a bus.

Neither Rose nor Gina, nor anyone else I knew, came into sight, and I felt, when I disembarked outside a busy newsstand in the next town and climbed into another prearranged car with driver, that there could be no one on my tail. Tom Pigeon, who had designed "the simple exit for glassblowers," had begged me at least to take one of his dogs with me, if I wouldn't take *him*. Hadn't I been bashed enough? he asked. Hadn't I needed him to rescue me twice? Wasn't I now being insane to insist on traveling alone?

Yes, quite likely, I agreed. So give me advice.

Thanks to him, then, I went to Lynton on the North Devon coast unmolested, and in the electoral register found the full address of Doctor Adam Force, in the Valley of Rocks Road.

The chief disappointment to this successful piece of research was that there was no one in the house.

I knocked and rang and waited and tried again, but the tall gray old building had a dead air altogether and an empty-sounding reverberation when I tried the back door. The neighbors weren't helpful. One was out, and one was deeply deaf. A passing housewife said she thought Doctor Force worked in Bristol during the week and came to Lynton only for the weekends. Not so, contradicted a shuffling old man angrily waving a walking stick; on Tuesdays, Doctor Force could be found up Hollerday Hill, at the nursing home.

The old man's anger, explained the housewife, was a form of madness. Doctor Force went up to Hollerday Phoenix House every Tuesday, insisted the walking stick.

My driver—"Call me Jim"—long-sufferingly reversed and returned to the town's center when the double bull's-eye more or less left us both laughing. Doctor Force worked in Bristol half the time *and* opened up his Valley of Rocks dreary house on Sundays and Mondays, *and* went up to Hollerday Phoenix House on Tuesdays. A small girl with plaited blond hair pointed out the road to Hollerday Phoenix House, then told us not to go there because of the ghosts.

Ghosts?

The Phoenix House was haunted, didn't we know?

The Town Hall scoffed at the idea of ghosts, afraid of deterring holiday visitors in spring and summer.

That useful person, 'A Spokesman,' explained that the mansion built by Sir George Newnes on Hollerday Hill had been totally arsonized in 1913 by persons still unknown and later blown up as part of an army exercise. The Phoenix House recently built close to the grown-over ruins was a private nursing home. There were positively no ghosts. Doctor Force had patients in the nursing home whom he visited on Tuesdays.

My driver, who believed in the supernatural, cravenly balked at driving up to the Hollerday Phoenix House, but swore he would wait for me to walk there and back, which I believed, as I hadn't yet paid him.

I thanked 'A Spokesman' for his help. And could he describe Doctor Force, so I would know him if I saw him?

"Oh yes," 'A Spokesman' said, "you'd know him easily. He has very blue eyes, and a short white beard, and he's wearing orange socks."

I blinked.

"He can't see red or green," 'A Spokesman' said. "He's color-blind."

CHAPTER 7

I took the quiet old back way through the woods, climbing the overgrown gently sloping carriage road that thoughtful Sir George Newnes had had blasted through rock to save his horses having to haul a coach up a heart-straining incline to his house.

On that January Tuesday I walked alone through the trees. Traffic motored sparsely along a modern road on the other side of the hill, raising not even a distant hum on its way to the new complex that had risen on the memory of the old.

There were no birds where I walked; no song. It was dark even in daylight, the close-growing evergreens crowding overhead. My feet trod noiselessly on fallen fir needles and in places there were still bare upright slabs of raw gray blasted rock. At-mospherically the hundred-year-old path raised goose bumps. There were ruins of a tennis court where long ago people had laughed and played in another world. *Eerie,* I thought, was the word for it, but I saw no ghosts.

I came down to Hollerday Phoenix House from above, as "A Spokesman" had foretold, and saw that much of the roof was covered with large metal-framed panes of glass, which opened and closed like roofs of greenhouses. The glass of course inter-ested me—it was thick float glass tinted to filter out ultraviolet A and B rays of sunlight—and I thought of the departed days of sanataria, where people with tuberculosis most unromantically coughed their lives away in the vain hope that airy sunshine would cure them.

Hollerday Phoenix House spread wide in one central block with two long wings. I walked around to the impressive front door and found that the building I entered at the conclusion of the spooky path was definitely of the twenty-first century, and in no way the haunt of apparitions.

The entrance hall looked like a hotel, but I saw no farther into the nursing home's depths because of the two white-coated peo-ple leaning on the reception desk. One was female and the other grew a coat-colored beard, and did indeed wear orange socks.

They glanced briefly my way as I arrived, then straightened with resigned professional interest when I presented with cuts and bruises that actually, until they peered at me, I had forgotten.

"Doctor Force?" I tried, and white-beard satisfactorily answered, "Yes?"

His fifty-six years sat elegantly on his shoulders, and his well-brushed hair, along with the beard, gave him the sort of shape to his head that actors got paid for. Patients would trust him, I thought. I might have been pleased myself to have him on my case. His manner held authority in enough quantity to show me I was going to have difficulty jolting him the way I wanted.

Almost at once I saw, too, that the difficulty was not a matter of jolting him but of following the ins and outs of his mind. All through the time I was with him I felt him swing now and then from apparently genuine and friendly responses to evasion and stifled ill will. He was quick and he was clever, and although most of the time I felt a warm liking for him, occasionally there was a quick flash of antipathy. He was powerfully attractive overall, but the charm of Adam Force, it seemed to me, could flow in and out like a tide.

"Sir," I said, giving seniority its due. "I'm here on account of Martin Stukely."

He put on a sorry-to-tell-you expression, and told me that Martin Stukely was dead. At the same time there was a rigidity of shock on his facial muscles: it wasn't a name he'd expected to hear up Hollerday Hill in Lynton. I said I knew Martin Stukely was dead.

He asked with suspicion, "Are you a journalist?"

"No," I said. "A glassblower." I added my name, "Gerard Logan."

His whole body stiffened. He swallowed and absorbed the surprise and eventually pleasantly asked, "What do you want?"

I said equally without threat, "I'd quite like back the videotape you took from the Logan Glass showroom in Broadway on New Year's Eve."

"You would, would you?" He smiled. He was ready for the question. He had no intention of complying, and was recovering his poise. "I don't know what you are talking about."

Doctor Force made a slow survey from head to foot of my deliberately conservative suit and tie and I felt as positive as if he had said it aloud that he was wondering if I had enough clout to cause him trouble. Apparently he realistically gave himself an honest but unwelcome answer, as he suggested not that I buzz off straight away, but that we discuss the situation in the open air.

By open air it transpired he meant the path I'd just ascended. He led that way and sneaked a sideways glance to measure my discomfort level, which was nil. I smiled and mentioned that I hadn't noticed any ghosts on the prowl on my way up.

Should he be aware of small damages to my face and so on, I said, it was as a result of Rose Payne being convinced either that I had his tape in my possession, or that I knew what was on it. "She believes that if she's unpleasant enough, I'll give her the tape or the knowledge, neither of which I have." I paused and said, "What do you suggest?"

He said promptly, "Give this person anything. All tapes are alike."

"She thinks your tape is worth a million."

Adam Force fell silent.

"Is it?" I asked.

Under his breath Force said what sounded like the truth, "I don't know."

"Martin Stukely," I murmured without hostility, "wrote a check for you with a lot of zeros on it."

Force, very upset, said sharply, "He promised never to say . . ."

"He didn't say."

"But . . ."

"He died," I said. "He left check stubs."

I could almost feel him wondering "*What else* did Martin leave?" and I let him speculate. In the end in genuine-looking worry he said, "How did you find me?"

"Didn't you think I would?"

He very briefly shook his head and faintly smiled. "It didn't occur to me that you would bother to look. Most people would leave it to the police."

He would have been easy to like all the time, I thought, if one could forget Lloyd Baxter's epileptic fit, and a missing bank bag full of money.

"Rose Payne," I said distinctly, again . . . and somewhere in Adam Force this time her name touched a sensitive reaction. "Rose," I repeated, "is convinced I know where your videotape is, and as I said before, she is certain I know what's on it. Unless you find a way of rather literally getting her off my back, I may find her attentions too much to tolerate and I'll tell her what she's anxious to know."

He asked, as if he hadn't any real understanding of what I'd said, "Are you implying that I know this person, Rose? And are you also implying that I am in some way responsible for your . . . er . . . injuries?"

I said cheerfully, "Right both times."

"That's nonsense." His face was full of calculation as if he weren't sure how to deal with an awkward situation, but wouldn't rule out using his own name, Force.

On the brink of telling him why I reckoned I could answer my own questions, I seemed to hear both Worthington and Tom Pigeon shrieking at me to be careful about sticks and wasps' nests. The silence of the dark fir forest shook with their urgent warnings. I glanced at the benevolent doctor's thoughtful face and changed my own expression to regret.

Shaking my head, I agreed with him that what I'd said was of course nonsense. "All the same," I added after quizzically checking with my two absent bodyguards, "you did take the tape from my shop, so please can you at least tell me where it is now."

He relaxed inwardly a good deal at my change of tone. Worthington and Tom Pigeon went back to sleep. Doctor Force consulted his own inner safeguards and answered the question unsatisfactorily.

"Just suppose you are right and I have the tape. As Martin could no longer keep the information safe, there was no longer any need for it. Perhaps, therefore, I ran it through to record a sports program from first to last. That tape might now show horse racing and nothing else."

He had written to Martin that the knowledge on the tape was dynamite. If he'd wiped the dynamite out with racing, boasting he'd poured millions down the drain (or past the recording head), he still surely had whatever he needed for a clone.

No one would casually wipe out a fortune if not sure he could bring it back. Nobody would do it *on purpose,* that was.

So I asked him, "Did you obliterate it on purpose, or by mistake?"

He laughed inside the beard. He said, "I don't make mistakes."

The frisson I felt wasn't a winter shudder from a daunting fir forest but a much more prosaic recognition of a familiar and thoroughly human failing: for all his pleasant manner, the doctor thought he was God.

He stopped by a fallen fir trunk and briefly rested one foot on it, saying he would go back from there as he had patients to see. "I find business is usually completed by this point," he went on and his voice was dismissive. "I'm sure you'll find your own way down to the gate."

"There are just a couple of things," I said. My voice sounded flat, the acoustics dead between the trees.

He took his foot off the log and started to go back up the hill. To his obvious irritation I went with him.

"I said," he commented with a stab at finality, "that we'd completed our conversation, Mr. Logan."

"Well . . ." I hesitated, but Worthington and Tom Pigeon were quiet, and there wasn't even a squeak from the dogs. "How did you get to know Martin Stukely?"

He said calmly, "That's none of your business."

"You knew each other but you weren't close friends."

"Didn't you hear me?" he protested. "This is not your concern."

He quickened his step a little, as if to escape.

I said, "Martin gave you a large chunk of money in return for the knowledge that you referred to as dynamite."

"No, you're wrong." He walked faster, but I easily kept up with him stride for stride. "You completely do not understand," he said, "and I want you to leave."

I said I had no intention of leaving anytime soon, now that I saw beside me the likely answer to multiple riddles.

"Did you know," I asked him, "that Lloyd Baxter, the man you abandoned to his epileptic fit in my showroom, is the owner of Tallahassee, the horse that killed Martin Stukely?"

He walked faster up the slope. I stayed close, accelerating.

"Did you know," I asked conversationally, "that in spite of the onset of an epileptic seizure, Lloyd Baxter was able to describe you down to the socks?"

"Stop it."

"And of course you know Norman Osprey and Rose and Gina are as violent as they come . . ."

"No." His voice was loud, and he coughed.

"And as for my money that you whipped with that tape . . ."

Adam Force quite suddenly stopped walking altogether, and in the stillness I could clearly hear his breath wheezing in his chest.

It alarmed me. Instead of pretty well bullying him I asked him anxiously if he were all right.

"No thanks to you." The wheezing continued until he pulled from a pocket in his white coat the sort of inhaler I'd often seen used for asthma. He took two long puffs, breathing deeply while staring at me with complete dislike.

I was tempted to say "Sorry," but in spite of his charming ways and pleasant looks he'd been the cause of my being chucked to both the black masks in Broadway and to a piece of hose in a Taunton backyard, and if that were all, I'd count myself lucky. So I let him wheeze and puff his way up the rest of the incline. I went with him to make sure he didn't collapse on the way, and inside the reception area I checked him into a comfortable chair and went to find someone to pass him on to, for safekeeping.

I heard his wheezy voice behind me demanding my return, but by then I'd hurried halfway down one of the wings of the building and seen no human being at all, whether nurse, patient, doctor, cleaner, flower arranger or woman pushing a comforts cart. It wasn't that there weren't any beds in the rooms that lined the wing. In all the rooms there were beds, tray tables, armchairs and bathrooms, but no people. Each room had glass French doors opening to a well-swept area of garden tiles and parts of the glass roof were as wide open as they would go.

I stopped briefly at a room marked PHARMACY, which had an open skylight and a locked door of openwork grating to the passage. There was a host of visibly named pharmacy items inside, but still no people.

There had to be someone *somewhere,* I thought, and through the only closed door, at the end of the wing, I found a comparative beehive coming and going.

Twenty or more elderly men and women in thick white toweling bathrobes were contentedly taking part in comprehensive physical assessments, each test being brightly presented in play-school lettering, like "Your blood pressure measured here" and "Where does your cholesterol stand today?" A very old lady walked fast on a "jolly treadmill," and on the wall of a separate hard-sided booth was the notice "X rays here. Please keep out unless asked to step in."

Results were carefully written onto clipboards and then filed into computers at a central desk. An air of optimism prevailed.

My entrance brought to my side a nurse who'd been drawing curtains around a cubicle simply called UROLOGY. Squeaking across a polished floor on rubber soles, she smilingly told me I was late, and said only, "Oh dear," when I mentioned that the good Doctor Force might be gasping his last.

"He often does have attacks when he has visitors," the motherly nurse confided. "When you've gone, I expect he'll lie down and sleep."

The good Doctor Force was planning nothing of the sort. Registering annoyance like a steaming boiler, he wheezed to my side and pointed to a door coyly labeled "Here it is," then "Way out too." I explained as if harmlessly that I'd only come to find help for his asthma and he replied crossly that he didn't need it. He walked towards me with a syringe in a metal dish, advancing until I could see it was almost full of liquid. He picked up the highly threatening syringe and then jabbed it towards me and the exit; and this time I thanked him for his attention and left.

The door out of the medical examination hall led past lavish changing rooms to a generous lobby, and from there to a forecourt outside.

Unexpectedly I found the Rover waiting there, Jim, my driver, nervously pacing up and down beside it. He held the door open for me while explaining that his concern for my welfare had overcome his natural instincts. I thanked him with true feeling.

Doctor Force followed me out and waited until I was in the car and went indoors only after I'd given him a cheerfully innocent farewell wave, which he did not return.

"Is that the guy you came to see?" asked Jim.

"Yes."

"Not very friendly, is he."

I couldn't identify exactly what was wrong with that place, and was little further enlightened when a large bus turned smoothly through the entrance gate and came to a gentle halt. The title AVON PARADISE TOURS read black and white on lilac along the coach's sides, with smaller letters underneath giving an address in Clifton, Bristol.

Jim drove rapidly downhill until we had returned to, in his eyes, the supernatural safety of the town center. He did agree, though, subject to no further mention of things that go bump in the night, to drive around Lynton simply to enjoy it as a visitor.

Truth to tell, I was dissatisfied with myself on many counts and I wanted time to think before we left. I badly missed having my own car and the freedom it allowed; but there it was, I had indeed broken the speed limit often and got away with it before I'd been caught on the way to the dying gardener, and I could see that if Policewoman Catherine Dodd had a permanent toe in my future, I would have to ration my foot on the accelerator.

Meanwhile I persuaded Jim to stop in a side road. From there, Town Hall map in hand, I found my way to North Walk, a path around a seaward side of a grassy cliff, cold in the January wind and more or less deserted.

There were benches at intervals. I sat for a while on one and froze, and thought about the Adam Force who was color-blind, asthmatic, volatile and changeable in nature, and who visited an obscure nursing home only to do good. A minor practitioner, it seemed, though with a string of qualifications and a reputation for sparkling research. A man wasting his skills. A man who took a visitor outside to talk on a noticeably cold day and gave himself an asthmatic attack.

I trudged slowly around soaking up the spectacular views of the North Walk, wishing for summer. I thought of inconsequential things like coincidence and endurance and videotapes that were worth a million and could save the world. I also thought of the jewel I had made of glass and gold that not only looked truly old, but couldn't be distinguished from a three-thousand-five-hundred-year-old original. A necklace worth a million . . . but only one had that value, the genuine antiquity in a museum. The copy I had made once and could make again would be literally and only worth its weight in eighteen-carat gold, plus the cost of its colored glass components, and as much again, perhaps, for the knowledge and ability it took to make it.

Like many an artist of any sort, I found that it was to my own self alone that I could admit to the level I'd reached in my trade. It was also thanks to my uncle Ron's embargo on arrogance that I let the things I made achieve birth without trumpets.

That the existence of the tape explaining how to make the

necklace was in common knowledge among jockeys in the changing rooms didn't trouble me. I'd made it myself. It had my voice and hands on it, describing and demonstrating step by step what to do. I'd recorded it the way my uncle Ron had taught me in my teens. The actual gold necklace I'd made was in my bank, where I normally kept the tape as well. I'd better check on that, I supposed. I'd lent the instruction tape to Martin and didn't care if he'd shown it to anyone else, although I dearly wished he had returned it before it disappeared, along with all the others from his den.

I made a fairly brisk return to the end of the walk to find Jim striding up and down again and trying to warm his fingers. I thought perhaps he might not want to double the experience on the following day, but to my surprise, he agreed. "Tom Pigeon'll set his dogs on me if I don't," he said. "He phoned me just now in the car to check on you."

I swallowed a laugh. I prized those bodyguards, not resented them.

Jim apologized for not being in the same class as Worthington and Tom at kickboxing.

"I can bash heads against walls," he said.

I smiled and said that would do fine.

"I didn't know anything about you when I picked you up," Jim confessed. "I thought you were some useless sort of git. Then Tom tells me this and that on the phone and where Tom says he'll put his fists, you can count on mine."

"Well, thanks," I said weakly.

"So where do we go tomorrow?"

I said, "How does Bristol grab you? A hospital area, best of all?"

He smiled broadly, transforming his face in one second from dour to delighted. He knew his way around Bristol. Up Horfield Road we would find a hospital, or on Commercial Road down by the river. No problem at all. He drove an ambulance there one year, he said.

Jim said to count him out when it came to fists or feet, but no one could catch him in a car. We shook hands on it, and I acquired bodyguard number three, one who could slide around corners faster than Formula One.

Jim took me home and, apparently on Tom Pigeon's urging, came indoors with me and checked all ten rooms for uninvited occupants.

"You need a smaller pad," he judged, finishing the inspection of the window locks. "Or . . ."—he looked sideways—"a swarm of children."

Catherine arrived at that moment on her motorbike. The driver gave her a leer, and I had to explain . . . a swarm of children. Police Constable Dodd seemed not to think it a bad idea.

Much amused, the driver left. Catherine fussed over my fresher crop of trouble and said she'd been bored by the class reunion from registration to wrap.

I said, "Next time ditch the boredom and come home."

The words slid out as if on their own. I hadn't intended to say "home." I'd been going simply to offer the house as a refuge, I explained. She nodded. It was later, holding her in bed, that I thought of Sigmund Freud and his telltale slip.

Bristol was wet with drizzle.

My driver—"Call me Jim"—was short and stout and pronounced himself shocked that I preferred quiet in the car to perpetual radio.

Quite reasonably he asked where we were going exactly in the city. To find a phone book, I replied, and in the yellow pages singled out Avon Paradise Tours without trouble. They advertised that they operated adventures throughout Cornwall, Devon and Somerset and all points to London.

Jim, with his ambulance memory, more useful than any paper map, drove us unerringly to their lilac headquarters and with a flamboyant gesture drew the busy bus depot to my attention like a rabbit from an abracadabra top hat.

Once they understood what I was asking, the women in the Avon Paradise Tours office were moderately helpful but reluctant to say too much in case they broke house rules.

I did understand, didn't I?

I did.

They then opened the harmless floodgates and told me all.

On Tuesdays members of a Bristol area Health Clubs Association went on a scenic bus tour to the Hollerday Phoenix House nursing home in Lynton for medical checkups and advice on healthy living. Doctor Force, who ran the clinic because he lived in Lynton, was paid jointly by the health clubs and Avon Paradise Tours for his one day's work per week. After extra consultation together, the office staff admitted they'd been told Doctor Force had been "let go" (given the sack, did I understand?) by the research lab he used to work for.

Which research lab? They didn't know. They shook their heads in general, but one of them said she'd heard he'd been working on illnesses of the lungs.

Another phone book—listing all things medical—borrowed from the Avon Paradise ladies, had me trying all the remotely possible establishments, asking them via Paradise Tours phone if they knew a Doctor Force. Doctor Force? Unknown, unknown, unknown. The forever unknown Doctor Force had me looking out of the window at the distant sheen of the River Avon at high tide and wondering what to try next.

Illnesses of the lungs.

Check stubs. A lot of zeros. The payee . . . Bellows. In Martin's handwriting, it had meant nothing to Bon-Bon and nothing to me.

There wasn't any listing for Bellows in the Bristol area phone book, nor had Directory Inquiries ever heard of it.

Martin, though, had written BELLOWS boldly in unmistakable capital letters.

Lungs were bellows, of course.

My mind drifted. Rain spattered on the window. The ladies began to fidget, implying I'd overstayed my time.

BELLOWS.

Well . . . Maybe, why not?

Abruptly I asked if I might borrow their office telephone again and with their by-now rather grudging permission I spelled out Bellows in phone dial numbers, which resulted in 2355697. I punched them in carefully. There was nothing to lose.

After a long wait through maybe a dozen rings I was about to give up, when a brisk female voice hurriedly spoke, "Yes? Who is that?"

"Could I speak to Doctor Force, please," I said.

A long silence ensued. I was again about to disconnect and call it a waste of time when another voice, deep and male, inquired if I were the person asking for Doctor Force.

"Yes," I said. "Is he there?"

"Very sorry. No. He left several weeks ago. Can I have your name?"

I wasn't sure how to answer. I was beginning to learn caution. I said I would phone back very soon, and clicked off. To the Paradise ladies' curiosity I offered only profound thanks and left promptly, taking Jim in tow.

"Where to?" he asked.

"A pub for lunch."

Jim's face lightened like a cloudless dawn. "You're the sort of customer I can drive for all day."

In the event he drank one half pint of cola, which was my idea of a good hired driver.

The pub had a pay phone. When we were on the point of leaving I dialed BELLOWS again and found the male voice answering me at once.

He said, "I've been talking to Avon Paradise Tours."

I said, smiling, "I thought you might. You probably have this pub's public phone booth's number in front of your eyes at the moment. To save time, why don't we meet? You suggest somewhere and I'll turn up."

I repeated to Jim the place suggested, and got a nod of recognition. "Thirty minutes," Jim said, and twenty-two minutes later he stopped the car in a no-waiting zone near the gate of a wintry public park. Against the united teaching of Worthington, Tom Pigeon and Jim not to go anywhere unknown without one of them close, I got out of the car, waved Jim to drive on, and walked into the park on my own.

The drizzly rain slowly stopped.

The instructions for the meeting had been "Turn left, proceed to statue," and along the path, by a prancing copper horse, I met a tall, civilized, sensible-looking man who established to his own satisfaction that I was the person he expected.

CHAPTER 8

H E SPOKE AS if to himself. "He's six feet tall, maybe an inch or two more. Brown hair. Dark eyes. Twenty-eight to thirty-four years, I'd say. Personable except for recent injury to right side of jaw which has been medically attended to and is healing."

He was talking into a small microphone held in the palm of his hand. I let him see that I understood that he was describing me in case I attacked him in any fashion. The notion that I might do that would have made me laugh on any other day.

"He arrived in a gray Rover." He repeated Jim's registration number and then described my clothes.

When he stopped I said, "He's a glassblower named Gerard

Logan and can be found at Logan Glass, Broadway, Worcestershire. And who are you?"

He was the voice on the telephone. He laughed at my dry tone and stuffed the microphone away in a pocket. He gave himself a name, George Lawson-Young, and a title, Professor of Respiratory Medicine.

"And 2355697?" I asked. "Does it have an address?"

Even with modern technology he didn't know how I'd found him.

"Old-fashioned perseverance and guesswork," I said. "I'll tell you later in return for the gen on Adam Force."

I liked the professor immediately, feeling none of the reservations that had troubled me with Force. Professor Lawson-Young had no ill will that I could see, but on the contrary let his initial wariness slip away. My first impression of good-humored and solid sense progressively strengthened, so that when he asked what my interest in Adam Force was I told him straightforwardly about Martin's promise to keep safe Doctor Force's tape.

"Martin wanted me to keep it for him instead," I said, "and when he died the tape came into my hands. Force followed me to Broadway and took his tape back again, and I don't know where it is."

Out on the road Jim in the gray Rover drove slowly by, his pale face through the window on watch on my behalf.

"I came with a bodyguard," I said, waving reassurance to the road.

Professor Lawson-Young, amused, confessed he had only to yell down his microphone for assistance to arrive at once. He seemed as glad as I was that he would not have to use it. His tight muscles loosened. My own Worthington-Pigeon-driven alertness went to sleep.

The professor said, "How did you cut your face so deeply?"

I hesitated. What I'd done in the backyard of 19 Lorna Terrace sounded too foolish altogether. Because I didn't reply Lawson-Young asked again with sharper interest, pressing for the facts like any dedicated newsman. I said undramatically that I'd been in a fight and come off worst.

He asked next what I'd been fighting about, and with whom, his voice full of the authority that he no doubt needed in his work.

Evading the whole truth, I gave him at least a part of it. "I wanted to find Doctor Force, and in the course of doing that I collided with a water tap. Clumsy, I'm afraid."

He looked at me intently with his head on one side. "You're lying to me, I'm sorry to say."

"Why do you think so?"

"It's unusual to fight a water tap."

I gave him a half-strength grin. "OK then, I got hit with one that was still on a hose. It's unimportant. I learned how to find Adam Force, and I talked to him yesterday in Lynton."

"Where in Lynton? In that new nursing home?"

"Phoenix House." I nodded. "Doctor Force's clinic looks designed for children."

"Not for children. For mentally handicapped patients. He does good work there with the elderly, I'm told."

"They seemed pretty happy, it's true."

"So what's your take-away opinion?"

I gave it without much hesitation. "Force is utterly charming when he wants to be, and he's also a bit of a crook."

"Only a bit?" The professor sighed. "Adam Force was in charge here of a project aimed at abolishing snoring by using fine optical fibers and microlasers. . . ." He briefly stopped. "I don't want to bore you. . . ."

My own interest, however, had awoken sharply as in the past I'd designed and made glass equipment for that sort of inquiry. When I explained my involvement, the professor was in his turn astonished. He enlarged into detail the work that Force had been busy with and had stolen.

"We'd been experimenting with shining a microlaser down a fine optical fiber placed in the soft tissues of the throat. The microlaser gently warms the tissues, which stiffens them, and that stops a person from snoring. What Adam Force stole was our results of the trials to find the optimum laser light wavelength needed to penetrate the tissues and heat them to the precise temperature necessary . . . do you follow?"

"More or less."

He nodded. "A reliable way of abolishing snoring would be invaluable for severe sufferers. Adam Force stole such data and sold it to a firm of marketers whose business it is to advertise and inform prospective buyers of goods available. Force sold our latest but incomplete data to people we had dealt with occasionally before and who had no reason to suspect anything was wrong. Adam produced the right paperwork. It was weeks before the theft was discovered and really no one could believe it when we went to the marketers and they told us they had already bought the material and paid Adam Force for what we were now trying to sell them."

"So you sacked him," I commented.

"Well, we should have. He must have thought we might, but he was crucial to our research program." The professor, however, looked regretful, not enraged.

I said, "Let me guess, you basically let him off. You didn't prosecute him because you all liked him so much."

Lawson-Young ruefully nodded. "Adam apologized more or less on his knees and agreed to pay the money back in installments, if we didn't take him to court."

"And did he?"

In depression the professor said, "He paid on the dot for two months, and then we found he was trying to sell some even more secret information . . . and I mean *priceless* information in world terms. . . ." He stopped abruptly, apparently silenced by the enormity of Adam Force's disloyalty.

Eventually he went on. "He repaid us for our generosity by stealing the most recent, the most dynamite-laden data in our whole laboratory, and we are certain that he is offering this work to the highest bid he can raise around the world. This is the information recorded on the tape Force took back from you, and it is this tape we have been praying you would find."

I said with incredulity, "But you didn't know that I existed."

"We did know you existed. Our investigators have been very diligent. But we weren't sure you hadn't been indoctrinated by Adam, like your friend Stukely."

"Martin?"

"Oh yes. Force can be utterly charming and persuasive, as you know. We think it likely he also swindled Stukely of a fairly large sum of money, saying it was to be applied to our research."

"But," I protested, "Martin wasn't a fool."

"It is quite likely that Stukely had no idea that the contents of the tape had been stolen. Believe me, you don't need to be a fool to be taken in by a con man. I wouldn't consider myself a fool, but he took *me* in. I treated him as a friend."

I said, "Wherever did Martin meet Doctor Force? I don't suppose you know."

"I actually do. They met at a fund-raising dinner for cancer research. Adam Force was there raising money on behalf of the charity, and Stukely was there as a guest of a man for whom he raced, who was also a patron of the charity. I too as it happens am a patron, and I also saw Martin Stukely briefly on that evening."

I vaguely remembered Martin mentioning the dinner but hadn't paid much attention. It was typical of Martin, though, to make friends in unexpected places. I had myself, after all, met him in a jury room.

After a while Lawson-Young said, "We searched absolutely everywhere for proof that Adam had in his possession material that belonged to the laboratory. We know . . . we're ninety percent certain . . . that he recorded every relevant detail onto the videotape that he entrusted to the care of Martin Stukely."

There was nothing, I heard with relief, about trying to make me reveal its whereabouts through the use of black-mask methods or threats of unmerciful dentistry. I was aware, though, that the former tension in the professor's muscles had returned, and I wondered if he thought I was fooling him, as Adam Force had done.

I said simply, "Force has the tape. Ask him. But yesterday he told me he'd recorded a sports program on top of your formulae and conclusions, and all that remained on the tape now was horse racing."

"Oh God."

I said, "I don't know that I believe him."

After a few moments the professor said, "How often can you tell if someone's lying?"

"It depends who they are and what they're lying about."

"*Mm,*" he said.

I glanced back in my mind to a long line of half-truths, my own included.

"Discard the lies," George Lawson-Young said, smiling, "and what you're left with is probably the truth."

After a while he repeated, "We've searched absolutely *everywhere* for proof that Adam had in his possession material that belongs to the laboratory. We believe that he recorded every relevant detail onto the videotape because one of our researchers thought he saw him doing it, but as he works in an altogether different field he believed Adam when he said he was making routine notes. Adam himself entrusted a tape into the care of Martin Stukely at Cheltenham races. When Stukely died we learned from asking around that his changing room valet had passed the tape on to Stukely's friend, as previously planned." He paused. "So as you are the friend, will you tell us where best to look for the missing tape? Better still, bring it to us yourself . . . as we believe you can."

I said baldly, "I can't. I think Force has it."

Lawson-Young shivered suddenly in the cold damp wind, and my own thoughts had begun to congeal. I proposed that we find somewhere warmer if we had more to say and the professor, after cogitation and consultation with his microphone, offered me a visit to his laboratory, if I should care to go.

Not only would I like to go, I felt honored to be asked, a re-action clearly visible on my face from the professor's own return expression. His trust however didn't reach as far as stepping into my car, so he went in one that arrived smoothly from nowhere, and I followed with Jim.

The professor's research laboratory occupied the ground floor of a fairly grand nineteenth-century town house with a pillared entrance porch. Antiquity stopped right there on the doorstep: everything behind the front door belonged to the future.

George Lawson-Young, very much the professor on his own turf, introduced me to his team of young research doctors whose chief if not only interest in my existence lay in my having long ago invented a way of making perfect glass joins between tiny tubes of differing diameters so that liquid or gasses would move at a desired speed from one tube to the next.

They hadn't much else of my work there, but the words Logan

Glass etched on mini pipettes and a few specialized test tubes got me accepted as a sort of practitioner rather than simply a sightseer. Anyway, my ability to identify things like vacutaires, cell separators, tissue culture chambers and distillation flasks meant that when I asked what exactly had been stolen the second time by Adam Force, I got told.

"Actually, we now think it was the third thing," a young woman in a white coat murmured sorrowfully. "It seems likely that he also took out of here the formula of our new asthma drug aimed at preventing permanent scar tissue occurring on the airways of chronic asthmatics. Only recently did we realize what had happened, as at the time, of course, we believed his assurances that he was borrowing some finished work from last year."

The nods all around were indulgent. In spite of all, there were friendly faces for Adam Force. It was the professor himself, whose eyes had opened, who told me finally what I'd been in need of knowing all along.

"The videotape made and stolen by Adam Force showed the formation of a particular tissue culture and its ingredients. The tissue culture was of cancer cells of the commoner sorts of cancer like that of the lung and the breast. They were concerned with the development of genetic mutations that render the cancer cell lines more sensitive to common drugs. All common cancers may be curable once the mutated gene is implanted into people who already have the cancer. The tape probably also shows photographs of the chromatography of the different components of the cancer cell genetic constituents. It is very complicated. At first sight it looks like rubbish, except to the educated eye. It is, unfortunately, quite likely anyone might override the 'Don't record on top of this' tab."

He lost me halfway through the technical details, but I at least understood that the tape that could save the world contained the cure for a host of cancers.

I asked the professor, "Is this for real?"

"It's a significant step forward," he said.

I pondered, "But if Force is going around asking millions for it, is it worth millions?"

Somberly, Lawson-Young said, "We don't know."

Adam Force had said the same thing, "I don't know." Not a lie, it seemed, but a statement that the process hadn't yet been extensively tested. The tape was a record of a possibility, or of an almost certainty whose worth was still a gamble.

I said, "But you do have backup copies of everything that's on that tape, don't you? Even if the tape itself should now show horse racing?"

Almost as if he were surrendering to an inevitable execution, the professor calmly stated the guillotine news. "Before he left with the videotape, Adam destroyed all our at-present irreplaceable records. We *need* that tape, and I hope to God you're right that he's lying. It's two years' work. Others are working along these lines, and we would be beaten to the breakthrough. We'd more likely *lose* the millions we might have earned."

Into a short silence the telephone buzzed. George Lawson-Young picked up the receiver, listened and mutely handed it to me. The caller was Jim in a high state of fuss.

He said with lively alarm, "That medic you saw yesterday, the one with the white beard?"

"Yes?"

"He's here in the street."

"Bugger him . . . What's he doing?"

"Waiting. He's in a car parked fifty yards up the road, facing towards you, and there's a big bruiser sitting next to him. He's got another car waiting and facing towards you, but coming the other way. It's a classic squeeze setup, with you in the middle. So . . . what do you want me to do?"

"Where exactly are you?" I asked. "To reach you, do I turn left or right?"

"Left. I'm four cars in front of White-Beard, pointing towards the door you went in at. I'm parked there, but there's a parking warden creeping about. I'm in a no-parking zone here, which White-Beard isn't, and I can't afford another ticket, it's not good for my business."

"Stay where you are," I said. "Move only if you have to, because of the parking warden. Doctor Force saw you and your car yesterday. It can't be helped."

Jim's voice rose. "White-Beard's got out of his car. What shall I do? *He's coming this way . . .*"

"Jim," I said flatly, "don't panic. Also don't look at Doctor Force if he comes near you and don't open the window. Keep on talking to me, and if you have anything near you that you can read, read it aloud to me now."

"Jeez."

Lawson-Young's eyebrows were up by his hairline.

I said to him, "Adam Force is in the road outside here, alarming my driver." And I didn't say that on our last encounter the doctor had seen me off with a poisonous-looking syringe.

Jim's voice wobbled in my ear with the opening paragraphs of the Rover's instruction manual and then rose again an octave as he said, "He's outside my window, he's rapping on it . . . Mr. Logan, what shall I do?"

"Keep on reading."

I gave the receiver to the professor and asked him to continue listening, and without wasting time I hurried from the part of the laboratory where we'd been standing, along the hallway and out into the street. Along to my left Adam Force stood in the roadway tapping hard on the window of the gray Rover on the driver's side and clearly getting agitated at the lack of response from Jim.

I walked fast along the sidewalk, and then, strolling the last part, crossed the road and came up quietly behind Doctor White-Beard and, as I'd done to Victor at Taunton station, said, "Hello," at his shoulder.

Worthington and Tom Pigeon wouldn't have approved. Adam Force spun around in astonishment.

"Are you looking for me?" I asked.

Inside the car Jim in great agitation was stabbing with his finger towards the lab's front door and the road beyond. Traffic in this secondary road was light, but one of the approaching cars, Jim was indicating to me, was ultra-bad news.

"Adam Force," I said loudly, "is too well known in this street,"

and with a total lack of complicated advance planning, and with
unadulterated instinct, I grabbed the charming doctor by the
wrist, spun him around and ended with him standing facing
the oncoming car with his arm twisted up behind him, held in
the strongest grip resulting from years of maneuvering heavy
molten glass.

Adam Force yelled, at first with pain and then, also, with bar-
gaining surrender. "You're hurting me. Don't do it. I'll tell you
everything. Don't do it. . . . God . . . Let me go, *please.*"

In between the two phases, from defiance to entreaty, a small
object fell from the hand I'd gripped. It lay in the gutter quite
close to a storm-drain grating, and I'd have paid it no attention
were it not for Force trying hard to kick it down through the
grating into the sewer, to be forever lost.

I didn't know what he meant when he said "everything," but
I didn't in the least mind learning. He screeched again under my
jerking pressure and I wondered whatever Professor Lawson-
Young was making of it, if he were still listening. The advancing
car stopped at the sight of Adam Force's predicament and the
four cars behind it exercised their horns, the drivers impatient,
not knowing what was going on.

"Everything," I prompted Force from behind his ear.

"Rose," he began, and then thought better of it. Rose would
frighten anyone.

I jerked his arm fiercely to encourage him and, with some dismay, I saw the big bruiser, now lumbering out of his car to come
to his aid, to be Norman Osprey, with his gorilla-type shoulder

development. Over my shoulder I could see the second car of the classic squeeze moving towards me. In consequence of these unwelcome surprises I jerked my captive's arm yet again, then feared to break or dislocate his shoulder. There were tears of real pain in the doctor's eyes.

Imploring for release, he half said, half sobbed, desperately, "I got the cyclopropane gas for Rose . . . I took it from the clinic's pharmacy . . . I can't see red from green, but I'm sure of orange . . . now let me go."

It was hard to hear him distinctly because of the street noises and the blaring horns, and his "everything" only confirmed what had already seemed likely, but I kept the pressure on just long enough for him to shriek out the answer I badly wanted to the question, "How come you know Rose?"

To him it seemed unimportant. He answered impatiently, "Her sister Gina came with her mother-in-law to my clinic; I met Rose at Gina's house."

Satisfied, I was faced with a fast, unharmed disengagement. The cars had advanced until they were radiator to radiator and going nowhere. The driver of the second was hurriedly disembarking, and to my horror, I saw that it was Rose. Uninvolved cars made a constant cacophony. The busy parking warden, notebook to the ready, spotted the fracas from a distance and veered back towards Jim and his zone infringement.

Norman Osprey, a mountain on the move, charged towards Force and myself to release the doctor and maybe continue with the entertainment Tom Pigeon and his dogs had interrupted at Broadway.

Not seeing anything except straight ahead, the warden and Norman the bookmaker bumped into each other violently, which slowed their pace and purpose while they cursed their mutual carelessness.

Jim unhelpfully kept his eyes fixed faithfully down on his instruction manual, as I'd told him, and went on steadfastly reading.

I tried screaming at him to gain his attention, but uselessly, and in the end I let out the loudest possible London-rain taxi whistle, which pierced even Jim's concentration.

"Window," I shouted.

He at last understood, but it took him eons to switch on the ignition and press the window-lowering button. Rose started running. The warden unwound herself from Norman Osprey. Car horns deafened because of the blockage of the highway.

I shouted at my driver, "Jim, get the car out of here. I'll phone you."

Jim suddenly proved his stunt-driving skills weren't a rumor. With not much more than two hand spans' clearance he locked the wheels of his Rover and circled like a circus horse bumping over the sidewalk, brushing me and my captive strongly out of the way with the rear wing and leaving us standing where the car had been, with the white-bearded doctor no longer in agony but still not going anywhere while I held him gripped. Jim's taillight flashed briefly at the first corner as he slid around it and left the scene.

Everyone else seemed to be running and shouting to no real purpose. I let go of Force's wrist while at the same time shoving him heavily into the joint arms of the warden and Osprey, with a bounce-off weight that unbalanced them all.

In that disorganized few seconds I bent down, scooped up the small object Force had dropped and *ran,* ran as if sprinting off the starting blocks on an athletic track. It was only the unexpectedness of my speed, I thought, that made the difference. I ran, dodging cars and irate drivers, swerving around Rose's grasp like a player evading a tackle in a football game, and believing—making myself believe—that I was fit enough to outrun them all, as long as no busybody stranger tripped me up.

I didn't have to test fate too much. The front door of the laboratory house swung open ahead of me, with George Lawson-Young, still with the telephone clutched in his hand, coming out under the pillared porch, looking my way and beckoning me to safety. I fairly bolted through his heavy shining black-painted door, and ended breathless and laughing in his hall.

He closed the door. "I can't see what there is to laugh about," he said.

"Life's a toss-up."

"And today it came up heads?"

I *liked* the professor. I grinned and held out to him the small object I'd salvaged from the gutter, asking him with moderate urgency, "Can you find out what this contains?"

He looked with shock at what I'd brought him, and I nodded as if in confirmation that I'd got it right. He asked a shade austerely if I knew what he was with great care holding.

"Yes. It's a sort of syringe. You can put the needle into any liquid drug and suck it into the bubble," I said. "Then you push the needle into the patient and squeeze the bubble to deliver the drug. Veterinarians sometimes use them on horses that are upset by the sight of an ordinary hypodermic syringe."

He said, "You're right. You seem to know a lot about it."

"I was with Martin once . . ." I broke off. So much of my life seemed to have touched Martin's.

Lawson-Young made no comment about Martin but said, "These little syringes can be used too on manic patients, to make them manageable and calm them down."

Phoenix House treated patients with mental illnesses. Adam Force had access to a well-stocked pharmacy.

George Lawson-Young turned away from me and, holding the tiny balloon with great care, led the way back to that part of the laboratory that held the gas chromatograph.

The thumbnail-sized balloon was full still of liquid, and was also wet outside from lying in the gutter. George Lawson-Young laid it carefully in a dish and asked one of his young doctors to identify the baby balloon's contents as soon as possible.

"Should it be one of several forms of poison," he warned me, "it might be impossible to find out what it is."

"It surely had to be something already in the Phoenix House pharmacy," I said. "It was only yesterday afternoon that I met Force. He hadn't much time to mobilize anything too fancy."

The balloon's contents raised little but smiles.

It took the young research doctor barely ten minutes to come back with an identification. "It's insulin," he said confidently. "Plain ordinary insulin, as used by diabetics."

"Insulin!" I exclaimed, disappointed. "Is that all?"

Both the young research doctor and the professor smiled indulgently. The professor said, "If you have diabetes, the amount of insulin in that syringe might send you into a permanent coma. If you *don't* have diabetes, there's enough to kill you."

"To *kill?*"

"Yes, certainly." Lawson-Young nodded. "That amount was a lethal dose. It's reasonable to suppose it was intended for you, not your chauffeur, but I can hardly believe it of Adam." He sounded shattered. "We knew he'd steal, but to kill . . ." He shook his head. "Are you *sure* that syringe came from him? You didn't just find it lying in the road?"

"I'm positive he was holding it in his hand, and I dislodged it."

The professor and I by that time were sitting on swiveling chairs in the professor's personal officelike room section of the laboratory.

"Actually," I murmured, "the big question is *why?*"

George Lawson-Young couldn't say.

"Do me a favor," he finally begged. "Start from the beginning."

"I will phone my driver first."

I used my mobile. When Jim answered his car phone he sounded first relieved that I was free and talking to him, and second, anxious that he was going to be late home for his wife's risotto, and third, worried about where he was going to find me safe and on my own. I was glad enough that he proposed to wait for me. The professor, taking the phone, gave Jim pinpointing instructions for one hour's time, and suggested to me that I waste none of it.

"It's a tale of two tapes," I tentatively began.

"Two?" said the professor.

"Yes, two," I replied, but then hesitated.

"Do go on, then." The professor was in a natural hurry.

"One was filmed here and stolen by Adam Force," I said. "He persuaded Martin Stukely to keep it safe for him, so that it couldn't be found."

"We had obtained a Search and Seizure Order from the court and had already started searching everywhere for it," said Lawson-Young, "including in Adam's own home, but we didn't ever think of it being in the care of a jockey."

"That must be why he did it," I said. "But as I understand it, Martin thought Force's tape would be safer still with me, a friend who hasn't four inquisitive children." And no talkative or quarrelsome wife, I could have added. But, I thought, would Martin have really given me the tape if he knew the contents were stolen?

The professor smiled.

I continued, "Martin Stukely received the stolen tape from Force at Cheltenham races and gave it into the temporary care of his valet while he went out to ride a horse called Tallahassee, in the race from which he didn't return."

He nodded. "When Martin Stukely died his valet, Eddie, gave the tape to you, as he knew that's what Martin intended.

"Eddie the valet," the professor went on, "was eventually one of the people that our investigators talked to and he said he didn't know anything about any stolen laboratory tape. He said he thought he was handling a tape that you yourself had made, which explained how to copy an ancient and priceless necklace."

"That's the second tape," I said. "It's also missing."

"Eddie had seen your duplicate of the necklace in the jockeys' changing rooms. And incidentally"—George Lawson-Young's smile illuminated his little office—"he said your copy of the necklace was stunning. Perhaps you will show it to me one day, when all this is over."

I asked him what he would consider "over," and his smile disappeared. "For me it will be over when we find the tape of our work."

He was aware, I supposed, that it was comparatively easy to make duplicates of videotapes. And that the knowledge recorded on them was like the contents of Pandora's box; once out, it couldn't be put back. The stolen tape itself might now show racing. The records of the cancer research might already be free in the world, and would never again be under the professor's control. For him, perhaps, it was already over.

For me, I thought, it would be over when Rose and Adam Force left me alone . . . but abruptly, out of nowhere, the specter of the fourth black mask floated into my consciousness. It wouldn't be over for me until his mask came off.

As casually as I could I mentioned Number Four to the professor, fearing he would discount my belief, but instead he took it seriously.

"Add your Number Four into all equations," he instructed, "and what do you get in the way of answers? Do you get a reason for Force to want you dead? Do you get a reason for anyone to attack you? Think about it."

I thought that that method must be what he used in nearly all research: if I added in an X factor, an "unknown," into all I'd seen and heard and hadn't wholly understood, what would I get?

Before I could really learn the technique, one of the young doctors came to tell me and the professor that Adam Force was standing on the sidewalk opposite with a thin woman with brown hair—my friend Rose. Doctor Force was staring at the entrance of his former workplace as if deciding how best to storm the Bastille. The young doctor, on the other hand, seemed to enjoy devising an escape from the fortress.

The professor said thoughtfully, "Adam knows his way round this house and its environs at least as well as any of us. He'll have stationed the other man, the one we can't see now, at the rear door into the mews. So how do we get Mr. Logan out of here without Adam Force being aware of it?"

The brilliant researchers came up with several solutions that required Tarzan-like swinging over an abyss, but with civil regard for each other's brains, they voted unanimously for the exit I actually took.

The glowingly pretty female doctor whose idea I followed gave me life-threatening directions. "Go up the stairs. Beside the top of the staircase, on the sixth floor, there's a bolted door. Unbolt it. Open it. You'll find yourself on the roof. Slide down the tiles until you meet a parapet. Crawl along behind the parapet there, so that the man in the mews doesn't see you. Crawl to the right. Keep your head down. There are seven houses joined

together. Go along behind their parapets until you come to the
fire escape at the end. Go down it. There's a bolt mechanism that
lets the last part of the iron ladder slide down to the pavement.
When you're down, shove the last part of the ladder up again
until it clicks. My car is parked in the mews. I'll drive out in half
an hour. You should be on the ground there by then, out of
sight of Doctor Force. I'll pick you up and go to meet your
driver. When I pick you up, lie on the floor, so that my car looks
empty except for me."

Everyone nodded.

I shook hands with George Lawson-Young. He gave me multiple contact numbers and mentioned with a grin that I already
had the phone number of the lab. He would expect me to find
the stolen tape. Deduction and intuition would do it.

I said, "What a hope!"

"Our only hope," he added soberly.

The author of my escape and a couple of her colleagues came
up to the top floor with me in high good spirits and unbolted the
door to the roof.

Cheerfully, but in whispers because of the man in the mews
far below, the researchers helped me slide down the gently sloping roof tiles to reach the parapet along the edge. Seeing me
safely on my knees there, they happily waved good-bye and
bolted the top-floor door behind me.

It was true I could have crawled along on my hands and knees,
but I would have been visible to Norman Osprey waiting below.
She, my savior, being tiny, hadn't realized that I was almost double
her body size. To be invisible I would have to go on my stom-

ach, as the height of the parapet was barely the length of a fore-arm.

I sweated and trembled along on my stomach within the para-pet's scanty cover and had to freeze my nerves and imagination to zero in order to cross crumbling bits of old mortar. It was a long way down to the ground.

Dusk gathered in unwary corners and made matters worse.

The seven houses seemed like fifty.

When at last I reached the fire escape, I'd begun to think that falling over the parapet would be less terrifying than inching along so precariously behind it.

At least, I thought grimly, if Adam Force had ever been up on the laboratory house's roof, he wouldn't expect me to have gone up there myself.

My dear pretty savior, on picking up my shaky self, remarked critically that I'd taken my time on the journey. My dry mouth found it impossible to reply. She apologized that the recent rain had drenched the roof and wet my clothes. Think nothing of it, I croaked. She switched on the headlights and the heater. I grad-ually stopped shivering—both from cold and from fear.

We found Jim at the rendezvous in his usual state of agitation. My savior, handing me over, reported that the fun escape had been a great success. She wouldn't accept anything for petrol. She did accept an absolutely heartfelt hug of gratitude, and a long, long kiss.

CHAPTER 9

I MADE A detour to talk to Bon-Bon on my way home and found her tears fewer and her memory recovering. When I asked her questions, she sweetly answered. When I suggested a course of action, she willingly agreed.

By the time Jim decanted me yawning to my hill house we were both very tired and he still had a few miles to go. Far and away the most orthodox of my three self-appointed minders, he also lived nearest. His wife, he said, had told him to apply to drive me regularly until I got my license back. I was considering the cost, and he was considering a ban on radio and music. We had agreed to let each other know.

On that Wednesday, Catherine's transport stood on its frame

outside the kitchen door. Inside the kitchen, when Jim had driven away, the warm welcoming smell of cooking seemed as natural as in the past with other women it had been contrived.

"Sorry about this." She pointed with her elbow at half-scrambled eggs. "I didn't know when you were coming back, and I was hungry."

I wondered how much care had gone into saying "back" instead of "home."

She gave me a careful look, her eyebrows rising.

"I got a bit wet," I said.

"Tell me later." She cooked more eggs while I changed, and we ate in companionable peace.

I made coffee for us both and drank mine looking at her neat face, her blond curving hair and her close-textured skin; and I wondered without confidence what I looked like to her.

I said, "I saw Doctor Force again today. . . ."

Catherine smiled. "And was he still charming and good-looking and filling everyone with belief in humanity?"

I said, "Well, not exactly. He quite likely meant to bump me off, if he got a chance." I yawned, and bit by bit, without exaggeration, told her about my day.

She listened with concentration and horror.

I collected her coffee cup and put it in the sink. We were still in the kitchen, which thanks to my mother had a pair of large comfortable chairs near an efficient heater.

We sat together, squashed into one of the chairs, as much for support for the spirits as for physical pleasure.

I told her about the professor and his X-factor method of

research. "So now," I finished, "I go over everything that anyone has said and done, add in X and see what I get."

"It sounds difficult."

"Different, anyway."

"And when you find him? Blackmask Number Four?"

"He gives me nightmares," I said.

I smoothed her hair. She felt right in my arms, curling there comfortably.

If I added Blackmask Four into the picture when he'd first blown into my awareness of his existence I had to remember every separate blow of that encounter on the Broadway sidewalk and, I realized with distaste, I had to go back and listen again in my mind to every word of Rose's.

She'd shouted, "Break his wrists . . ."

Catherine stirred in my arms and cuddled closer, and I discarded Rose in favor of bed.

CATHERINE WOKE EARLY and went off before dawn to her morning shift, and I walked down in the dark to Logan Glass thinking of the past two days in Lynton and Bristol and wondering, like Professor Lawson-Young, if Doctor Force still possessed and could produce for sale the irreplaceable data he'd stolen.

Strictly speaking, none of it was truly the business of a provincial glassblower, but my fast-mending skin reminded me still that not everyone agreed.

Also, strictly speaking, none of it was truly the business of a dead steeplechase jockey, but his wife and children had been assaulted by gas and comprehensively robbed of their video machines.

The dedicated professor depended, he'd hopefully said, on my deductive abilities, but to my mind he was staking his shirt on a nonrunner, as Martin would have put it.

I had come to see the hunt for the videotape as sorties up a series of roads leading nowhere: as a starburst of cul-de-sacs. The professor believed that one of the roads would eventually lead to his treasure, and I thought of Lloyd Baxter and Ed Payne and Victor and Rose and Norman Osprey and Bon-Bon and Adam Force, all as blind-alley roads. I thought of all they'd said and done, and the professor was right, if I could discard the lies, I'd be left with the truth.

Far more absorbing of my time and mental energy was his assertion that if I included factor X (Blackmask Four) in all my insoluble sums, I would find them adding up.

Although I arrived at work half an hour before the normal starting time, Hickory was there before me, obstinately trying again to make a perfect sailing boat. He'd made the boat itself much larger and had put in red and blue streaks up the mast and the whole thing looked lighter and more fun.

I congratulated him and got a scornful grunt in return, and I thought how quickly his sunny temperament could blow up a thunderstorm, and hoped for his sake as well as for our competent little team's, that it would blow over just as fast. Meanwhile I tidied the shelves in the stockroom end of the furnace room, where Hickory had currently raised the melted-glass temperature to 2400 degrees Fahrenheit. To give Hickory his due, he handled semi-liquid glass with a good deal of the panache he would need on the way to general recognition. I privately thought, though, that he would get stuck on "pretty good" and never reach "marvelous," and because he understood deep down where his limit lay, and knew I could do better, his present feeling of mild resentment needed patience and friendly laughter if he were either to stay or to leave on good terms.

Irish and Pamela Jane arrived together, as they often did, and this time were arguing about a film they'd seen that had a bad glassblower in it. They asked Hickory what he thought and embroiled him so intensely in the argument that with a fatally noisy bang Hickory's precious new sailing boat cracked apart into five or six pieces. It had been standing free on the marver table, the outer surfaces cooling more rapidly than the superhot core. The stresses due to unequal rates of contraction had become too great for the fragile glass. The pieces had blown away from each other and lay on the floor.

All three of my helpers looked horrified. Hickory himself glanced at his watch and said bleakly, "Three minutes, that's all it took. I was going to put it in the oven . . . God damn that *stupid* film."

No one touched or tried to pick up the fallen pieces. They were still near to their liquid heat and would incinerate one's fingers.

"Never mind," I said, shrugging and looking at the sad bits, "it happens." And I didn't need to remind them that practice glass was cheap. It did happen to everyone. It happened to the best.

We worked conscientiously all morning, making swooping birds for mobiles, which always sold fast. Pamela Jane, loving them particularly, was the one who fixed their strings the following morning early and who at noon would carefully pack them in boxes in such a way that they would pull out easily to fly.

Hickory, who could make neat little birds, recovered his good humor by the time Worthington drew up outside in Marigold's Rolls. Marigold herself, in a dramatic black-and-white-striped caftan, issued from her glossy car with mascara-laden eyelashes batting hugely up and down like a giraffe's. She had come, she announced, to take me to lunch in the Wychwood Dragon. She had a favor to ask, she said.

Worthington, always a step behind Marigold when on active bodyguard duty, looked the more richly suntanned from the skiing trip. He had spent most of the time on the slopes, he said with satisfaction, while Marigold's wardrobe had swelled by three enormous suitcases. And a good time had clearly been had by both.

Her intense vitality as usual stirred anyone in Marigold's vicinity to giggles and, as on other days, she and Hickory were soon indulging in batting a sexual ball to each other with gleeful freedom.

Marigold in enjoyment stayed for half an hour—a century for her—during which time Worthington drifted me with a gentle tug on the arm into the furnace end of the room, and told me with the unhappiest of expressions that the underground fraternity of bookmakers were forecasting my destruction, if not death.

"Rose is still actively prowling round here, looking for vengeance, because she can't understand why you aren't on your knees to her. They are *laughing* at her because you and Tom and I have walked away from two of her best-planned smasheroos, and there's no way she's going to put up with such a loss of face. So you just look out, because I hear that someone in Broadway has binocs on you now, reporting every twitch you make straight back to Rose."

"Binocs?"

"Bins. Where have you been all your life? Binoculars. Race glasses. But seriously, Gerard, Tom Pigeon says it's no joke."

I promised to be careful, but who could live forever in a state of alarm? I said, "I suppose I'd better tell you, then, that Adam Force and Rose did try to do me in yesterday. At least, I think so."

He listened grimly and asked the unanswerable: "Where's Rose now?"

Marigold and Hickory, having enjoyed their flirting as much because of their twenty-year age difference as in spite of it, gave each other a pecking kiss on the cheek in farewell, and Marigold and I made a head-turning entrance into the Wychwood Dragon dining room. The Dragon herself swept in full sail between the tables to fetch up by Marigold's side, two splendid ladies eyeing each other for supremacy.

I counted it a draw for outrageous clothes and an easy win for Marigold in the mascara stakes, and nearly two hours slid by before Marigold, tiring of the underlying contest, told me the reason for her invitation to me for lunch.

She declaimed to start with (unnecessarily), "I am Bon-Bon's mother!"

"Ah," I said. I knew.

"At Christmas," Marigold continued, "Martin gave his wife a videocamera from the children, and he was going to give her a necklace from himself as well."

I nodded. "But she preferred warm winter boots."

"The silly girl has no taste."

"But she gets cold feet."

Marigold considered fashion far more important than comfort. "Martin said you had made a spectacular necklace once, and that you could make the same one again. So . . . for Bon-Bon, will you do it now? As a present from me, of course. And I'd like to see it first."

She waited an uncharacteristically long time for my answer, gazing hopefully into my face. I didn't know in fact what to say. I couldn't insult her by telling her it would cost more than the woolly boots and the video camera combined, though she would need to know, but the videotape describing how to make it and listing the detailed ingredients in grams was not only missing but might have come into Rose's field of things to die for. When I had said I would make a necklace for Bon-Bon, I hadn't known Rose.

After too long a pause Marigold asked, "What's the problem? Can't you do it?"

When an answer of some sort became essential I said, "Does Bon-Bon give the necklace idea her blessing?"

"She doesn't know about it. I want her to have a lovely surprise to cheer her up. I thought of buying her something in Paris, but then I remembered what Martin wanted you to do, so will you?"

She was so seldom presented with a negative that she couldn't understand my hesitation. I put together my most persuasive smile and begged for a little time. She began to pout, and I remembered Martin, laughing, saying that the Marigold pout meant the knives were out.

Hell, I thought, I wished he were alive. He'd been dead twenty-one days and I'd found each one a quandary without him.

I said to Marigold, "The necklace I made is in a strongbox in the bank down the road here. I do agree that you should see it before we go any further."

The pout cleared away to a broad smile of understanding, and although we could easily have walked the distance, Marigold grandly summoned Worthington, equally grandly paid for our lunch, and outshone the poor Dragon all the way to the Rolls.

In the bank Marigold had the manager bowing to the floor while minions were sent scurrying to bring my locked box into the private room where contents could be checked. I opened the metal box and laid the flat blue velvet folder containing the copy of the Cretan Sunrise onto the bench-shelf, opening it for her opinion.

I hadn't seen the antique original except lit behind glass, so I couldn't completely compare them, but in the chill light of the bank's viewing room the duplicate I'd made gleamed as if with inner life, and I gave way to such a bout of self-regard as would have caused my uncle Ron to bury his head in his hands in shame.

Marigold exclaimed "Oh!" in astonishment, then drew in a breath and said, "Oh, my dear," and couldn't decide whether or not she liked it.

The necklace designed three thousand five hundred years ago was a matter of twenty flat pieces, each made of aquamarine-colored and dark blue glass streaked together with melted gold. About two inches, or five centimeters, long, by a thumbnail wide, each flat shining piece bore the imprint of a flower. When worn, the long pieces, strung loosely together around the neck by their short sides, spread out in rays like a sunrise, the imprinted flowers, outermost, lying flat on the skin. In a way barbaric, the whole thing was antiquely magnificent, and definitely heavy. I didn't blame delicate Bon-Bon for not wanting to wear it.

Marigold, regaining her breath, asked if Martin had seen it.

"Yes." I nodded. "He thought it would suit Bon-Bon, but she wanted the boots more." I'd lent the necklace to him without conditions, and he'd shown it around in the jockeys' changing room. Dozens of people had seen it.

Marigold, incredibly brought again to speechlessness, said nothing at all while I reenclosed the necklace into darkness and put the velvet folder back in the metal strongbox. There were the other papers there that I checked yet again—will, insurance policy, deeds of the hill house, all the conventional paper trail of living, but of an instructional videotape, still not a sign.

I searched carefully once more through the pile of envelopes.

There was no tape. Nothing. I reflected with irony that even if one followed the instruction tape, it wouldn't be enormously easy to fabricate. I kept it partly because of the difficult hours it had cost me.

The bank minions relocked everything and gave me back my key, and Marigold grandly commanded Worthington to drive us all back to Logan Glass. Apart from her instruction to her chauffeur she remained exceptionally quiet on the very short journey, and also, as I'd noticed in the Wychwood dining room, her gin intake had dropped to scraping zero.

Back at Logan Glass she paraded up and down the brightly lit gallery as if she'd never been in there before, and halted finally in front of Catherine's wings before addressing all of us, Worthington, Irish, Hickory, Pamela Jane and myself, as if we'd been a junior class in prep school. She said we were lucky to be in a studio that stood so high already in the world's estimation. She was going to give us all a huge jump forward in reputation because, "Gerard"—she blew me a kiss—"with the help of all of you, of course, is going to make a marvelous necklace for me, which I'm going to call the Marigold Knight Trophy, and I'm going to present it each year to the winner of a steeplechase run at Cheltenham on every New Year's Eve in memory of my son-in-law, Martin Stukely . . . and *there*"—she spread her arms wide—"what do you think of *that*?"

Whatever we thought, we gazed silently in awe.

"Well, Gerard?" she demanded. "What do you say?"

I didn't say, "Over the top. In fact, out of sight," but I thought it.

"You see," Marigold went on triumphantly, "everyone benefits. People will flock to your door, here."

Apart from terrible trouble with insurance, the one dire probability ahead in her scheme was that someone somewhere would try to exchange the modern for the antique, with Marigold embroiled in legal pincers.

"I think it's a *beautiful* idea," Pamela Jane told Marigold, and the others, smiling, agreed. Even Worthington raised no security alarms.

Marigold, delighted with the scheme she had thought up within ten minutes, filled in the details rapidly. She would consult the Cheltenham Race Trophy Committee immediately . . . Gerard could start work at once . . . the press should be alerted . . .

I hardly listened to those plans. Almost anything would be a better trophy than a copy of a jewel worth a million. The obituary for Martin that I hadn't yet fashioned would be more suitable. Glass trophies were common in racing and I would be elated in general to be commissioned to make one.

Irish with enthusiasm clasped Marigold's hand and shook it vigorously, to the lady's surprise. Hickory beamed. The trophy necklace idea swept the polls at Logan Glass, but the Cheltenham committee might not like it.

The Cheltenham committee were given little time more to remain unconsulted. Marigold used my telephone to get through to an influential high-up whom she galvanized into visiting Logan Glass at once.

An hour later, Marigold, irresistible to many a powerful man, greeted the man from Cheltenham, Kenneth Trubshaw, with a familiar kiss and explained her intention even before introducing Irish, Hickory and Pamela Jane.

I got a nod from the smoothly urbane member of the racecourse's upper echelon. He knew me by sight, but we hadn't until then talked. Marigold with arms raised put that right.

"Darling, you know Gerard Logan, of course?"

"Er . . . Yes, of course."

"And it's Gerard who's made the *fabulous* necklace which you *must see,* which is down in the bank here. . . ."

Everyone looked at a watch, or the clock on the showroom wall. The bank had closed its doors five minutes earlier and Marigold looked frustrated. Time had ticked away too quickly.

I suggested diffidently that Mr. Trubshaw, not to have wasted entirely his short journey, might care to see a few other things I'd made and although Marigold protested, "Darling, there's more *gold* in the necklace and it's going to be a Gold Trophy race. . . ."

Kenneth Trubshaw, though perhaps more courteous than interested, took the first few brisk uncommitted steps into the gallery. Then, to my great relief, he paused, and stopped, and went back a pace, and finished thoughtfully in front of Catherine's wings.

"How much is this one?" he asked. "There's no price on it."

"It's sold," I said.

My assistants all showed astonishment.

"Pity," commented Trubshaw.

"There isn't enough gold," Marigold complained.

"Um," I said. "I did a horse jumping a fence, once. The fence was solid gold; so were the horse's hooves. The rest of the horse was crystal, and the ground, the base of the piece, was black glass, with tiny gold flecks."

"Where is it now?" Kenneth asked.

"Dubai."

He smiled.

"What about the necklace?" Marigold demanded, cross.

Her Kenneth appeased her gently. "I'll come over and see it tomorrow, but this young man has more than a necklace to show us. These wings, for instance . . ." He stood in front of them, his head on one side. He asked me, "Couldn't you make that again? If this one's sold?"

"Part of what I sell is a guarantee of one-of-a-kind," I apologized. I wasn't sure I could, even if I wanted to, repeat the wings. The climbing powerful splendor of their construction had come from the subconscious. I hadn't even written up my notes.

Could I instead, then, he asked, make a tribute to Martin Stukely?

I said, "I could make a leaping horse with golden streaks. I could make it worthy of Cheltenham."

"I'll come tomorrow," the trophy chairman said and embraced Marigold in farewell with smiling enthusiasm.

Marigold having agreed earlier with her daughter to take me back to Bon-Bon's house, she, Worthington and I made tracks to the Stukely gravel, arriving at the same moment as Priam Jones, who was carefully nursing the expensive tires he'd bought to replace those wrecked on New Year's Eve. Priam, Bon-Bon had reported, had after all decided not to sue the town for erecting sharp-toothed barriers overnight, but had already transferred his disgust to Lloyd Baxter, who'd ordered his horses, including Tallahassee, to be sent north to a training stable nearer his home.

Bon-Bon came out of the house in a welcoming mood, and I had no trouble, thanks to her maneuvering it privately on my behalf, in talking to Priam Jones as if our meeting were accidental. Priam looked like the last of the cul-de-sacs.

"Bon-Bon invited me to an early supper," Priam announced with a touch of pomposity.

"How splendid!" I said warmly. "Me too."

Priam's face said he didn't care to have me there too, and things weren't improved from his point of view when Bon-Bon swept her mother into the house on a wardrobe expedition and said over her departing shoulder, "Gerard, pour Priam a drink, will you? I think there's everything in the cupboard."

Bon-Bon's grief for Martin had settled in her like an anchor steadying a ship. She was more in charge of the children and had begun to cope more easily with managing her house. I'd asked her whether she could face inviting Priam to dinner, but I hadn't expected the skill with which she'd delivered him to me in secondary-guest capacity.

The children poured out of the house at that moment, addressing me unusually as "Uncle Gerard" and Priam as "Sir." They then bunched around Worthington and carried him off to play "make believe" in the garage block. Priam and I, left alone, made our way, with me leading him through the house, to Martin's den, where I acted as instructed as host and persuaded Priam with my very best flattery to tell me how his other horses had prospered, as I'd seen one of his winners praised in the newspapers.

Priam, with his old boastfulness reemerging, explained how no one else but he could have brought those runners out at the right moment. No one, he claimed, knew more about readying a horse for a particular race than he did.

He smoothed the thin white hair that covered his scalp but showed pink skin beneath and conceded that Martin had contributed a little now and then to his training success.

Priam at my invitation relaxed on the sofa and sipped weak scotch and water while I sat in Martin's chair and fiddled with small objects on his desk. I remembered Priam's spontaneous tears at Cheltenham and not for the first time wondered if on a deeper level Priam was less sure of himself than he acted. There were truths he might tell if I got down to that tear-duct level, and this time I'd meet no garden hose on the way.

"How well," I asked conversationally, "do you know Eddie Payne, Martin's old valet?"

Surprised, Priam answered, "I don't know him intimately, if that's what you mean, but some days I give him the silks the jockeys will be wearing, so yes, I talk to Eddie then."

"And Rose?" I suggested.

"Who?"

"Eddie Payne's daughter. Do you know her?"

"Whyever do you ask?" Priam's voice was mystified, but he hadn't answered the question. Eddie and his daughter had first worn black masks, I thought, but could Priam have been Number Four?

I said with gratitude, "You were so kind, Priam, on that wretched day of Martin's death, to take back to Broadway that tape I so stupidly left in my raincoat pocket in Martin's car. I haven't thanked you properly again since then." I paused and then added as if one thought had nothing to do with the other, "I've heard a crazy rumor that you swapped two tapes. That you took the one from my pocket and left another."

"Rubbish!"

"I agree." I smiled and nodded. "I'm sure you took back to my place in Broadway the tape I'd been given at Cheltenham."

"Well, then." He sounded relieved. "Why mention it?"

"Because of course in Martin's den, in this very room, in fact, you found tapes all over the place. Out of curiosity you may have slotted the tape I had left in the car into Martin's VCR and had a look at it, and maybe you found it so boring and unintelligible that you wound it back, stuck the parcel shut again, and took it back to me at Broadway."

"You're just guessing," Priam complained.

"Oh, sure. Do I guess right?"

Priam didn't want to admit to his curiosity. I pointed out that it was to his advantage if it were known for a certainty what tape had vanished from Logan Glass.

He took my word for it and looked smug, but I upset him again profoundly by asking him *who* that evening, or early next

morning, he had assured that the tape he'd delivered to Broadway had nothing to do with an antique necklace, whether worth
a million or not.

Priam's face stiffened. It was definitely a question he didn't
want to answer.

I said without pressure, "Was it Rose Payne?"

He simply stared, not ready to loosen his long-tight tongue.

"If you say *who*," I went on in the same undemanding tone,
"we can smother the rumors about you swapping any tapes."

"There's never any harm in speaking the truth," Priam
protested, but of course he was wrong, the truth could be dis-
believed, and the truth could hurt.

"Who?" I repeated, and I suppose my lack of emphasis went
some way towards persuading him to give the facts daylight.

"When Martin died," he said, "I drove his things back here, as
you know, and then as my own car was in dock having the . . .
er . . . the tires, you see, needed replacing . . ."

I nodded without judgment or a smile.

Priam, encouraged, went on. "Well . . . Bon-Bon said I could
take Martin's car, she would have said yes to anything, she was
terribly distraught, so I just drove Martin's car to my home and
then back to Broadway, with Baxter's bag and your raincoat, and
then I drove myself home again in it. In the morning, when I
came in from morning exercise with the first lot of horses, my
phone was ringing, and it was Eddie Payne . . ." Priam took a
breath, but seemed committed to finishing. "Well . . . Eddie asked
me then if I was sure the tape I'd taken back to your shop was

without doubt the one he'd given you at Cheltenham, and I said I was absolutely certain, and as that was that, he rang off."

Priam's tale had ended. He took a deep swallow of whisky, and I poured him a stronger refill, a pick-you-up from the confessional.

Eddie himself had been to confession. Eddie hadn't been able to face Martin's funeral. Eddie was afraid of his daughter Rose, and Eddie had put on a black mask to do me a good deal of damage. If Tom and the Dobermans hadn't been passing, Eddie's sins would have involved a good deal more of deep-soul shriving.

It had taken such a lot of angst for Priam to answer a fairly simple question that I dug around in what I'd heard to see if Priam knew consequences that I didn't.

Could he have been Blackmask Four? Unknown factor X?

Ed Payne had probably told Rose that the tape stolen from Logan Glass at the turnover of the new century had to do with a necklace. Rose had not necessarily believed him. Rose, knowing that such a necklace existed, but not realizing that the tape, if found, wasn't itself worth much and certainly not a million, may have hungered for it fiercely enough to anesthetize everyone around at Bon-Bon's house with cyclopropane, and gather up every videotape in sight.

I had thought at the time that it had been a man who had sprung out from behind the door and hit me unconscious, but on reflection it could have been Rose herself. Rose, agile, strong and determined, would without question lash out when it came to attacking a man. I knew all about that.

Thoughtfully I asked Priam, as if I'd forgotten I'd asked him before, "How well do you know Rose Payne?"

"I don't know her," he replied at once, and then, more slowly, revised the assertion and watered it down. "I've seen her around."

"How well does she know Adam Force, would you say? Do you think Doctor Force would be foolish enough to lend her a cylinder of gas from a nursing home he visits?"

Priam looked as shocked as if I'd run him through with swords, but unfortunately from my own point of view he didn't actually flag-wave any signs of guilt. He didn't feel guilty; almost no one did.

Bon-Bon's "early supper" proved to be just that, slightly to Priam's disappointment. He preferred grandeur, but everyone sat around the big kitchen table, Marigold, Worthington, the children, Bon-Bon, me and Priam himself. I also acted as waiter, as I often did in that house, though Daniel, the elder boy, carried empty dishes sometimes.

"Gerard," he said, standing solidly in front of me between courses, to gain my attention, "Who's Victor?"

I paid attention very fast and said, "He's a boy. Tell me what you've heard."

"Is it still the same?" Daniel asked. "Do we get the gold coins?"

"No, of course not," Bon-Bon scolded. "That was a game."

"So is this," I promised her, "so do let's play the same way."

I dug in a pocket and found some loose change, surprised I had any left after the twenty or more coins they'd won several days earlier.

"What about Victor?" I asked. I put a coin flat on the table and Daniel said, "There are two things," so I put down a second coin.

"You're teaching these children all wrong," Marigold berated.

Theoretically I might agree with her but Daniel unexpectedly spoke up. "Gerard told Worthington and a friend of his that you have to pay for what you get."

Marigold's disfavor spread to her chauffeur, but Daniel, not understanding, simply waited for me to listen.

"Go on," I said. "Two pieces of treasure. And they'd better be worth it." I grinned at him. He put his chubby hand flat over the coins and said directly to me, "He wants to tell you a secret."

"When did he say that?" I took him seriously, but the other adults laughed.

Daniel picked up one of the gold coins. Mercenary little devil, I thought.

Daniel said, "He phoned here. Mommy was out in the garden, so I answered it. He said he was Victor. He didn't want to talk to Mommy, but only to you. You weren't here, but I told him you were coming for supper so he said to tell you he would try again, if he could."

Daniel's hand hovered in the air over the second coin. I nodded philosophically and he whisked it away in a flash.

"That's disgraceful!" Marigold told me severely. "You're teaching my grandson all sorts of bad habits."

"It's a game," I repeated, and one for eleven-year-olds. Bright though he was, I thought Daniel had done a good piece of work.

"Early supper" ended at seven-thirty, an hour before the younger children's bedtime. Marigold, her mercurial spirits restored, gave Daniel a forgiving good-night hug that swallowed him in caftan, and after coffee, three large slugs of Grand Marnier and a giggly chat on the telephone with Kenneth Trubshaw involving the sponsorship of gold trophies, Marigold floated out to the Rolls in clouds of goodwill and let Worthington solicitously install her in the back seat and drive off to her home.

Priam Jones felt less than decently treated. He let Bon-Bon know, while thanking her for her hospitality, that as a racehorse trainer of prestige, and especially as her husband's ex–chief employer, he would have enjoyed more attention and consideration. He bestowed an even cooler farewell nod to me and in irritation gave his new tires a harsh workout in his departure across the gravel. Poor Priam, I thought. It couldn't be much fun being *him*.

Victor kept me waiting a long time. Bon-Bon, going upstairs to read stories to the children, gave me a kiss good night and waved me to the den for the evening; but it was after eleven o'clock when the fifth caller on the line spoke with the familiar cracked voice of Taunton.

"Gerard? I'm in a public phone box. Mom thinks I'm in bed. She threw away your mobile number. I can't use the e-mail. Auntie Rose has taken my computer . . . I'm absolutely sick of things. I want to see you. Tell me where. I'm running out of money."

There were indeed too many time-over warning clicks. He was feeding small coins, I supposed, because he hadn't any others. In a short period of peace I said, "I'll come to Taunton station. Same train, on Sunday."

"No. Tomorrow. *Please,* tomorrow."

I agreed, and the line went dead.

YOU'RE RAVING MAD, that's what you are," Tom Pigeon said at seven in the morning, when I told him. "Today's Friday. The boy should be in school."

"That's probably why he was so insistent. He could skip school without his mother knowing."

"You're not going," Tom said positively; and then, a few seconds later, "We'll get Jim to drive us; he's got an estate car for the dogs. Where are you?"

"At the Stukelys'. Can you pick me up here?"

"Last Sunday, five days ago," Tom said with mock patience, "dear Rose tore your face open in Taunton with the tap end of a garden hose."

"Mm," I agreed.

"And the day before yesterday, I hear, you nearly got yourself killed."

"Well . . ."

"How about staying at home?"

I smiled at the silly idea.

CHAPTER 10

By FRIDAY JIM'S wife had told him I was accursed by demons and he should no longer drive me. Our lateness on Wednesday had burned her risotto.

Jim and I however came to a mutual understanding and shook hands on it. He would drive when I needed him in bodyguard status, there would be no radio, and I would pay him double.

Despite this slightly crabby start, Jim drove Tom, me and the dogs cheerfully to Taunton and stopped in the no-parking zone outside the station. I remembered too late that the weekday timetable was different from Sunday's, and the expected train had come and gone, leaving Victor stranded.

He wasn't on the platform.

Giving Tom the news and receiving a promise to sit and wait, I hurried along the road until 19 Lorna Terrace was in sight. No Victor. Back to the station—and I found him there, cold and anxious, in the waiting room.

He stood up looking thin and stressed, my arrival not enough to bring out smiles. I'd spent part of the journey adding Victor into every event that Blackmask Four could have attended without disguise, and feeling I was nowhere near as good as George Lawson-Young at this factor-X stuff, I couldn't make X fit Victor anywhere.

"I'm late because I didn't come on the train," I briefly explained. "What's the matter?"

"I want . . ." He sounded as desperate as he looked. He began again. "Auntie Rose has moved into our house. . . . I hate her. I can't bear her, and Mom won't speak to me unless I do what Auntie Rose says; because Mom's that scared of her. And my dad, when he gets out, won't come home while she's there. I know he won't, so where can I go? What can I do? I don't know anyone except you to ask, and that's a laugh really, considering your face. . . ."

"Did you try your grandfather?"

Victor said hopelessly, "He's shit scared of Auntie Rose. Worse than Mom."

I said, "Last Sunday . . ." and he interrupted.

"I'm sorry. I'm really sorry about your face. I thought you wouldn't come today. . . . I thought you hadn't come."

"Forget about last Sunday," I said. "Concentrate on Adam Force instead."

"He's great," Victor said without fervor, and then with a frown, added, "Everyone says so. He sometimes used my computer. That's how I got his letter. He thought he had deleted the file but I found it in the cache memory."

It explained a lot.

I asked, "How long has he known your auntie Rose?" and this time I got an answer.

"About as long as he's known Mom. Months, that is. Mom went on the bus trip to his clinic, and he got hooked on her. He was a real cool guy, I thought. He came round for her when Dad was at work. So when Auntie Rose finds out, she goes round to the hotel where Dad's working and says if he comes home quick he'll catch them at it in Dad's own bed; so Dad goes round and Doctor Force has gone by then, but Dad gives Mom a hell of a beating, breaking her nose and about six of her ribs and things, and Auntie Rose goes round to the cops and tells on Dad. So they put him away for twelve months. Then, last Sunday," he said miserably, "Auntie Rose takes Adam Force off Mom, which she meant to do all along, I reckon, and now he does what she tells him, and it's queer, but I'd say she *hits* him pretty hard most days; and then I've seen them kissing after that."

He spoke in puzzlement, and Worthington, I thought, could explain a thing or two to Victor. Fatherly, steady and worldly, Worthington, a great fellow, simply *couldn't* be Blackmask Four. And Victor? Surely not Victor, though Blackmask Four hadn't been bodily substantial, like Worthington, but lithe, like Victor. But Victor *couldn't* have bashed me about then, and asked me for help now.

Not Victor, not Worthington, but what about Gina? Was she muscular enough? I didn't know for sure, and, I decided reluctantly, I would have to find out. I'd been through almost the whole register of cul-de-sacs and failed to find anyone that fitted a factor X. Yet there had indeed been a fourth black-masked attacker. I had felt the hands. I'd felt the blows. I'd seen the eyes within the mask. Blackmask Four was real.

According to the professor, there was a question I wasn't asking, and if I didn't ask the right question, how could I expect to be told the right answer? But *what* was the right question? And whom should I ask?

With a mental sigh I took Victor out of the station, and to his obvious pleasure reunited him with Tom and his three black canine companions. He told Tom that that day, the Sunday that we'd spent on the moor, had been one of his happiest ever. Happiest, that was, until his auntie Rose had ruined it.

He played with the dogs, plainly in their good graces, and spoke to them instead of us. The black ears heard him say, "I'll bet people can still run away to sea."

I said after a while, "I'll go round to Victor's house, and if his mother's in I'll ask her if he can spend the weekend with us."

Tom protested, "I'll go."

"We'll both go," I said, and in spite of Victor's fears we left him with Jim, and, taking the dogs with us, knocked on the door of the roughly repaired entrance to 19 Lorna Terrace.

Gina Verity came to our summons and failed to close her mended door against us fast enough. Tom's heavy shoe was quicker.

In the five days since the previous Sunday, Gina had lost her looks, her serenity and her confidence. She stared at my slashed and mending jaw as if it were one straw too many. She said helplessly, "You'd better come in," and with sagging shoulders led me down the now familiar passage to the kitchen. We sat, as before, at the table.

Tom and the dogs stood on guard outside the house because Gina didn't know when either her sister or Adam Force would return.

"I would like to invite Victor to stay for the weekend," I said.

Gina lit cigarette from cigarette, as before. "All right," she agreed in a dull sort of way. "Pick him up from school." She thought it over. "Better not let Rose find out, she wouldn't let him go with you."

Gina's left-hand fingers were stained nearly orange with nicotine. The right-hand fingers were white. I stretched forward and lifted first her right hand and then her left, putting them down again gently. The muscles were flabby, with no tone. Too apathetic to complain, she merely looked at her own hands one by one, and said, "What?"

I didn't reply. Blackmask Four's left hand hadn't been as intensely yellow as this one, even seen under the streetlights and even while actively punching. With those strongly muscled arms, Blackmask Four had been male.

Gina had not been Blackmask Four. The certainty was unarguable.

Time to go.

Out in front of the house Tom's equivalent of my alarm whistle set up a howling, growling, barking clamor, which the dogs only ever did at their owner's prompting.

Gina immediately stood and shrank away from the table, her eyes wide with unmistakable fear. "It's Rose," Gina said. "She's come back. She always makes dogs bark. They don't like her. She makes their hair stand on end."

Mine too, I thought. The deep-throated Dobermans went on proving Gina right.

"Go," Gina said to me, her tongue sticking on the words. "Go out. Out through the backyard . . . and out through the gate and down the lane. Go, go. Hurry." Her urgency was for my own safety as much as hers.

It might have been prudent to go, but I'd never been a wise devotee of the "He who fights and runs away lives to fight another day" school of thought. Running away from Rose . . . I supposed that I'd already escaped three times from her traps, and once from Adam Force . . . With that amount of good luck, I thought, I might remain a bit longer undestroyed.

I stayed sitting at the table, though with chair pushed back and one knee over the other, while the front door creaked open and the purposeful footsteps came along the passage.

Not only Rose had come, but Adam Force with her. Rose had recognized Tom and his sidekicks, but the doctor was pinning his negative emotions entirely on me. He'd set me up two days ago as an insulin-dosed car crash hit-and-run victim—a scheme that had gone wrong. My presence in that house shook him.

Rose, interestingly, had bloomed as fast as Gina had faded. Her dry skin and frizzy hair seemed lubricated, and she was alight with what (thanks to Victor's run-through) I could only interpret as satisfied sex.

Adam Force, good-looking and charming though he still might be, was to my mind a con man sliding towards self-inflicted destruction. If he'd kept anywhere a copy of what he'd stolen from Professor Lawson-Young's laboratory, Rose in the end would have it. Rose would acquire whatever she set out to get, man, tape or power.

Rose had definitely worn one of the black masks, but Adam Force hadn't. He hadn't known who I was when I turned up at Phoenix House.

I said lazily, rising to my feet, "We'll not have a repeat of last Sunday. I came to see Gina, principally, but I came also to leave a message for Rose."

They listened attentively, to my amazement.

I said, "The fourth of your band of black-masked thugs has whispered in my ear."

The possibility of my untruth being accurate froze Rose long enough for me to go forwards along the passage and into the Dobermans' territory of safekeeping. Tom, eyebrows up, joined in step beside me once we were out in the road, and, unpursued, we walked along and around the bend towards the station, the dogs following in silence.

"However did you manage to get out of there unharmed?" Tom asked. "I was sure you would whistle."

"I told them a lie."

He laughed. But it hadn't been funny. Adam Force's sharply focused calculating assessment of me from neck to ankles had been too much like a matter of adding up the amount of deadly substance needed per kilo of body weight to finish me off. A lethal amount of insulin . . . a syringeful of "good-bye" threat, a cylinder of cyclopropane gas, a prelude to any sort of injected extinction . . . Rose would inflict instant damage, but Adam Force would more deliberately kill.

In a normal kitchen, though Rose could always slash with knives, Adam Force wouldn't have at hand any poison, his weapon of choice. He would need more time than he had.

I kept a good distance from Rose on my way out, but it was the white beard and orange socks, the gracious manners and the Phoenix House pharmacy, the hunger for a million and the belief of infallibility, these were the long-term dangers that I had most to fear.

There were two particular videotapes missing, and both had at some time been in my care. Did Rose have the one detailing the necklace? Did Force after all retain the cancer research he'd stolen? I might believe the answers to be yes and no, but how the hell could I find out for sure?

On the way back to Broadway we veered into Cheltenham to call on Kenneth Trubshaw, the trophy committee man, who'd said on Jim's car phone that he would be at home. Slightly surprised by our numbers, he nevertheless generously offered the warmth of the kitchen stove to my traveling companions, plus a large tin of crackers, and shepherded me alone into his much colder drawing room. It was a large room facing north, its daylight gray and carpet green, a combination I found depressing.

I gave him the book I'd taken along for the purpose, which contained a series of glossy colored eight-by-ten photographs, a long record of the work I'd done over maybe twelve years.

I explained that I couldn't in good faith repeat any of the items exactly, but I could make something similar, if he liked.

He laid the book flat on a big table and turned the pages slowly. It mattered to me quite a lot, I discovered, that he would like at least some of the pieces, even if half of them weren't suitable for racing trophies. Vases of odd shapes had recently been blown for trophies of all sorts, though. There was no ban these days on anything surreal.

Trubshaw finished turning the pages. Then he closed the book, to my severe disappointment, and with too serious a tightening of his mouth gave me his verdict.

"If you can lend me this book I'll put it before the committee when they meet tomorrow morning. I know dear Marigold wants action. I will telephone her when the decision's made."

I'll be damned, I thought. How did he look when he was altogether turning things down?

He said, "The leaping horse is the one I'd choose. Can you do anything like it? And I'll need to know how high it would be overall, and how heavy. The one in the photograph looks too big."

"Any size you like," I promised, and told him that the leaping horse in the picture belonged to one of the Leicester races Stewards and his wife.

While Kenneth Trubshaw exclaimed with surprise I recalled minute by minute as best I could the conversation I'd had on the Stewards' friends' viewing balcony, where Lloyd Baxter had first told me about a white-bearded man stealing my money along with the much traveled videotape.

Lloyd Baxter, with his epilepsy, couldn't be factor X. His body hadn't the shape or the agility of Blackmask Four.

Kenneth Trubshaw put his hand down on the book of photos and said thoughtfully, "Could you include enough gold to satisfy Marigold?"

"Yes. Any amount."

"Er . . . how? And would it be . . . well . . . enormously expensive?"

"Not very expensive."

Kenneth Trubshaw held definite reasons for concerning himself and his committee members with the subject of cost, but he hesitated for a measurable time before he waved me to a chair, and, sitting himself, said, "I don't know if you follow the background ins and outs of racing politics at all? I don't mean the form of horses or speculations about their fitness, I mean the question about whether the cost of a winner's trophy should be deducted from the prize money, as it usually has been until recently. Many owners refuse to take the trophy, preferring the whole prize to be given as money. It's being suggested that we

give the whole prize *and* the trophy in every case. Ask Marigold
if she is giving the trophy herself outright, or if she expects the
racecourse to pay for it. Warn her the debate exists." He stopped
slowly, not proud of his shunting of his dilemma onto me.

"Well . . . all right," I said. "But don't expect Marigold to
decide. She's terrific, but she leaves life's really serious decisions
to her chauffeur."

"You don't mean it!"

"Of course I do. Her chauffeur, Worthington, is worth his
weight in cut crystal ten times over."

Kenneth Trubshaw absorbed the news manfully and then with
relief went back to straight expense, saying, "The necklace
Marigold wants is very expensive, isn't it?"

I nodded. "Very. And that necklace, if on public show, is inviting thieves. The gold is genuinely solid in that case."

"Isn't solid gold always the real thing?" He looked quizzical.

I explained, "Well . . . you can paint hot glass with molten
eighteen-carat gold, that's seventy-five percent pure gold mixed
with other metals. You paint what you want to look gold when
it's finished. Then you anneal the work for a second time, but
only at 450 degrees Fahrenheit, and when it cools the second
time the gold you painted on will have adhered completely to
the glass, and it will look like solid gold, even if it isn't."

Kenneth Trubshaw was fascinated, but didn't want to be considered cheap. "Gold has to be gold," he said. "I want Marigold
to like it, of course. That is, if we decide on this sort of thing for
her trophy."

I made murmuring agreeing noises.

He asked curiously, "What of all those sculptures in the book was the hardest for you to make?"

"The most difficult was the gypsy's crystal ball."

It surprised him, as it did most people. He thought a crystal ball was blown up like a child's balloon.

"No," I said. "It's solid glass. And it's extremely difficult to make a perfectly round large ball of glass without air bubbles forming in it as it cools in an annealing oven."

He wanted me to enlighten him about annealing, and when I told him, he said, "Could you make a leaping horse taking off from a crystal ball?"

Nodding, I said, "It would be heavy . . . and difficult . . . but I could make sure it was unique."

He pondered for a while, walking to his tall sash windows and looking out into his sleeping winter garden.

"If we decide on giving you the commission, can you make drawings for us to choose from?"

"Yes," I said, "I could. But actually I'll probably make examples in glass. I'm more at home that way. Glass itself isn't expensive, and if you don't like the things I make, I can sell them in the shop."

He smiled with irony at my frugal business sense. My chances, I judged, weren't much more than fifty-fifty.

Kenneth Trubshaw collected my crew from his kitchen and lined them up in an elegant striped nineteenth-century hall. Carefully then he looked them over. I followed his gaze and also his mind: a tubby driver in a wrinkled gray suit, a thin anxious boy, a piratical-looking vigorous man with a black pointed little Elizabethan beard, and three large black Dobermans with watchful eyes and uncertain moods.

I said to Ken Trubshaw with a smile, "They're my barbed-wire fence. Don't expect them to be pretty as well."

He glanced my way, then said, "It isn't enough for you and Marigold to make, pay for and give a splendid trophy to the winning owner of a race in memory of Martin Stukely." He stopped for reconsideration. "At least, it's enough for that great lady Marigold, but not for you."

He opened his front door for my guys to leave. Tom Pigeon bowed to him with ceremony, his glimmering smile making a mockery of solemnity. His dogs crowded his ankles to give him honor, and the manager earned Tom's allegiance forevermore by bowing back to him in return.

The Trubshaw hand on my arm again made me stay, while the others trooped out to the car. He said, "Martin Stukely's darling widow may not realize that his good name is in doubt just now. Marigold certainly doesn't, nor does the racing public; nor, thank God, does the racing press. But you do, don't you? I saw it in your reaction to Marigold's enthusiasm for a race in his memory. You need, don't you, to scrub clean his honorable reputation first?"

I felt a chilled moment of disbelief that anyone else besides myself had perceived the possibility that Martin could have been knowingly dishonest.

There had been the moment when, reading through the contents of the slim hard-to-find drawer in his desk, I'd had to face the unwelcome photocopy of the letter he had written to

Force. Parts of that short note had reverberated in my awareness
ever since.

". . . your formulae and methods . . . record onto a videotape
. . . and give it to me at Cheltenham races."

Martin had known precisely what was on that tape. Had he
after all known all along that the formulae and methods had
been stolen? Kind George Lawson-Young had given his assured
conviction that Martin had been one hundred percent innocent
in his dealings with Force. Terrible doubts all the same remained,
and I didn't like finding them alive in the Cheltenham hierarchy.

I said to the racecourse trophy chairman, with a lightness I
wasn't altogether feeling, "Could you tell me what you mean?"

With disillusion, he did. "As I understand it, on the day he
died, Martin had possession of a videotape on which were
recorded medical secrets of practically unlimited value. Medical
secrets stolen by a Doctor Force, who had been known to Martin
Stukely for some time. You yourself were to keep that tape
hidden."

I took a steadying breath and asked who had told him all that.
"Private investigators working for the laboratory from where
the secrets were stolen interviewed all sorts of people at Cheltenham." He looked at me curiously. "I also heard from Marigold
that you had been attacked by a pack of thugs outside your shop.
The bookmakers had all heard it was the doing of Rose Payne,
the racecourse valet's daughter, and she has a bit of a reputation
for being violent. One of the bookmakers, a man called Norman
Osprey, who looks a bit like Elvis Presley, he was boasting about

the hammering they gave you. But it seems you didn't give them any tapes anyway."

He waited for me to comment, but I didn't have much to say.

He smiled. "Apparently, the valet thought that what he'd given you was a tape you yourself had filmed, explaining how to make a striking necklace, a copy of an antique. It seems that all the jockeys, and Ed Payne as well, had seen both the necklace and its how-to-make-it instruction tape in the changing room. Ed Payne told his daughter Rose that he had given you a tape and so she tried to find it by stealing every tape she could lay her hands on, including by attacking Martin Stukely's family with knock-out gas."

"Rose herself?" I asked.

Kenneth Trubshaw didn't know. That was also the end of his up-to-dateness, except that, in the Cheltenham Stewards' opinion, Martin Stukely had very likely known that the scientific knowledge he'd promised to hide had been stolen from a research lab.

"And at present," I said with regret, "all those tapes are still missing. Whoever has them isn't telling."

"I'm told you yourself are looking for them."

"Who tells you all these things?" I really wanted to hear, but it seemed to be a matter of general supposition and logic.

"I'll tell you something myself," I said, and I gave him Victor's latest purple home-life news.

"Doctor Force and Rose deserve each other." He laughed in his throat. "That will do nicely for tomorrow morning's committee." He walked with me to Jim's car. "Give my warmest regards to Marigold. I'll be in touch."

He shook my hand with sincerity.

He said, "Find those tapes and clear Stukely's name."

So simple, I thought.

WHEN I DISEMBARKED at Bon-Bon's house, she herself with Daniel by her side came out to meet us.

"There's a message from Catherine Dodd for you," Bon-Bon said to me. "She has the evening free. She wants you to go to your house, if you can."

I thanked her, but she, like me and also Tom, was watching with fascination the flash of understanding between Victor, fifteen, and the four-years-younger Daniel. Alienation seemed more normal for that age bracket, but those two discovered immediately that they spoke computer language with a depth that none of the rest of us could reach. Victor climbed out of Jim's car and went indoors with Daniel as if the two of them were twins. Cyber twins, perhaps.

Bon-Bon would keep Victor for the night, instead of Tom, she said, amused, following the boys into the house, and Jim drove Tom, the dogs and myself back to Tom's house first, and then on to mine.

"I never thought we'd come back in one piece." Tom left me with that bright thought and a positively jaunty wave, and I would have cast *him* as Blackmask Four if I hadn't twice owed him a rescue from crippling injury, and perhaps my life.

Catherine's motorcycle graced its customary spot outside the kitchen door, and she herself came out when she heard Jim's car arrive. There was no difficulty in interpreting her reaction to my return, and Jim drove away with a vast smile (and double cash), promising his service again, "day or night."

Coming home to Catherine had become an event to look forward to. I'd never asked her to take me to see her own living space, and when I did, that evening, she laughed and said, "I'll take you there tomorrow. It's better by daylight."

She asked me how my day had been, and I asked about hers. She frowned over Victor's troubles and was encouraging about a glass trophy horse. It was all very *married,* I thought, and we'd only known each other for three weeks.

"Tell me about the police," I said, as we squashed companionably into one of the oversize chairs.

"What about them?" She was slightly defensive always about her job, but this time I especially wanted to know.

"The priorities," I said. "For instance, on that New Year's Day, you in your plainish clothes and the hobo lying on the doorstep, you were both there to frighten thieves off, weren't you, not to arrest them?"

She shifted in my arms. "Not really," she replied. "We like to get our man."

I knew better than to tease her. "Tell me about your partner, the hobo."

"He's not really a hobo," she replied, smiling. "His name is Paul Cratchet. He's a big guy but misleadingly gentle. Paul's a good detective. Many a villain has been surprised by his hand on their collar. He's known as Pernickety Paul at the station because he is so fussy over his reports."

Smiling, I inquired plainly, "What events get most police attention?"

"Accidental deaths, and murder, of course. Especially murder of a police officer. The murder of a fellow police officer, I'd say, gets people going most."

"But after that?"

"Any physical assault."

"Especially of a police officer?"

She twisted her neck and searched my purposefully straight face for levity. Satisfied, she nodded. "Especially of a police officer."

"And next?"

"Aggravated theft. That's when a weapon is used, or a severe physical threat, or violence as a means to achieve theft. It's called robbery."

"And then?"

"Actually, and in general," Catherine said, "if someone's bleeding, then police officers will come at once. If goods are stolen, but no one's hurt, the officers will probably come in the morning after the nine-one-one call. If cars are stolen, the police will take the registration number and promise to inform the owner if the car is found."

"And that's that? That's all for cars?"

"More or less. It depends. They're usually found burnt out."

"And who," I asked mildly, "would I go to if I found some stolen property?"

"Are you talking about those old videotapes again?"

"Yup. Those old tapes."

"Well . . ." She let a good few seconds pass, then said, "I did inquire about this . . ."

"It sounds bad news," I said.

Catherine sighed. "The tapes themselves are worth practically nothing. You said they hadn't even any covers. The information recorded on them, on both of them, even if they're totally different from each other, is called intellectual property. It has very little priority in police thinking. How to make a copy of an antique necklace? You must be joking! Industrial secrets, even medical secrets? Too bad. No one is going to waste much police time looking for them. There would be slightly more interest in your bag of cash, *if* you could identify a single note of it for sure. It would be much more likely, after three weeks, that it's been spent and dispersed. It was a fair amount to you personally, but not much in world terms, do you see?" She stopped as an entirely opposite thought struck her, then said, "Does this dreadful Rose still believe you know where to find the tapes?"

"Don't worry about it."

"But does she?" Catherine was insistent. "Does she, Gerard?"

I told her, smiling, "I now think she's had the necklace tape almost from the beginning, and if she has, she knows I haven't got it." And Rose knows, I thought, that I could repeat it any day.

"But the other one?" Catherine begged. "The one stolen from the lab?"

"Yes." I felt lighthearted. "I could make a guess. Let's go to bed."

I awoke first in the morning, and lay for a while watching Catherine's calm gentle breathing. At that moment, it filled me with total contentment . . . but would I feel the same in ten years? . . . and would she? When she stirred and opened her eyes and smiled, ten years didn't matter. One lived *now,* and now went along as a constant companion, present and changing minute by minute. It was *now,* always, that mattered.

"What are you thinking about?" she asked.

"Same as you, I dare say."

She smiled again, and asked simply if I had plans for us both on her free Saturday. Relaxed, I offered the comfortable new chair in Logan Glass, and accepted a pillion ride to get there.

Hickory had again arrived before me and was again intent on a perfect sailing boat. He greeted me like the good friend of time gone by, tentatively asking if I could assist him, as he was finding it difficult on his own.

With uncomplicated pleasure I stripped down to a working singlet and helped Hickory, bringing a gather out of the tank when he needed it and holding the hot glass ready for his use. Hickory typically kept a running commentary for Catherine's sake and flirted with her mildly, and seldom, I thought, had I more enjoyed a frivolous start to the morning.

Hickory this time remembered to put the finished boat in the annealing oven, and if he accepted Catherine's unstinted praise with smugness, he had at least taken a satisfactory step forward in his training.

Irish arrived and brewed tea. Pamela Jane tidied and refilled the tubs of colored powder that we would use during that session, to restock the shelves. The rest of the regular Saturday morning unwound in work from nine to twelve o'clock.

At a few minutes past noon the shop embraced first Bon-Bon and the two boys, Daniel and Victor, for whom glassblowing had temporarily become a greater draw than e-mail.

Not long after them, Marigold swooped in, batting the eyelashes, grinning at Hickory, smothering Daniel in a bright pink gold-smocked cloudlike dress and telling Bon-Bon at the top of her voice that "Darling Trubby" would be with them right away.

"Darling Trubby," Kenneth Trubshaw, swam through the bright pink experience and emerged with lipstick on his cheek. The trophy chairman of Cheltenham races was carrying my book of photographs, and besides being apparently unnerved by the chattering din, he eyed my half-undress with a degree of disbelief and suggested that the Wychwood Dragon might be better for a business meeting.

"Darling Trubby, what a *great* idea!" Marigold's immediate enthusiasm resulted in herself, Kenneth Trubshaw, Bon-Bon, Catherine, myself, and of course Worthington (Marigold insisted) occupying a quiet corner of the dining room to listen to the opinions of that morning's meeting of the Cheltenham Racecourse Company's trophy committee.

Irish was dispatched down the hill to fill the two boys with hamburgers and Cokes, and Hickory and Pamela Jane were left in peace to deal with that less demanding breed, the January tourist.

When six of us were neatly seated and listening, Kenneth Trubshaw began his spiel. "First of all, dear Marigold," he said, "everyone on the committee wants me to thank you for your splendid generosity. . . ." He gave flattery a good name. Marigold glowed. Worthington caught my eye and winked.

"The committee voted . . . ," the chairman came at last to the point. "We decided unanimously to ask you, Gerard Logan, to design and make a Martin Stukely memorial of a horse rearing on a crystal ball, like the one in the book. If it pleases Marigold and the committee . . ." His final words got temporarily lost in a bright pink Marigold hug, but came out the other side with provisos about cost. To Marigold, cost was a bore. Worthington bargained, and I telephoned a jeweler who promised enough gold.

"Can you make it today, darling Gerard?" Marigold enthused. "It's barely three o'clock."

"Tomorrow would be difficult," I said. "Next week would be better. Today, I'm sorry, is impossible." Sooner rather than later, I thought, to keep her happy.

The Marigold pout appeared, but I wasn't going to help it. I needed time for thinking if it were to be a good job, and a good job was what I needed to do for Bon-Bon, for Marigold, for Cheltenham racecourse and for Martin himself.

"I'll do them tomorrow," I said. "The crystal ball and the rear-ing horse. I'll do them on my own, alone except for one assistant. They will be ready on Monday for the gold to be added, and on

Tuesday afternoon I'll join them together onto a plinth. By Wednesday the trophy will be finished."

"Not until then?" Marigold protested, and urged me to think again.

"I want to get it right for you," I said.

And also I wanted to give my enemies time.

CHAPTER 11

MARIGOLD OBJECTED TO my wanting no audience to the making of the rearing horse and the crystal ball. Kenneth Trubshaw understood, he said.

"Darling Trubby," substantial, gray-haired and very much a businessman, mentioned to me the one quiet word, "Fees?"

"Worthington and I," I said, "will fix a price with Marigold, then you can haggle if you like."

He shook my hand wryly. "The Leicester Steward whose wife owns several of your things is also a Steward of Cheltenham, and he told our committee this morning that five years ago we could have bought this trophy for peanuts."

"Five years ago," I agreed. "Yes, you could."

"And he said," Trubshaw added, "five years from now works by Gerard Logan will at least cost double again."

Uncle Ron would have loved it. Well . . . so did I. It was surviving the next five *days* that caught my attention.

By midafternoon everyone had collected and split apart again. Bon-Bon and Marigold left the boys in my care while they browsed the antique shops, and Worthington and Kenneth Trubshaw developed a strong mutual regard in a stroll.

In the workshop, Victor, utterly impressed, watched Hickory show off with two gathers of red-hot glass that he rolled competently in white powder and then colored powder and tweaked into a small wavy-edged one-flower vase. Pamela Jane expertly assisted in snapping the vase off the punty iron and Hickory with false modesty lifted it into an annealing oven as if it were the Holy Grail.

Daniel, for whom the workshop was a familiar stamping ground, mooned around looking at the shelves of bright little animals, pointing out to me the scarlet giraffe his father had promised him the day before he died. That story was most unlikely, I thought, remembering Martin's absentmindedness towards all his children, but I gave Daniel the giraffe anyway, a gift that would have displeased his grandmother.

Giving to Daniel, though, always reaped a worthwhile crop. This time he wanted me to go outside with him, and, seeing the stretched size of his eyes, I went casually, but at once.

"What is it?" I asked.

"There's a shoe shop down the road," he said.

"Yes, I know."

"Come and look."

He set off, and I followed.

"Victor and I came down here with Irish, looking for hamburgers," he said, "but we came to the shoe shop first."

The shoe shop duly appeared on our left, a small affair mostly stocked with walking shoes for tourists. Daniel came to an abrupt halt by its uninspiring window.

"I should think it might be worth two gold coins," he said.

"For two gold coins it had better be good."

"See those sneakers?" he said. "Those up there at the back with green-and-white-striped laces? The man with that gas, those are his laces."

I stared disbelievingly at the shoes. They were large with thick rubberlike soles, triangular white flashed canvas sections and, threaded in precision through two rows of eyeholes, the fat bunched laces of Daniel's certainty.

He said again, "The man who gassed us wore those shoes."

"Come into the shop, then," I said, "and we'll ask who bought some like them."

He agreed, "OK," and then added, "It might cost two more gold coins, to go into the shop."

"You're an extortionist."

"What's that?"

"Greedy. And I've no more coins."

Daniel grinned and shrugged, accepting fate.

The shop had a doorbell that jingled when we went in, and

contained a grandfatherly salesman who proved useless from our point of view, as he was standing in for his daughter whose baby was sick. She might be back some day next week, he vaguely thought, and he knew nothing about previous sales.

When we went back into the street, Bon-Bon, away up the hill, was beckoning Daniel to her car, to go home. Only the fact that she had already loaded Victor, having offered him another night's computer hacking, persuaded her son to join her, and presently, when Marigold and "Darling Trubby" had gone their separate ways, only Catherine and my little team were left, and those three, as it was Saturday afternoon, were setting things straight as if for a normal winter Sunday of no action. They departed with my blessing at four-thirty, leaving only myself and Catherine to lock up: and I gave her too a bunch of keys for the future.

I also told police officer Dodd about the laces, which sent her on a brief reconnaissance only, as first of all she said she needed another officer with her if she were to question the shop owner, and second, the grandfather salesman had shut up shop and left it dark.

Catherine, like Martin before her, grew minute by minute more interested in the technical details and the chemical complexities of bright modern glass. Old glass could look gray or yellow, fine to my eyes but dingy on racecourses.

Catherine asked which I would make first, the horse or the ball, and I told her the horse. I asked her whether, even though they would not be on duty the next day, she could persuade her

Pernickety Paul hobo partner to come and walk up and down Broadway with her a couple of times? She naturally asked why.

"To mind my back," I joked, and she said she thought he might come if she asked him.

"He might be busy," I said.

"I doubt it," she replied. "He seems rather lonely since his wife left him."

We rode her motorbike to a hotel deep in the country and ate there and slept there, and I avoided Blackmask Four and explained to my increasingly loved police officer, before I kissed her, that she and the hobo might find handcuffs a good idea on the morrow. "He always carries them," Catherine said.

In the morning she said, "All this walking up and down Broadway . . . is it the tapes?"

"Sort of." I nodded. I didn't mention life or death. One couldn't somehow.

All the same, I woke Tom Pigeon, who woke his dogs, who all growled (Tom included) that Sunday was a day of rest.

I phoned Jim. At my service all day, he said. His wife was going to church.

Worthington was already awake, he said, and had I noticed that Sundays weren't always healthy for Gerard Logan?

"*Mm.* What's Marigold doing today?"

"I've got the day free, if that's what you're asking. Where do you want me to turn up when? And most of all, why?"

I hesitated over the last answer but replied in order: "Wychwood Dragon lobby, soon as possible, on account of fear."

"Whose fear?"

"Mine."

"Oh yeah?" His laugh traveled with bass reverberation. "You'll be alone in that workshop of yours, is that it? In that case, I'll be with you soon."

"I won't exactly be alone. Catherine and her partner officer will probably be in the town, and in the workshop there will be Pamela Jane, who's going to assist."

"The girl? Why not that bright young man, what's his name . . . Hickory?"

"Pamela Jane doesn't argue."

Worthington's deep voice arrived as a chuckle. "I'm on my way."

I made one more phone call, this time to the home of George Lawson-Young, apologizing for the eight-thirty wake-up.

"The hour doesn't matter"—he yawned—"if you bring good news."

"It depends," I said, and told him what he might expect.

He said, "Well done."

"More to do."

"I wouldn't miss it." His smile came across the air. "I'll see you later."

Catherine and her motorcycle took me to Logan Glass, where local inhabitants could have seen a display of affection to wag tongues for a week. I unlocked the doors, being there intentionally before Pamela Jane, and again read the notes I'd made (and filed in the locked bookcase) last time I'd tried my hand at a rearing horse.

This one would take me about an hour to complete, if I made the whole trophy, including plinth and ball. At a little less than half a meter high, it would weigh roughly twenty kilos, heavy because solid glass itself weighed a good deal, let alone the added gold. Marigold had with wide-sweeping arms insisted on magnificence. It was to be Martin's memorial, she proclaimed, and she had been exceedingly fond of her son-in-law. Both Bon-Bon and Worthington thought this much-to-be-publicized admiration a little retrospective, but "Darling Trubby" might think the trophy handsome in the sun.

I had filled the tank with clear crystal and put ready at hand the punty irons I'd need, also the small tools for shaping muscles, legs and head. Tweezers too, essential always. I set the furnace temperature to the necessary 1800 degrees Fahrenheit.

By then I "saw" the sculpture complete. A pity they hadn't wanted Martin himself on the rearing horse's back. I saw him there clearly now, at last. Perhaps I would repeat the horse with Martin riding. Perhaps one night . . . for Bon-Bon, and for the friend I'd lost and still trusted.

While I waited for Pamela Jane to arrive, I thought about the wandering videotape that had raised so many savage feelings, and like curtains parting, the deductive faculty Professor Lawson-Young had put his faith in continued to open vistas in my mind. I had at last added in his factor X, and the mask had dropped from Blackmask Four.

Out of doors it started raining.

I stood looking at the furnace and listening to its heart of flame. Looking at the raisable trapdoor that kept 1800 degrees Fahrenheit at bay. Irish, Hickory, Pamela Jane and myself were so accustomed to the danger of the extreme heat roaring within the firebricks that taking care was automatic, was second nature.

I knew at last the sequence of the roads in the cul-de-sacs. I listened in my mind to Catherine's list of punishable crimes and their penalties, and reckoned that Rose and Adam Force should, if they had any sense at all, just leave the videotapes where they rested and save themselves the grief of prosecution.

Thieves never had any sense.

I'd surrounded myself with as many bodyguards as I could muster that Sunday simply because neither Rose nor Adam Force had shown any sense or restraint so far, and because the making of the trophy horse left me wide open to any mayhem they might invent. I could have filled the workroom with a crowd of onlookers and been safe . . . safe for how long?

I knew now where the danger lay. I couldn't forever look over my shoulder fearfully, and, however rash it might seem, I saw a confrontation as the quickest path to resolution.

If I were disastrously wrong, Professor Lawson-Young could say good-bye to his millions. The breakthrough that would save the world in the cure for cancer would be published under someone else's name.

WHEN MY ENEMIES came, it wasn't just time, I found, that I had given them, as much as an opportunity to outthink me.

I was still listening to the furnace when sounds behind me announced the arrival of Pamela Jane. She had entered through the side door, though usually she came in through the front.

"Mr. Logan . . ." Her voice quavered high with fright, and besides, she normally called me Gerard.

I turned at once to see how bad things were, and found that in many unforeseen ways they were extremely bad indeed.

Pamela Jane, dressed for work in her usual white overalls cinched around the waist, was coming to a standstill in the center of the workshop, trembling from a situation far beyond her capabilities. Her raincoat lay dropped in a bundle on the floor and her wrists were fastened together in front of her by sticky brown packing tape. Simpler and cheaper than handcuffs, the tape was equally immobilizing, and more effective still in Pamela Jane's case as the charming Adam Force held a full syringe in one hand and, with the other, had dragged down a clutch of female overalls to reveal a patch of bare skin below the needle. Thin and frightened, she began to cry.

A step or two behind Pamela Jane came Rose, every muscle triumphant, her whole face a sneer. She too came quietly, in soft shoes, and fast.

Rose, strong, determined and full of spite aimed powerfully my way, held in a pincer grip the upper arm of Hickory. My bright assistant stood helplessly swaying, his eyes and his mouth stuck out of action by strips of brown packing tape. The same tape had been used to bind his hands behind his back and also to form a makeshift hobble between his ankles.

Roughly steadying Hickory's balance loomed the bookmaker

Norman Osprey, more bully beef than beauty, but arithmetically as fast as a computer chip. Just inside the side door, keeping guard and shifting uncomfortably from foot to foot, was, of all people, Eddie Payne. He wouldn't meet my eyes. He took instructions steadfastly from Rose.

The actions of all four intruders had been whirlwind fast, and I had arranged little in any way of retaliation. All the bodyguards were simply to roam the street outside. Catherine and her hobo were to patrol their normal disjointed beat. Rose and her cohorts had somehow slid past them in the rain.

I was wearing, as usual, a white singlet which left my arms, neck and much of my shoulder area bare. The heat from the furnace roared almost unbearably beyond the trapdoor, if one weren't used to it. I put my foot and my weight sideways on the treadle, which duly opened the trap and let a huge gust of Sahara heat blow out over Norman Osprey's wool suit and reddening face. Furious, he made a snatch towards hurling me onto the trapdoor itself, but I sidestepped and tripped him, and unbalanced him onto his knees.

Rose yelled to Norman, "Stop it, you stupid asshole, we don't want him damaged this time; you know bloody well we'll get nowhere if he can't talk."

I watched as Rose tugged my blindfolded assistant across a good length of floor, with Norman Osprey holding him upright in a fierce grip. Hickory stumbled and felt tentatively forwards step by step until he reached the chair I'd bought for Catherine. At that point Rose revolved Hickory roughly until he fell into the chair on his side and had to struggle to turn and sit upright.

Behind me now I could hear the distressed breathing of Pamela Jane, and also the unmistakable heavy wheeze of Adam Force's asthma. He said nothing at all about his near miss with insulin at Bristol. He definitely needed an inhaler but had no free hands.

Rose said to Hickory with malignant satisfaction, "Now you sit there, buddy boy, and it will teach you not to put your nose in where it isn't wanted." She redirected the pleased venom back my way while Hickory tried hard to talk but produced only a throttled tenor protest.

"Now you," she told me, "will hand over everything I want. Or your friend here will get holes burned in him."

Pamela Jane cried out, "Oh no, you *can't!*"

"You shut up, you silly little bitch," Rose acidly told her, "or I'll spoil your soppy looks instead."

Whether or not he was aware of Rose's speed in standing on the treadle part of the floor that raised the flap of the furnace, Hickory was unable to protest more vigorously than to shrink ever deeper into the chair. He did understand, though, the diabolical choice she was thrusting under my nose.

As if she could read his mind, she said in the same sharp tone, "You, what's your name, Hickory? You'd better pray that this boss of yours won't let you burn. Because I'm not fooling, this time he's going to give me what I want."

She picked up one of the long punty irons and pushed it into the tank of molten glass. Her movement was ungraceful rather than smooth with constant practice, but somewhere, sometime, she had watched a glassblower collect a gather from a tank. She withdrew the iron with a small blob of red-hot glass on the end of it, and revolved the rod so that the glass stayed adhered to it and didn't fall off.

Pamela Jane moaned at the sight and all but fell onto the doctor's needle.

"Gerard Logan," Rose said to me with emphasis. "This time you will do what I tell you, now, at once."

Extraordinarily she sounded less sure of herself than screaming "Break his wrists" into the Broadway night, and I remembered Worthington's judgment that as I would beat her at the tennis match of life, so she would never again face me on the actual court. Yet here she was, visibly pulling together the sinews and nerves of resolution.

I'd seen Martin summon his mental vigor when going out to race on a difficult horse, and I'd seen actors breathe deeply in the wings when the play ahead dug deep into the psyche. I understood a good deal about courage in others and about the deficiencies in myself, but on that Sunday in January it was Rose's own mushrooming determination that pumped up in me the inner resources I needed.

I watched her as she in turn watched me, and it wasn't what she said that mattered at all, it was which of us would win the desperate battle for pride.

She plunged the cooling small ball of glass into the tank again and drew it out again, larger. She swung the iron around until the molten red-hot lump advanced to a too close spot under Hickory's chin. He could feel the heat. He shrank frantically away and tried to scream behind the adhering tape.

"Look out, for God's sake," I shouted automatically, and as if surprised, Rose swung the iron away from Hickory's face until he wasn't for the minute threatened.

"You see!" Rose sounded all of a sudden victorious. "If you don't like him burned you'll tell me where you've hidden the videotape I want."

I said urgently, "You'll disfigure Hickory if you're not careful. Glass burns are terrible. You can get a hand burned so badly that it needs amputating. An arm; a foot . . . You can smell flesh burning . . . you can lose your mouth, your nose."

"Shut up," Rose yelled, and again, at the top of her voice, "Shut up!"

"You can burn out an eye," I said. "You can sear and cauterize your guts."

Pamela Jane, who lived with the danger, was affected least of all in spite of her fluttery manner, and it was big Norman Osprey of the great muscular shoulders who sweated and looked ready to vomit.

Rose looked at her red-hot iron. She looked at Hickory and she glanced at me. I could more or less read her rapid mind. She had come to threaten me through my regard for Hickory and now here I was, a target again myself.

Beside Rose's powerful identity her companions' egos were

pale. Even Adam Force's good looks and persuasive smile faded to second rate in her presence, and I began to realize fully that her reputation in inspiring real abject terror, in men particularly, was in no way a myth. I felt the fringes myself, try though I might to counteract it. Her effect on her father sent him to the confessional at the best of times, and this being Sunday again I could barely imagine the turmoil churning in his good Catholic conscience.

To Norman Osprey no doubt one day was as good or bad as the next. His days were judged by the amount of muscle needed to achieve his own way, coupled with the fizzing ability to add, divide or multiply as if by instinct.

Adam Force's finger seemed to itch on the plunger set to activate the syringe's undisclosed contents. I wished to heaven that poor Pamela Jane would sniff back the tears and swallow the sobs, both of which seemed increasingly to irritate Doctor White-Beard; and as for Hickory, stuck with wide brown bands into silence and sightlessness, and deep in the soft armchair, I thought he would be staying exactly where Rose had put him until someone pulled him out.

Impressions flashed and passed. Rose stared at me with calculation, enjoying her certainty that she would defeat me pretty soon. I couldn't swear she wouldn't. This time there were no black masks or baseball bats. But to be faced bare-armed with molten glass was worse.

Suddenly and unexpectedly Rose said, "You came here this morning to make a trophy horse of glass and gold. I want the gold."

Wow! I thought. No one had brought gold into the equation before. Gold for the trophy hadn't been mentioned in Rose's hearing as far as I knew. I had ordered enough for the trophy, and a little over for stock, but a quantity worth holding up the stage-coach for, it was not.

Someone had misled Rose, or she had misunderstood, and her acquisitive imagination had done the rest.

Rose was still sure that, one way or another, I could make her rich.

Adam Force was admiring her with a smile and applauding her with his eyes.

If I could use this, well . . . *golden* . . . opportunity . . . I could but try . . . I did need time now, and if I made the trophy horse I could slow things nicely.

I said, "The gold isn't here yet. I'm fed up with the delay." The carefree but complaining tone I used nonplussed Rose into lowering the tip of the punty iron for the moment.

"If I don't get the trophy glass horse ready on time," I said, "the one that's ordered, that is, well . . ." I stopped abruptly, as if I'd teetered on the brink of a monster mistake. "Never mind," I said as if nervously, and Rose demanded I finish the sentence.

"Well . . . ," I said.

"Get on with it."

"Gold . . . ," I said. "I have to use it on the horse."

Pamela Jane, to her eternal credit, dried her tears in mid-sniffle and in horrified disgust told me frankly across the workroom that I should be thinking of freeing Hickory, not making a trophy for Cheltenham races.

"How can you?" she exclaimed. "It's *despicable*."

"A car from the jewelers is bringing the gold for the hooves, mane and tail," I said.

Rose wavered, and then demanded, "When?"

I said I wouldn't tell her.

"Yes, you will," she said, and advanced the hot iron in menace.

"Eleven o'clock," I said hastily. A good lie. "Let me make the horse," I suggested, and made it sound on the verge of pleading. "Then, when I've made the horse, I'll tell you where to look where I think the tape might be, and then you must promise to set Hickory free as soon as you have the gold."

Pamela Jane said helplessly, "I don't believe this."

She couldn't understand how easily I had crumbled. She couldn't see that her scorn was the measure of my success.

Rose looked at her watch, discovered she would have to wait an hour for the gold to arrive and did the unwise calculation that she could afford to wait for it.

"Get on and make the trophy," she instructed. "When the gold comes, you'll sign for it in the normal way, or your Hickory's for the slow burn, understand?"

I nodded.

"Get on with it, then." She looked around the workshop, assessing the state of things, and told Pamela Jane to sit deep in the other soft chair. There, while Adam Force held his threatening needle at her neck, Norman Osprey taped her ankles together.

Pamela Jane glared at me and said she wouldn't be assisting me with the horse, or ever again.

Rose consolidated this decision by telling her I'd always been a coward. I looked expressionlessly at Pamela Jane and saw the shade of doubt creep in, even while she listened to Rose pour on the disdain.

I hadn't meant to shape the trophy horse under the threat of Rose's hand on the punty irons. I had in fact mobilized the bodyguards to prevent it, and they hadn't. On the other hand a confrontation with Rose some day had been inevitable, and if it were to be *now* then I'd need to think a bit faster. I stood flat-footed, without drive.

Rose taunted, "I thought you were supposed to be good at glass."

"Too many people," I complained.

She peremptorily ordered Norman Osprey and Eddie Payne to go around the half-wall into the showroom, and with more politeness shifted Adam Force around after them. All three leaned on the half-wall, watching. Having pulled out one of the punty irons that I'd put to heat beside the active part of the furnace, Rose thrust it into the crucible—the tank—holding now white-hot glass, and drew it out, a reasonably sized gather, revolving it just speedily enough for it not to fall off onto the floor.

"Go on," she said. She shoved her lump of burning devastation towards my right arm and I retreated far enough for it not to char my skin.

It was no way to make a trophy of any sort. I needed to start the horse's body with several gathers of clear crystal and Rose,

with irons loaded with plum-sized tips that would destroy whatever they touched, hovered over Hickory's and Pamela Jane's
heads and threatened to melt off their ears, to make their roast-
ing flesh smell like meat cooking if I gave her the slightest cause.
I was to tell her all the time what I proposed to do next. There
were to be no sudden unforeseen moves on my part. Hickory
and Pamela Jane would suffer. Did I understand? Rose demanded.

I did.

I understood. So did Pamela Jane, and so did Hickory, who
could hear.

I told Rose I would need to take four or five gathers from the
tank, and while she had her own lump of destruction close to
Pamela Jane's ear I harvested enough glass to make a horse
standing on his hind legs a third of a meter high.

Pamela Jane closed her eyes.

I told Rose in advance that it was almost, if not totally,
impossible to make a horse of that size without an assistant,
which was partly because the body of the horse had to be kept
at working heat, after one had sculpted the muscles of the neck
and the upper legs while one added two pieces of glass for each
lower leg and foot, and others for the tail.

"Get on with it and don't whinge," she said. She was smiling
to herself.

People in circuses could keep a dozen plates spinning in the
air by twiddling sticks under them. Making that rearing horse in
Broadway felt much the same: keep the body and legs hot while

you sculpted the head. The resulting head wouldn't have won in a preschool contest.

Rose was enjoying herself. The less I blocked and opposed her the more certain she grew that I was on the way to capitulation. She liked it. She smiled again, a secretive dirty-little-girl underhand twist of the lips.

I looked at that smile and abruptly I personally understood what Worthington had described. Victory for Rose was never complete without the physical humiliation of a male adversary.

Victory over Gerard Logan, which Rose now saw as gloriously her own, wouldn't be sufficient for her in that place unless it included her inflicting some depth of burn.

I might shudder at such a prospect but Rose wouldn't. I might use plain muscle power in an all-out attempt to defeat her, but I wouldn't try to wreak havoc of molten glass on Rose. Nor on anybody. I lacked the brutality.

Neither, though, could I desert my team and run.

With tweezers I pulled the horse's front legs up and its rear legs down and held the whole body on an iron within the furnace to keep it hot enough to mold.

There were still things I could do, I thought.

Honorable exits.

Exits that were more or less honorable, anyway.

I managed to juggle body and leg pieces into a headless racer.

Exits, hell, I thought. Exit wasn't enough. Defeatism never got anyone anywhere.

I held two punty irons with difficulty and transferred enough glass from one to the other to attach and shape a mane, but it hadn't the elegance necessary for Cheltenham.

Worthington opened the gallery door and began to come in from the street. His eyes widened as fast as his comprehension as he spun a fast 180-degree turn and was on his way down the road before Rose could decide which had priority, chasing Worthington or keeping me penned.

When Worthington was out of anything but whistling distance she told Force and her father to lock the gallery door immediately and was furious because neither of them could find a key. I hoped to hell and back that Pamela Jane wouldn't report obligingly that she herself had a key to everywhere.

She gave me another uncertain stare and shut her mouth.

Rose stopped smiling, loaded her punty iron with a white-hot golf-ball-sized end of glass and held it close to Hickory.

I did my best to make and fix a tail to my increasingly non-thoroughbred creation. The tail and two hind feet formed a triangle to support the rearing horse. When I wanted a great result, this stage often went wrong. That day it all balanced like perfection.

Hickory wriggled desperately to get away from Rose's white-hot threat.

Pamela Jane saw me doing nothing to help Hickory while constructing only a toy, and went back to despising me.

I stuck the head on the neck and tweaked the ears forward. Finished, the object had four legs, head, mane and tail, and no grace whatever. I stood it upright on the marver table, where rearing, it was ready to start leaping into the future from a crystal ball.

In spite of the faults, Rose seemed impressed. Not impressed enough, however, to lower her guard, or her punty iron beside Hickory's head.

I glanced at the workshop clock.

A minute—tick tock, tick tock—was a very long time.

I said, "The gold will cover the hooves and the mane and the tail."

Tick tock, Tick tock.

Rose thrust her cooling punty iron back into the furnace and brought out a new white-hot gather, which she again held near Hickory's head.

"How long," she demanded, "until that gold gets here?"

Hickory wriggled violently, trying desperately to free himself from the sticky strips on his mouth and his eyes.

Pamela Jane, eyes closed, seemed to be praying.

Two minutes. Tick tock.

"The gold," I said, "will come in small bars. It has to be melted, then it has to cover the hooves and the mane and the tail . . ."

Hickory threw himself forward, trying to get out of his embracing chair. Rose didn't move her punty iron far enough away fast enough to avoid him, and one of his ears did touch her waving white-hot blob of glass.

Under the parcel tape, he couldn't scream. His body arched.

Rose jumped back, but Hickory's ear sizzled and now smelled of fried meat, and would never be perfect again.

Three minutes. Eternity. Tick tock.

Hickory's horror, plain and agonizing, had everyone staring. Rose should have jettisoned her iron and gone to his help, but she didn't.

Three minutes, ten seconds since I stood the rearing horse on the marver table.

Dangerous to wait any longer.

I picked up the big tweezers I'd used to form the horse's mane, and with them tore the parcel tape securing Pamela Jane's ankles. I pulled her up by her still-tied wrists, and Rose turned towards me from Hickory and yelled at me to leave her alone.

Pamela Jane had no idea what she should do, and dither could be fatal. I said to her urgently, *"Run,"* and she didn't, but hesitated, looking back to Hickory.

No time left. I lifted her up bodily and carried her.

Pamela Jane objected. Rose ordered me to put her down. I didn't, but aimed a bit unsteadily for the way into the showroom and shouted at the trio there leaning on the wall to get down behind it.

Rose came fast across the workshop after me, and drove at me, holding her hot glass–laden punty iron like a sword.

Half seeing her, half sensing the searing future, I twisted both myself and Pamela Jane roughly to let the iron miss us, like a bull-fighter, but Rose in fury dragged and stabbed and burned a long black slit through my white singlet.

No more time.

I lugged Pamela Jane around the half-wall to the showroom and threw her, screaming protests, to the ground, and I fell on top of her to pin her down.

The rearing horse had stood unannealed at maximum heat on the marver table for three minutes forty seconds when it exploded.

CHAPTER 12

THE HORSE EXPLODED into scorching fragments that flew like angry transparent wasps throughout the workshop and over the half-wall into the showroom beyond.

Adam Force, refusing to get down because it had been I who suggested it, had been hit twice, once in the upper arm, and once, more seriously, across the top of the cheekbone below the eye, taking away a chunk of surface flesh. Half fainting from shock, the doctor had dropped his syringe. Blood reddened his sleeve, but there was no spurting arterial flood.

It was the wreck of his good looks though, I thought, that would in the end grieve him most, and if he had peered into a looking glass at that moment, he would probably have collapsed altogether. The speed and sharpness of the flying glass fragment had opened a furrow that was bound to leave an untreatable scar, and like many facial cuts this one was bleeding copiously. Adam Force bled into his white beard, which was fast turning red.

Doctor Bright-Scarlet-Beard Force. Serve him right, I thought. A pity it would wash clean. Wash clean . . . other things would wash out too . . . an idea.

Glass cooled rapidly if it expanded and thinned. One could gently blow down an iron into semi-liquid glass so that it would expand until it looked like a soap bubble: a dollop of red-hot glass would cool to the cold shell of a brittle bubble in the few seconds it took to blow it from one state to the other.

The trophy horse, though, hadn't been blown on purpose from the inside, it had split violently apart along the internal stress lines caused by the pulling and stretching as the glass cooled, the outer regions cooling faster than the inner core. The splinters had still been fiercely hot when they'd dug into the first thing they met. Adam Force had been lucky not to lose an eye.

Norman Osprey, kneeling in spite of his antipathy towards the source of good advice, had survived the shattering of the horse with his skin intact, if not his temper.

Although pale and slightly shaking, the Elvis lookalike still clung to the doctrine of "Get Logan." In consequence he'd risen from his knees and planted his gorilla shoulders close inside the gallery-to-street door, making an exit that way a matter of hand-to-hand fighting and a toss-up whether I won or lost. A hand-to-hand fight against that visibly dramatic strength would have been daunting always but in my tottery state of that moment, even if I'd wanted to quit the scene, which I didn't, a win would have been impossible. As long as Norman Osprey thought he was usefully stationed where he was doing me no good, however, I could count him one less trouble to deal with, and be grateful.

Eddie, who seemed not to understand what had happened, was still on his knees beside the wall. Martin's valet who, with his stubborn misconceptions, had accompanied Rose on this whole unholy tape hunt, now looked as though he were begging absolution. To my mind he certainly failed to deserve it.

Pamela Jane heaved herself from under me in a troubled dilemma as she couldn't decide whether to thank me for saving her from razor-sharp damage since, in the chair, she'd been in a direct line to be peppered, or to revile me for leaving Hickory to take whatever came his way in the blast.

Pamela Jane, of course, had understood the physics of stress and strain in superheated glass, and she would now be sure I'd intended to shatter the horse from the moment I'd started to make it. She would be puzzling over the nonsense of the gold delivery, both the amount and the timing, because, as she confessed to me much later, it had all been so *unlike* me. She had believed every word I'd said to Rose, and now she felt a fool. "Dear Pam J," I contentedly said, "you were sincerely a great help."

That was afterwards. At the time, during the immediate aftermath of the destruction of the trophy horse, she still worried over the outcome for Hickory.

When I stood up and looked over the half-wall to see what shape Rose and Hickory were in, I found Rose bleeding down one leg but still shaking with determined fury while she shoved a clean punty iron into the tank and drew out a second one already tipped with white-hot hate.

Hickory, who had finally succeeded in flinging himself out of the chair altogether, lay facedown on the smooth brick floor trying to rub the adhesive off his mouth. Tears from the pain of his damaged ear seemed to be running helplessly down inside his nose, and he was trying to deal with that by sniffing.

Sharply aware that at some point somewhere Rose had succeeded in drawing a line of fire across my own lower back ribs, I felt I'd already had enough for one morning of the unequal combat.

Rose hadn't. Rose, it seemed, had energy in stock for a third world war. As she drew her loaded iron with speed from the fire, she told me that if I didn't get back at once into the workshop the burn to Hickory's ear would be only the beginning. She could have freed him. She could at least have helped him, but she didn't.

I went around the half-wall. Hickory still lay facedown on the floor, but instead of rubbing his face raw without results, he was now thrashing his legs instead. Hurting and helpless, he was in no immediate danger from Rose, who chose to advance on me, holding the silvery black five-foot-long punty iron loaded and ready to strike if I didn't dodge fast enough.

"Adam Force's videotape," she said. "Where is it?"

Short of breath from evading deep burns so long, I managed dry-mouthed to reply, "He said he'd rerecorded it with horse races."

"Rubbish." Rose advanced towards me with the white-hot ball of glass inexorably leading the way. Had we been armed the other way around, I could with two cuts of heavy scissors have sliced the ball into a pointed spear. The spear, if one thrust it fiercely, would burn a path right through a body, searing, cauterizing and killing. Rose had no spear but a ball was bad enough. Its effect would be the same.

With at least some sort of plan I backed away from Rose and her deadly fire, cursing that I couldn't reach the five or six punty irons lying idle to one side, irons I could at least have used to fence with, because Hickory with his shocking wound lay suffering in my way.

Rose began again to enjoy compelling me to retreat step by backwards step. Backwards past the furnace, its trapdoor shut. Backwards across the workshop, faster as she increased her pace.

"The videotape," she demanded. "Where is it?"

At last, *at last*, I saw Worthington again outside the gallery door, Worthington this time flanked by Tom Pigeon, Jim, Catherine and her hobo partner, Pernickety Paul.

Norman Osprey, suddenly not liking the odds, stood back to let them in and dived fast around them out into the street. I had a last glimpse of him as he set off down the hill with Tom and his three four-legged companions in pursuit.

The two plainclothes officers and, with Worthington and Jim, filled the doorway he'd left. Furiously seeing the advent of my friends as her last chance to make me remember her for life, Rose rushed recklessly at my abdomen. I sidestepped and dodged yet again and ran and swerved, and ended where I'd aimed for, beside the wide round pots of colored powders on the stock shelves.

It was the white color I wanted, the dust the Germans called *Emaill weiss.* I snatched off the lid and plunged my hand into the open pot, grabbed as much dust as I could in one handful and threw it at Rose's eyes.

Emaill weiss—white enamel ground to dust—contained arsenic . . . and arsenic dust made eyes blur and water and go temporarily and effectively blind. Rose, her eyes streaming, her sight gone, went on sweeping around with her petrifying length of death-bearing punty iron.

Eddie seemingly rose from his prayers and walked around the half-wall pleading with her to be still. "Rose, dear girl, it's over . . ."

But nothing would stop her. Blinded for a while she might be, but she lashed out with the killing iron at where she'd last seen me, trying still to penetrate my stomach or chest, then wildly slashing at where my head had been.

Missing me didn't stop her being more dangerous blundering about than if she could see me, and finally, disastrously, the unimaginably hot glass connected twice with living flesh.

There were screams chokingly cut off.

It was Eddie, her father, that incredibly she had hit first. She had seared the skin from his fingers as he had held them in front of his face to defend himself. There were crashes of iron against walls and a fearful soft sizzling as the worst of all calamities happened.

Pamela Jane hysterically threw herself into my arms and hid her face, but it wasn't she who had burned. From across the workshop, where the air again smelled of funeral pyre, Paul folded to the ground and lay motionless, his limbs sprawling in the haphazardness of death.

Catherine in a state of shock and anger stared hollow-eyed in disbelief. I stretched an arm towards her and hugged both girls as if I could never let them go.

Adam Force came to stand against the safe side of the wall into the workshop and begged Rose to stand still and let someone— like himself—come to help her and her father, with the only result that she changed direction towards his voice, lashing through the air in great sweeps of the punty iron.

Catherine, a police officer to the bone, stiffened after her first need for comfort and, with Rose following the sound of her voice, walked away from me and called her station urgently for backup. Stifling human terror, she spoke tightly on her personal radio. "Officer down," she said, pushing the transit button. "Red call. Red call. Officer in need of immediate assistance."

She reported the address of Logan Glass, and then and with less formality, and genuine extreme emotion, added, "Come at once. Dear God."

She dodged Rose's rushing speed and with incredible bravery knelt down beside her silent hobo partner. The plainclothes inhabitant of doorways, whose name to me had never been more than "Pernickety Paul," would catch no more villains. Pernickety Paul had taken a long white-hot direct hit through his neck.

I disentangled myself from Pamela Jane and half ran across the room away from Catherine and called to Rose, "I'm here, Rose. I'm over here and you'll never catch me."

Rose turned half circle my way and pivoted once more when I jumped past her again and yelled at her. She turned again and again and finally began to tire enough with her blurring eyes for Worthington and Jim to reach my side and for Catherine to come up behind us, and for the four of us to grab Rose at high speed and immobilize her still-slashing punty iron arm. I wrestled the iron a good safe way away from her, feeling the heat of it near my legs, but not on my skin, and *still* she went on struggling in Worthington's and Jim's grasp.

The police side of Catherine flowed in her like a strong tide. She sought and found the handcuffs carried by Pernickety Paul on a belt around his waist. She clicked them roughly onto Rose's wrists behind her back, the metal bands squeezed tight against her skin.

Rose kicked.

"Take my belt," Worthington shouted, and I unbuckled his pliable woven leather belt and tied it around one ankle and knotted it to the other, until she overbalanced and lay on her side on the floor, thrashing her legs still and cursing.

There was nothing about "going quietly" in the arrest of Rose Payne. An ambulance with paramedics and two cars full of bristling young police officers drew up outside the gallery and filled Logan Glass, crunching the fragments of the shattered horse to dust under their heavy boots. They talked with Catherine and fetched a blanket in which they rolled Rose like a baby in swaddling clothes and, with her struggling to the end, they manhandled her out through the showroom and gallery door and shoved her into the back of one of the police cars.

Spitting fury, she was soon joined there by the burly Norman Osprey, whose muscles had been no match for three sets of canine fangs. Tom told me later that the big man had sat in the road quivering with fear, his head and hands between his legs, begging for the police to rescue him from the black snarls circling around him.

In the workshop I watched as Catherine, dry-eyed, brought another blanket in from a police car to cover the silence of Paul.

MORE POLICE ARRIVED, some in uniform and others in plainclothes more suitable for a Sunday in front of the television than a trip to a fiery hell on earth. Off duty or not, some things demanded attendance. White overalls and gray plastic shoe covers were produced and soon the workshop took on the look of unreal science fiction.

I watched a policeman wearing surgical rubber gloves carefully lift the fallen syringe and place it gingerly in a clear plastic bag, which he sealed.

Methodically the police began to sort and list names, and it was the Dragon across the road who offered solace and recovery with a warm heart. One of the police officers removed the tape from Pamela Jane's wrists, took her personal details, and then with a solicitous arm helped her to the hotel.

I knelt beside Hickory. I told him I was going to remove the sticky strips from his eyes and mouth. I asked him if he understood.

Hickory nodded and stopped struggling against the floor.

As humanely as possible I pulled the tape from his eyes. It painfully came off with eyelashes attached and it was several minutes before his long-obstructed sight cleared and he was staring straight at me beside him.

"I'm going to take the tape off your mouth," I said.

He nodded.

One of the young police officers stretched a hand down over my shoulder and with a lack of sensitivity simply ripped the strong tape off. Hickory yelled and went on yelling, telling the police officer to free his taped-together hands, and to hurry up.

I left them for a moment and brought the first-aid box from the stock shelves to put a dressing on Hickory's ear, and after a good deal of chat, the paramedics and the police decided together that he should go to the hospital along with Eddie, who was now deep in shock with hands that had already blistered badly.

Catherine stood by the ambulance's open door watching Eddie being helped aboard for treatment.

I told her other things she ought to know, extra things about Blackmask Four that had come to me during the night, that I hadn't mentioned in the dawn.

She said thoughtfully, "Our superintendent is that man standing beside Paul. I think you'd better talk to him. I have to go to the police station. I'll come back here when I can. . . ."

She took me across the room, introduced me as the owner of the place and left me to deepen the frown of the top brass.

I shook hands with Superintendent Shepherd of the West Mercia police.

First of all he looked with disenchantment at my singlet, now no longer white and clean but grubby from constant contact with workshop clutter. He took in the singed piece of cloth hanging loose in the lower ribs area where Rose's relentless attentions had connected. He asked if the reddened skin beneath was painful and I tiredly said yes, it was, but I'd had worse burns in the past and would prefer to ignore it: but, I added to myself, burns had always before been accidentally self-inflicted.

I looked down at the blanket over Pernickety Paul, the fusspot who had cared like a father for Catherine's safety in the violent streets.

"He was a good policeman," I said.

The superintendent let a small silence ride by before mentioning comeuppance for the perpetrator. He would need me to proceed to the police station to make a statement which would be videotaped and in every way recorded. Judiciously he agreed I could cover the burns with dressings and restore my shirt on top, and then, reluctantly, he also agreed I could hang my coat over my shoulders so as not to freeze out of doors.

During this display of humanity George Lawson-Young arrived, and with his presence transformed the general police atmosphere from suspicion to common sense. He was the sort of deeply respected man that other men in authority instinctively trusted. When he greeted and treated me with noticeably high levels of deference, my standing with the super took a slow drift upwards. I thought he went so far after a while as to believe what I said.

George Lawson-Young asked me as if expecting the answer "Yes," "Did you work out the identity of the fourth man who assaulted you outside here on the sidewalk two weeks ago?"

"Yes."

He knew that answer in advance, as I had told him that morning on the telephone. I had used his search-and-discard method to sort out truth from lies, and to go carefully down the cul-de-sacs, but however flatly I said the name, it would cause consternation.

The professor, tall, tidy and nearsighted, made a slow visual inspection of the damage to the most familiar of faces turned his way. No one tried to hurry him, not even the superintendent.

Adam Force, his facial bleeding down from Niagara to a trickle, had wandered dizzily into the workshop from the show-room and was standing beside Hickory, looking down on him as, on his knees, Hickory cradled his mutilated ear.

When Adam Force saw the professor he looked as if he would prefer to evaporate rather than be in the same room as his onetime boss, and George, usually the most forgiving of men, produced a thoroughly baleful glare with no pity component for his expert practitioner of treason.

One of the policemen in white overalls asked Doctor Force his name and address while another took his photograph. The flash seemed to startle him and, with a blood-red rivulet still meandering down his cheek into his beard, he looked far from the assured physician I had first met on the hill at Lynton.

A spent Force, I thought ironically.

The photographer moved on, snapping under the direction of the Scene-of-Crime Officer. Nothing was to be missed. Pernickety Paul would have been proud.

It was George Lawson-Young, saying he was hoping I'd done enough for him for the next thousand years, who related to the superintendent step by step how the data stolen from his research laboratory had caused me so much pain and trouble.

Naming each person in turn to identify them for the policeman's sake, and referring back to me for confirmation when he needed it, George quietly threaded his way through the complexities of January 2000.

"Adam Force," he said, pointing at Dr. Bright-Scarlet-Beard, "worked for me but jumped ship and stole the cancer research that just may be worth millions and would certainly be to the advantage of the whole world."

I could see the superintendent begin to be skeptical but I nodded and he focused back on the professor.

"We knew," George went on, "that he had stolen the information, had transferred it to a videotape and had destroyed all other records of our research. Understandably, we searched everywhere for it, even engaging private investigators, after the police had shown little interest."

Superintendent Shepherd flinched not at all but continued listening intently.

"All our searches were in vain. We did not expect him to have entrusted the tape to the safekeeping of a jockey. Doctor Force had passed it to Martin Stukely but Stukely preferred to hand it on to his friend Gerard Logan here away from the fingers of his own children. As perhaps you know, Martin Stukely was killed at Cheltenham races on New Year's Eve. But the tape had already begun its tortuous journey by then. Adam Force tried to steal it back. Tapes were stolen from here, from Gerard's home and from the home of Martin Stukely."

"Were we informed of those thefts?" asked the policeman.

"Yes," I replied, "but the theft of a few videotapes for no apparent reason hardly brought the law out like today."

"Hmm," replied the superintendent, knowing it was true.

"One of your officers did come around here the following morning," I said, "but there was far more interest in the money stolen with the tape."

"Did Doctor Force steal the money as well?" asked the super, looking at Force.

"Yes," I replied. "But I think that was just an opportunist theft which he might have thought would somehow smokescreen the removal of the tape."

Doctor Force listened impassionately, his bloodied face giving away nothing.

"Anyway," continued the professor, who did not welcome the interruption, "somehow all the thefts failed to get back the tape they wanted, and Doctor Force, with assistance from Rose Payne and others, has been trying here to coerce Mr. Logan to reveal its whereabouts. He tells me he hasn't got it."

"And have you?" asked the voice of authority.

"No," I replied, "but I think I know who has."

They all looked at me. Adam Force, Lawson-Young, the superintendent and even Hickory, who had been listening with his good ear, they all waited expectantly.

Into this tableau swept Marigold, floating in emerald silk with gold tassels and brushing aside the young constable who tried to stand in her way. In her wake came Bon-Bon, Victor, Daniel and the other children like the tail of a kite.

Marigold demanded to see how her trophy was getting along, but was brought up sharply by the sight of the blanket-covered form in the workshop and the mass of evidence gatherers crawling cautiously around it on their hands and knees. Bon-Bon, realizing the enormity of the situation, swept her brood back out of the door, leaving just her mother and Victor inside, both of them stock-still, transfixed, living through their eyes.

"Gerard darling," Marigold exclaimed. "What is going on? And where is Worthington?"

"Marigold, my dear," I said wearily, "there's been a disaster. Please go across the road to the hotel and wait for me there."

She seemed not to hear, her eyes steadfastly on the blanket. "Where is Worthington?" Her voice began to rise. "Where's Worthington? Oh my God."

I took her in my arms. "Marigold, Marigold, he's all right. I promise. That's not Worthington."

She sobbed on my shoulder, near to collapse.

Victor turned to me and said, his voice barely more than a whisper, "It's not a game anymore, is it?"

The question needed no answer, and presently the young constable led him and Marigold across to the Wychwood Dragon.

"So who is Blackmask Four?" asked Lawson-Young into the silence when they had gone.

"Who?" said the superintendent. "What are you talking about?"

The professor told him. "Gerard was attacked by four people in black masks outside his shop here. Three of them were Rose Payne, her father Eddie Payne and Norman Osprey. Gerard told me earlier today that he had worked out the identity of the fourth, so," he turned to me and said with faith, "who is it and where is my research?"

"I don't think Blackmask Four has the tape," I replied.

"What!" exclaimed the professor. His shoulders dropped, his expectations had been so high and he took it now that I was leading him only to another cul-de-sac, another dead end.

I put him right. "My fourth assailant, Blackmask Four, was just a hired help and I'm not sure he even knew exactly what he was looking for." But he knew, I thought, how to inflict maximum damage to my wrists. "He is, however, a dab hand with a baseball bat and anesthetic gas."

"Who is it, for God's sake?" The professor was finding it difficult to stifle his impatience, as was the superintendent, yet it wasn't the easiest disclosure I'd ever made. Still . . .

"Who was the fourth man, Hickory?" I asked.

Hickory looked up from where he was kneeling on the floor, still holding a dressing to his ear.

"Why are you asking me?" he said.

"You bunched my fingers."

"Of course I didn't."

"I'm afraid you did," I said. "You held my hand against a wall ready for a baseball bat to smash my wrist."

"You must be crazy. Why would I attack you? Why you of all people?"

It was a piercing question and one with a complex answer. He didn't answer it. But we both knew what he had intended.

"Did you do it for money?" I asked.

I suspected that it was for more convoluted reasons than that. Something to do with my ability with glassblowing and his comparative lack of it. Envy was a strong emotion and, I reckoned, he wouldn't have needed a whole lot of persuasion to oppose me.

He still refused to admit it. "You're crazy, you are," he said, getting to his feet and turning away as if looking for some quick escape.

"The green-and-white laces," I said.

He stopped dead and turned back.

I went on, "You wore them here the day Martin Stukely was killed, and you wore them again the following day when you stole the tapes from his house, the day you hit me with the orange cylinder. Martin's eldest son, Daniel, saw the laces and told the police about them."

Hickory advanced a step or two, his ear clearly hurting.

His poise cracked.

"You're so fucking clever," he said. "I wish we *had* broken your wrists."

The superintendent stopped leaning on the half-wall and stood up straight.

But Hickory had only just started.

"You and your fancy ways and your condescending comments about my work. I hate you and this workshop. I'm a damn good glassblower and I deserve more recognition." He raised his chin and sneered.

"One day," he went on, "John Hickory will be a name worth knowing and people will smash fucking Logan Glass to get to mine."

Such a shame, I thought. He really did have some talent but, I suspected, it would never be allowed to develop as it should. Arrogance and a belief in skills he didn't have would smother those he did.

"And Rose?" I asked.

"Stupid bitch," he said, holding his hand to his throbbing ear, "bloody mad she is. Tie you up, she said; use you as a hostage, she said. Nothing about frying my effing ear. Hope she rots in hell."

I hoped she'd rot on earth.

"She promised me my own place," Hickory said. "Claimed she'd close you down. Her and that stupid father of hers." He began to realize the hole he was digging for himself. "They put me up to it. It was their fault, not mine."

He looked wretchedly at the rapt faces around him.

"It wasn't my fault. It was their idea."

No one believed him. It had been Hickory who had reported all to Rose. Hickory had had the "binocs" in Broadway.

"So where is the tape?" asked George Lawson-Young.

"I don't know," replied Hickory. "Rose said that it must have been in Stukely's house or in Logan's but I've sat through hours of bloody horse racing and glassblowing and, I'm telling you, there was no tape of medical stuff."

I believed him. Otherwise, I thought ruefully, I might have been saved a couple of beatings and Pernickety Paul would still be lying around in shop doorways.

A paramedic appeared and said that it was time to take Hickory to the hospital to dress his burn. The superintendent, roused into action, arrested Hickory. "You do not have to say anything . . ."

"Too bloody late," retorted Hickory, as he was led off to the ambulance by a white-overalled police officer and the paramedic.

The super turned his attention to Doctor Red-Beard Force, who had listened in silence throughout.

He said, his speech always in the pattern of officialese, "Well, Doctor Force, can you enlighten us as to the whereabouts of a videotape containing medical research results stolen from the professor here?"

Force said nothing. It seemed that he had at least learned one lesson from our discussion under the fir trees in Lynton.

"Come on, Adam, tell us." The professor, I saw, still had some vestige of friendship for the man before him dripping blood from his beard onto my smooth brick floor.

Force looked at him with disdain and kept silent.

In his turn, he too was arrested and taken away for wound

stitching and fingerprinting. "You do not have to say anything. . . ."
So he didn't.

In time the gallery, showroom and workshop began to clear.
The coroner's representative arrived and supervised the reloca-
tion of Paul to the local morgue. The other officers stopped
work to stand and watch the sorry procession of undertakers
and their highly regarded and valued burden move through the
gallery to the door. There were tears in my eyes as well as in
theirs. He had been a good man as well as a good policeman.

A few more photographs were taken and a few more pieces of
evidence were collected. Blue-and-white "Do Not Cross" tape
was strung about, doors were locked and guarded, and the
professor and I were gently eased out to the street into the gray
appropriate drizzle.

The superintendent again asked me to accompany him to the
police station to make a full statement, though this time, there
was more warmth in his manner. I agreed, but first, I asked, could
we all go over to the Wychwood Dragon Hotel as I was thirsty
and needed a jug of tea. I looked at my cheap watch. Amazingly
it was still morning though it felt to me more like teatime must
have come and gone.

They were in the residents' downstairs sitting room. Bon-Bon
and her four sat tightly side by side on the wide sofa in de-
scending height from the right. Coca-Colas had been bought and
a line of empty bottles with straws sat on a coffee table. Marigold
occupied a deep squashy armchair while Worthington perched

on its arm by her side. The manner in which Marigold clung to Worthington's hand reminded me of his flytrap warning. He didn't appear to protest.

The Dragon poured tea into large millennium souvenir mugs and told us that Pamela Jane, still badly shocked, had been given a pill by the police doctor and dispatched to bed upstairs.

Victor stood by the window unable to remove his eyes from Logan Glass opposite. I took my tea over and joined him.

Without turning his head he said, "I suppose my aunt Rose will be inside for a long time?"

"Yes," I said. "A very long time." For life, I thought, either in prison or a secure mental hospital. Police killers didn't get early parole.

He stood in silence a moment longer, then turned and looked me straight in the eye. "Good," he said. "It might give me and Mom a chance."

I turned and took Bon-Bon out into the hotel lobby. I needed her to do me a favor. Certainly, she said, and trotted off to the telephone box beneath the stairs.

I went back into the sitting room to finish my tea and soon after Bon-Bon returned with a smiling nod.

I thought about the events of the morning, and wondered if there had been another way.

Punty irons in anyone's hand had to be swung around carefully. In Rose's hands a punty iron tipped with semi-liquid glass had been literally a lethal weapon, and it had seemed to me that as it was me she was after, however weird and mistaken her beliefs, it was I who ought to stop her.

I'd tried to stop her with the shattering horse and I hadn't suc-ceeded. It had torn a hole in her lover and stoked her own anger, and I'd thought then, if I could blind her she would stop, so I'd thrown the powder, but blinding her had made her worse.

Paul had died.

If I hadn't tried to stop her, if instead I had surrendered at once to her as she'd demanded, then Paul would be alive. But, I re-flected, searching for comfort, I couldn't have given her the tape she demanded as I hadn't known exactly where it was.

I'd done my best, and my best had killed.

THE VOICE OF the superintendent brought me back to the present. He said he was eager to get to the police station to in-terview his prisoners and also that he was less eager, but duty demanded it, to visit Detective Constable Paul Cratchet's family. "Would the professor and Mr. Logan come with me now, please, sirs?" he said.

"Another cup of tea?" I replied.

The super was not happy. "Contrary to popular belief, the tea at the station house is quite drinkable. So, if you please."

I needed more time.

Settling into another deep armchair, I said, "Just a moment to sit down? I'm exhausted. How about something to eat before we go?"

"We have a canteen at the station. You can have something there." The voice of authority had spoken and there seemed little else to do but comply.

I rose slowly to my feet and with relief found my expected guest hurrying at last through the door.

"Hello, Priam," I said.

He looked past me towards the tall, elegantly suited George Lawson-Young. He flicked a glance at Bon-Bon as if to say, "Is this the one?"

"Priam," I repeated, "it's so good of you to come. Priam Jones, can I introduce Superintendent Shepherd of the West Mercia police."

Priam turned slowly my way and instinctively shook an offered hand.

"I'm sorry?" he said, puzzled. "I don't quite understand. Bon-Bon called me to say that she was with a potential racehorse owner and I should get down here pronto if I wanted the business. Interrupted a good lunch too, I can tell you."

He looked around him still searching for the elusive owner.

"Priam," I regained his attention, "that wasn't quite the truth. I asked Bon-Bon to make that call because I needed to talk to you." He wasn't pleased. Far from it.

"What's wrong with the bloody telephone if you needed a chat, although about what I can't imagine." He looked down at four sets of childhood eyes staring up at him. "*Hmp* . . . sorry."

I said, "I needed a chat about a videotape."

"Not that bl . . . er . . . videotape business again," he said. "I have told you already, I don't have any videotape."

Daniel said distinctly, "I know where there's a videotape."

"*Shhhh, darling,*" said Bon-Bon.

"But I *do* know where a tape is," Daniel persisted.

I had learned to take Daniel very seriously indeed.

I squatted down to his level on the sofa. "Where is the video-tape, Daniel?" I said.

"I think it must be worth at least three or four gold coins," he replied.

"What does he mean?" asked Professor Lawson-Young.

"It's a game we have been playing," I said. "I give Daniel trea-sure if he gives or finds me information." I turned back to Daniel. "I think it might indeed be worth three or four gold coins."

"A whole bagful of treasure," said the professor, "if it's the right tape."

Daniel looked positively delighted at the prospect.

"It's in Daddy's car," he said. "It's in the pocket on the back of Daddy's seat. I saw it there yesterday when Mommy brought us to your shop."

He looked at me questioningly and beamed when I told him, "Ten gold coins this time if the professor agrees."

George Lawson-Young, speechless, nodded his head until it seemed it might fall off.

Daniel said, "I like finding things for Gerard. I'll always look for things for him."

Priam shuffled uneasily beside me.

I said to him, "Why did you switch the tapes?"

"I told you . . . ," he started.

"I know what you told me," I interrupted. "It was a lie." Dis-card the lies, the professor had told me in Bristol, and I would be left with the truth. I asked again, "Why did you switch the tapes?"

He shrugged his shoulders. "I thought," he said, "that the tape Eddie Payne passed to you was one showing the hiding place of an antique necklace. Worth millions I'd heard from someone. I found it in your raincoat that night and I thought, with Martin dead, no one would know if I kept it."

Half-truths and misconceptions had woven a path to death and destruction.

Priam went on, "I took another tape from Martin's den, one with racing on it, and wrapped it in the paper and put it back in your raincoat pocket. When I played the original tape at home that night I discovered that it was all unintelligible mumbo jumbo with nothing about a necklace. So I just put it back in Martin's car when I drove it back to Bon-Bon's the next day."

He looked around him. "No harm done. You have the tape back. No need for the police."

No harm done. Oh God, how wrong he was.

IT WAS FOUR days before the police would allow me back into Logan Glass.

Broadway had been the center of a media circus. The Dragon from over the road had previously said, "You were always news in this town, lover" and, for filling her rooms, she allowed me use of her best suite and paraded her little glass animals along a shelf in the lobby with a notice offering duplicates for sale.

Marigold, her natural competitor in the matter of saris, caftans, eyelashes and "Darling," wandered in and out waiting for me to start again on her trophy. Worthington, who had been upgraded from her chauffeur to her arm-in-arm companion, was dispatched with me to collect the necklace from the bank. Marigold secured total victory over the Dragon by wearing it day and night and finally buying it from me outright at huge expense.

Rose, Norman Osprey, Doctor Force and Hickory had been remanded in custody while Eddie had been remanded in the hospital, his hands a mess.

Priam, not understanding the fuss, had been given police bail, which meant that his passport had been confiscated. "Most inconvenient," he had declared. "Why have I been treated like a common criminal?" Because he was one, Worthington had told him and anyone else who'd listen.

Professor George Lawson-Young had been given the tape from Martin's car. There had been a few ugly moments when the superintendent had tried to hang on to it as evidence. Having once lost the information it contained, Lawson-Young had no intention of allowing it out of his sight again. The police had reluctantly consented to his taking it away briefly to make a copy.

Catherine, cuddling in my arms every night, kept me up-to-date with the news from the police station.

Rose did little else but scream abuse, most of it in my direction it seemed.

Hickory blamed me, Rose and the world in general.

Doctor Force had said a little but denied most. He had revealed, however, that Martin Stukely had not been aware that the information on the tape had been stolen. Indeed the doctor had told Martin that he was protecting the research from others trying to steal the work from Force.

I was glad of that. Had I doubted it?

On Thursday we reopened. The showroom was busier than it had ever been on a weekday in January and sales boomed. But, in truth, there was far greater interest in the bloodstains, which had proved difficult to remove from between the bricks on the floor, than in the stock.

Pamela Jane had recovered sufficiently to return in time for the weekend although she preferred to work in the showroom and made rapid transits across the workshop to her locker only when she couldn't avoid it.

On Sunday, one week after the mayhem, I set out again to make the trophy horse.

Dependable Irish had agreed to act as my assistant and this time we had an audience of one. Catherine sat in her now familiar chair and watched as I again readied my tools and stripped down to my singlet.

I stood on the treadle to lift the door to the furnace and let the heat flood into the room.

Catherine took off her coat.

"Hang it in my locker," I said, tossing her the locker keys.

She walked to the far end of the workshop and opened a door on the tall gray cabinet.

"What's on this?" she said, holding up a videotape. "It has a label, 'How to make the Cretan Sunrise.' "

I moved swiftly to her side. She had by mistake opened Hickory's locker, and there inside we found not just the necklace instruction tape but also, tucked into a brown paper bag, a pair of bright laces, green-and-white-striped.

I laughed. "A tale of three tapes and one of them was under my nose all the time."

"Three tapes?" she asked. "Two were bad enough."

"There were three," I replied. "The only really important, valuable and perhaps unique tape was the one Force made from the stolen cancer research results. He gave it to Martin, who via Eddie gave it to me. Priam swapped it, mistakenly thinking it a treasure finder's dream to millions. When he found that it wasn't, he simply left it hidden in Martin's car. It's the tape that Rose and Doctor Force have been trying so hard to find."

"And the necklace tape?" Catherine asked. "This one?"

I said, "I had lent the necklace instruction tape to Martin and it remained in his den at his house until Hickory stole it with all the others. Hickory kept it because, to him, the tape had some value. He thought he could make a copy of the necklace and obviously kept the tape in his locker."

"What's the third tape then?" she asked.

"The tape," I went on, "that Priam took from Martin's den before Hickory's theft. He put it in my raincoat pocket and it's that tape that Force stole at midnight on New Year's Eve thinking it was his cancer tape. I would have loved to see his face when he played it and found horse racing instead."

I MADE THE TROPHY horse. With Irish's help I gathered the glass from the furnace and again formed the horse's body, its legs and tail. But this time I took time and care and applied the knowledge and talent both learned and inherited from my uncle Ron. I molded a neck and head of an intelligent animal, prominent cheekbones and a firm mouth. I gave it a mane flowing as if in full gallop and then applied it seamlessly to the body.

I had started out to make a commercial work for Marigold and Kenneth Trubshaw and his Cheltenham Trophy Committee.

In the event I made a memorial to a trusted and much missed friend. A memorial worthy of his skill and his courage.

The leaping horse stood finally on the marver table and Irish and I lifted it quickly but carefully into one of the annealing ovens. There it would cool slowly and safely, allowing the strains and stresses to ease gradually. This one was not for shattering.

I WENT WITH CATHERINE to the funeral of Pernickety Paul, but I abandoned her at the church door to her colleagues, uniformed or not. A small bunch of plainclothes enveloped her and mourned with her and it was a thoughtful and subdued police officer who mounted her motorcycle, paused before starting the engine, and said blankly to her future passenger, "The private cremation's tomorrow and there are drinks in his memory in the pub this evening. I've been given leave for the rest of the day, so where do you want to go now?"

"To bed," I said without hesitation, and added that surely Pernickety Paul would have approved.

Catherine shed sorrow like melting snow.

I said, "I haven't seen where you live, remember? So how about now then?"

She smiled with a touch of mischief and then kicked down on the starter and invited me to step aboard.

Her home was maybe five minutes' walk or less than a one-minute motorcycle ride along a straight gray road from the district police station. She stopped outside a single-storied semi-detached bungalow in a row of identical stuccoed boxes, and I knew within a second blink that this was not the place for me. Going there had been a mistake but, as Catherine was my transport, I would smile and pretend to like it.

I actually did both, and not from politeness's sake.

Inside, the plainclothes's one-floor living space had been allied to *Alice's Adventures in Wonderland,* where a more-than-life-size March Hare and a same-size Mad Hatter sat at the kitchen table and stuffed a dormouse into a teapot. A white rabbit consulted a watch by the bathroom door, and a red queen and a cook and a walrus and a carpenter danced a quadrille around the sitting room. All the walls, everywhere, were painted with rioting greenery and flowers.

Catherine laughed at my expression, a mixture no doubt of amusement and horror.

"These people," she said, "came to me from a closing-down fun fair when I was six. I've always loved them. I know they're silly but they're company." She suddenly swallowed. "They have helped me come to terms with losing Paul. He liked them. They made him laugh. They're not the same now, without him. I think I've been growing up."